THE HUMAN ENCOUNTER
WITH DEATH

STANISLAV GROF, M.D., worked with psychedelic drugs at the Psychiatric Institute in Prague before joining the Maryland Psychiatric Research Center in 1967. Author of over sixty articles in this field and the book *Realms of the Human Unconscious: Observations from LSD Research*, he is now scholar-in-residence at the Esalen Institute in Big Sur, California.

JOAN HALIFAX, Ph.D., is a medical anthropologist, specializing in psychiatry and religion. She is presently working with the mythologist Joseph Campbell. She has done research at Columbia University, the Musee de l'Homme in Paris, the University of Miami School of Medicine, and the Maryland Psychiatric Research Center.

The Human Encounter With Death

STANISLAV GROF, M.D.,

JOAN HALIFAX, Ph.D.

With a Foreword by
Elisabeth Kübler-Ross

 *A Dutton Paperback*

E.P. DUTTON · NEW YORK

Grateful acknowledgment is made to the following:

For permission to use copyrighted material from *Memories, Dreams, Reflections* by C. J. Jung, edited and recorded by Aniela Jaffe, translated by Richard and Clara Winston. Copyright © 1963 by Random House, Inc. Reprinted by permission of Pantheon Books, a Division of Random House, Inc.

For permission to use copyrighted material, an excerpt from "I Died at 10:52 A.M.," by Victor D. Solow, *The Reader's Digest,* October 1974. Copyright © 1974 by the Reader's Digest Association, Inc. Used with permission.

For permission to use copyrighted material from the *American Journal of Psychiatry,* Vol. 124, pp. 84–88, 1967. Copyright © 1967, the American Psychiatric Association. Reprinted by permission.

For passages from *Glimpses of the Beyond* by J. B. Delacour, Delacorte Press, 1974.

This paperback edition of
The Human Encounter With Death
first published 1978 by E. P. Dutton, a Division of
Sequoia-Elsevier Publishing Co., Inc., New York.

Library of Congress Cataloging in Publication Data
Grof, Stanislav, 1931–
 The human encounter with death.

 Bibliography: p.
 Includes index.
 1. Death—Psychological aspects. 2. Lysergic
acid diethylamide. I. Halifax, Joan, joint author.
II. Title.
BF789.D4G76 1977 155.9'37 76-55419
ISBN: 0-525-47492-7

Published simultaneously in Canada
by Clarke, Irwin & Company Limited,
Toronto and Vancouver

10 9 8 7 6 5 4 3 2 1

CONTENTS

FOREWORD BY
ELISABETH KÜBLER-ROSS

The Human Encounter With Death is the latest of many recent publications in the newly evolving field of thanatology. It is, however, a quite different kind of book—one that belongs in every library of anyone who seriously tries to understand the phenomenon we call death.

Anyone interested in psychosomatic medicine and its correlations, as well as those involved in the clinical use of the psychedelic experience, should read this book. It is a Pandora's box of information as well as a good historical review. The author, who is an already well-known and talented writer and an extremely bright and well-read researcher, actually takes you on a fascinating journey through *The Egyptian Book of the Dead,* through LSD experiences and its possible application, through near-death experiences associated with drownings and accidents, to the many different points of views and theoretical interpretations of the subjective experiences of the dying. This book is long overdue in our drug-oriented society.

As Grof, himself, states, the experiences of dying individuals cover a wide range, from the abstract to aesthetic sequences—from reliving traumatic and positive childhood memories and episodes of death and rebirth to profound archetypal and transcendental forms of consciousness.

This work is not really a summary of human encounters with death; in fact it deals very little with the natural experiences of dying patients. It is written almost exclusively by a man whose real contribution is the better understanding of the use, application, and understanding of psychedelic drugs, altered states of consciousness, and special reference to the time of transition we call death. He deals with the phenomenon of pain and its alteration with LSD; the transformation of unsuccessful suicide patients after jumping from the Golden Gate Bridge; the changing values of individuals who have ''been on the other side''—whether through the use of drugs, spontaneous cosmic experience or a close death encounter.

It is interesting to note that of Karlis Osis' 35,540 reported cases of ''death observations,'' only 10 percent of dying patients seem to have been conscious in the hour preceding death. It is my personal opinion that our heavy emphasis on ''drugging'' patients prior to their deaths is a great disservice to them and to their families. Patients who were not heavily medicated in their final hours were able to experience these blissful states prior to their transition, resulting in a knowledge (rather than a belief) of a waiting, loving presence of another being, of an existence (rather than a place) of peace and equanimity, of a state of well-being and wholeness —transcending all fear of death.

The vision with a predominantly nonhuman content is also typical, as it represents the in-between phase of the patient's weaning off earthly interpersonal relationships, prior to the contact with the ''guiding hands'' that will help all of us in the transition from this plane to the next one.

It may be reassuring for those who lost a loved one through suicide that the survivors of these near-death experiences were not riddled with guilt and shame—which we tend to impose on them—but rather with a sense of new hope and purpose in being alive.

Grof's and Halifax's *Human Encounter With Death,* together with Osis' pioneering work and Raymond A. Moody's published and soon-to-be published material, will help the many sceptics to reevaluate their position, to raise questions rather than to reject the new area of research in existence after physical death. They should ask themselves why there are so few differences in the stories of these people, and why there is this recurrence of certain motifs and themes in remote countries, and different time periods, and cultures, and religions.

ACKNOWLEDGMENTS

The authors would like to express their gratitude and appreciation to all those colleagues and friends at the Maryland Psychiatric Research Center in Catonsville, Maryland, who contributed to the Spring Grove studies of psychedelic therapy with individuals dying of cancer. The results of this research endeavor represented the most powerful stimulus for the inception of the interdisciplinary analysis of the death experience which constitutes this book.

The person whose enthusiasm, energy, and dedication were essential for the launching of the programs of LSD and DPT psychotherapy with cancer patients was Walter Pahnke, M.D., Ph.D.; his background in medicine, psychology, and religion, combined with his unique personality, made him the ideal person to head the research of psychedelic therapy with the dying. Walter himself died a tragic death in July 1971, before he could see the completion of his projects.

We would like to give special notice to William Richards, Ph.D., who contributed to both the LSD and DPT studies in the role of therapist as well as conceptual thinker. In various stages of research other

staff members of the Maryland Psychiatric Research Center participated in the cancer project as psychedelic therapists. Grateful acknowledgment is made to Sanford Unger, Ph.D., Sidney Wolf, Ph.D.,
Thomas Cimonetti, M.D., Franco DiLeo, M.D., John Rhead, Ph.D.,
John Lobell, and Lockwood Rush, Ph.D. The latter, together with
Richard Yensen, Ph.D., and Mark Schiffman, operated the media
department at the center. As a result of their commitment and enthusiasm, much of the case material described in this book has been pre-
served in the form of videotape records. Another member of the research team at the Maryland Psychiatric Research Center, Helen
Bonny, contributed to the studies in a unique combination of roles as
musical advisor, co-therapist, and research assistant. In addition, we
would like to extend our gratitude to Nancy Jewell, Ilse Richards, and
Karen Leihy for their sensitive and dedicated participation in the project as nurses and co-therapists; all three showed extraordinary interest,
enthusiasm, and initiative in their work and accepted with great understanding all the extra duties imposed on them by the unusual nature of
psychedelic therapy with cancer patients.

Special appreciation is due Albert A. Kurland, M.D., director of the
Maryland Psychiatric Research Center and assistant commissioner for
research of the Maryland State Department of Mental Hygiene. Although his responsible position and complex administrative duties
made it impossible for him to participate in actual clinical work on the
project, his role as coordinator, facilitator, and advisor was crucial.
Charles Savage, M.D., associate director of the Maryland Psychiatric
Research Center, deserves respectful acknowledgment for the invaluable support and encouragement he granted to the projects over the
years.

The experimental programs of psychedelic therapy could not have
been carried out without the unique understanding and cooperation of
Louis E. Goodman, M.D., attending surgeon and head of the Oncology Clinic at Sinai Hospital. Also, several other members of the medical staff of this hospital deserve appreciation for their interest, help,
and willingness to provide their resources for this unexplored and

highly sensitive area. Among these we gratefully acknowledge Adolph Ulfohn, M.D., and Daniel Bakal, M.D.*

Special acknowledgment should be granted to the agencies that provided the necessary funding for the Spring Grove research endeavors, namely the Department of Mental Hygiene of the State of Maryland and the National Institutes of Health. Especially significant was the help of the Mary Reynolds Babcock Foundation, whose financial support at a most critical time allowed these activities to be expanded in depth. We also remember with gratitude the administrative and financial help of the Friends of Psychiatric Research, Inc.

We are indebted to our many friends and colleagues who have helped us put the clinical data and observations into a broader interdisciplinary perspective. Among these we particularly appreciate the contribution and catalyzing influence of Margaret Mead, Ph.D., and Mary Catherine Bateson, Ph.D. In July 1973, they invited us to a symposium entitled "Ritual: Reconciliation in Change" that they had conceived and coordinated. During long and stimulating discussions with thirteen other participants that took place for nine days at Burg Wartenstein in Austria, some of the ideas expressed in this book originated while others crystalized and took a more concrete form. We also extend our sincerest thanks to Lita Osmondsen, president of the Wenner-Gren Foundation, which sponsored the Austrian symposium, for making this unique interdisciplinary exchange possible, as well as for her extraordinary hospitality.

Our theoretical thinking in the area of death and dying has been deeply influenced by the work of Russell Noyes, M.D., professor of psychiatry at the University of Iowa, who drew our attention to the

* It seems appropriate in this context to clarify a point of basic importance: The results of the Spring Grove studies have been described in a number of papers read at professional meetings and published in scientific journals; these articles are included in the bibliography of this book. Those of the above researchers who co-authored these papers are responsible only for the information and conclusions that were expressed in that form. The interdisciplinary excursions in this book extend far beyond the framework of the original clinical papers. The speculations and opinions expressed in this volume are entirely our responsibility (S. G. and J. H.).

phenomenology of near-death experiences and the subjective concomitants of clinical death. The invaluable data provided by Noyes made it possible for us to recognize that the inner cartography developed in LSD research is applicable to this area. This was an important step in developing a deeper understanding of the universal and central significance of the death experience. David Rosen, M.D., of the Langley-Porter Neuropsychiatric Institute in San Francisco, made it possible for us to study the data from his research of survivors of suicidal jumps from the Golden Gate Bridge long before this material was published. We hereby acknowledge our gratitude to both of these researchers.

One person has to be mentioned in a special category. Since our first encounter several years ago, our meetings with Joseph Campbell have been a rare combination of intellectual feast, apotheosis of art, spiritual event, and joyous reunion. His influence on our lives as a teacher and dear friend has been paramount. By sharing with us in his special way his encyclopedic knowledge and deep life-wisdom, he has opened our eyes to the relevance of mythology for a deeper understanding of human life and death.

We are both grateful to Esalen Institute at Big Sur Hot Springs, California, for giving us ideal conditions in which to develop our concepts and work on a series of books. Within the framework of Esalen we have been able to create an ongoing experimental educational program for professionals; the intense interactions with our guest faculty and participants in these unusual events have been a rich source of ideas and professional inspiration. Our sincerest thanks are extended to Michael Murphy, Richard Price, Janet Lederman, Andrew Gagarin, Julian Silverman, and all our other friends at Esalen. Of these, Rick Tarnas gave us invaluable help in various stages of the writing and editing of the manuscript.

Those whose contribution to this volume was absolutely essential cannot be mentioned by name; we are deeply indebted to them and remember them with utmost gratitude. Many hundreds of psychiatric patients and LSD subjects who during their psychedelic sessions explored the realms of death in this modern version of a rite of passage volunteered their experiences and the knowledge that they acquired during their inner journeys. Our most valuable teachers were persons suffering from cancer and facing the imminence of biological death, for whom symbolic encounters with death in their psychedelic sessions were an immediate preparation for their last journeys. Their contributions to this volume are inestimable; without the gracious sharing on the part of these courageous individuals and their families, this volume could not have been written.

Esalen Institute
Big Sur, California
October 1976

THE HUMAN ENCOUNTER WITH DEATH

1.

THE CHANGING FACE
OF DEATH

Death is one of the few universal experiences of human existence. It is the most predictable event in our lives, one that is to be expected with absolute certainty. Yet the nature of death is immersed in deep mystery. Since time immemorial the fact of our mortality has stimulated human fantasy and found incredibly varied expression in the realms of religion, art, mythology, philosophy, and folklore. Many extraordinary works of architecture throughout the world have been inspired by the mystery of death: the monumental pyramids and sphinxes of Egypt and its magnificent tombs and necropolises; the mausoleum in Halicarnassus; * the pre-Columbian pyramids and temples of the Aztecs, Olmecs, and Mayans; and the famous tombs of the great Moghuls, such as the Taj Mahal and the Monument of Akbar the Great. According to

---

* The mausoleum of Halicarnassus was the tomb of Mausolus of Caria, a provincial governor of the Persian Empire who died in the year 353 B.C. It was built by a group of sculptors at the request of his devoted sister and widow, Artemisia, and became one of the seven wonders of the ancient world because of its unusual form, rich decoration, and exquisite finish. The mausoleum consisted of thirty-six columns resting on a high base and supporting a marble pyramid capped by a four-horse chariot.

recent research, even the legendary Minoan palace in Crete was not a royal residence but, rather, a gigantic necropolis.*

The enigmatic nature of death opens a wide range of possibilities for individual and collective imagination. To take only a few examples from Western culture, people have seen death as the Grim Reaper, Terrible Devourer, Abominable Horseman, Senseless Automaton, Implacable Punisher, Gay Deceiver, Passionate Lover, Sweet Pacifier, and Great Unifier. The emotions associated with these images cover a broad spectrum, from a profound sense of horror to feelings of ecstatic rapture.

Different concepts of death and associated beliefs have a deep influence not only on the psychological state of dying people but also on the specific circumstances under which they leave this world and on the attitudes of their survivors. As a result of this, dying and death can be understood and experienced in many different ways. From this point of view it is interesting to compare the situation of a person facing death in contemporary Western civilization with that of individuals in ancient cultures or from preindustrial countries.

Most non-Western cultures have religious and philosophical systems, cosmologies, ritual practices, and certain elements of social organization that make it easier for their members to accept and experience death. These cultures generally do not see death as the absolute termination of existence; they believe that consciousness or life in some form continues beyond the point of physiological demise. Whatever specific concepts of afterlife prevail in different cultures, death is typically regarded as a transition or transfiguration, and not as the final annihilation of the individual. Mythological systems have not only detailed descriptions of various afterlife realms, but frequently also complex cartographies to guide souls on their difficult posthumous journeys.

---

* According to Dr. Hans Georg Wunderlich, professor of geology and paleontology from Stuttgart, the palace of King Minos at Knossos had never been intended for the living but was a necropolis where a powerful sect practiced elaborate burial rites, sacrifices, and ritual games. Wunderlich expounded his provocative theory in his book, *The Secret of Crete*.

The intensity of this belief in the postmortem journey found its expression in a variety of funeral rites. Most researchers interested in death customs emphasize that the common denominators of these procedures seem to be the basic ambivalence of the survivors toward the dead and the belief in an afterlife. Many aspects of funeral rites represent an effort to facilitate and hasten the transition of the deceased to the spirit world. However, the opposite tendency can be observed with almost equal frequency—namely, the ceremonial establishment of the relationship between the quick and the dead to obtain safety and protection. Specific aspects of many rituals conducted after death can be simultaneously interpreted in terms of helping the dead in their posthumous journeys as well as preventing them from returning.

A special variation of the belief in the continuation of existence after death is the concept of reincarnation. In addition to the element of disembodied existence following the death of an individual, it also involves an eventual return to material existence in a different form in the phenomenal world as we know it. The belief in reincarnation occurs in such diverse cultural and religious frameworks as philosophies and religions of India, cosmologies of various North American Indian tribes, Platonic and Neoplatonic philosophy, the Orphic cult and other mystery religions of ancient Greece, and early Christianity.* In Hinduism, Buddhism, and Jainism this belief is connected with the law of karma, according to which the quality of individual incarnations is specifically determined by the person's merits and debits from preceding lifetimes.

It is not difficult to understand that a firm conviction concerning the

* Since it is generally assumed that the belief in reincarnation is incompatible with Christianity and alien to it, it seems appropriate to elaborate on the above statement. The concept of reincarnation existed in Christianity until it was attacked in 543 A.D. by the Byzantine emperor, Justinian, together with other teachings of the learned father, Origen, and finally condemned by the Second Council in Constantinople in 553 A.D. Origen, considered the most prominent of all Church Fathers with the exception of Augustine, stated explicitly in his work, *De Principiis:* "The soul has neither beginning nor end. . . . Every soul comes to this world strengthened by the victories or weakened by the defeats of its previous life. Its place in this world as a vessel appointed to honor or dishonor is determined by its previous merits or demerits. Its work in this world determines its place in the world which is to follow this."

continuity of consciousness or life beyond the framework of an individual's biological existence—or even an open-minded attitude toward such a possibility—can alter the experience of aging, the concept of death, and the experience of dying itself. In the extreme, the relative values attributed to life and death can be completely reversed in comparison with prevailing Western concepts. The process of dying can then appear to be even more important than living. This is true, for example, in the case of some of the philosophical or religious systems that involve a belief in reincarnation. Here, the period of dying can be of paramount significance, because the attitude of the dying individual determines the quality of the entire future incarnation, and the nature and course of the next existence is an actualization of the manner of death. In other systems, life is experienced as a state of separation, a prison of the spirit, and death is a reunion, liberation, or return home. Thus for the Hindu death is an awakening from the world of illusion (*maya*) and an opportunity for the individual self (*jiva*) to realize and experience its divine nature (Atman-Brahman). According to Buddhist scriptures, suffering is an intrinsic aspect of biological existence; its deepest cause is the force that is responsible for the life process itself. The goal of the spiritual path is to extinguish the fire of life and leave the wheel of death and rebirth.

In some cultures dying means moving a step up the social or cosmological hierarchy into the world of ancestors, powerful spirits, or demigods. In others it is a transition into a blissful existence in the solar realms or in the presence of gods. More frequently, the afterlife is clearly dichotomized; it involves hells and purgatories as well as heavens. The posthumous journey of the soul to a desirable destination is fraught with perils and ordeals of various kinds. It is essential, for a successful completion of the journey, to be familiar with the geography and rules of the other world. Thus many of the cultures that believe in an afterlife have developed complicated and elaborate procedures that familiarize the individual with the experience of dying.

In all ages and in many different cultures, ritual events have existed in which individuals have experienced a powerful symbolic encounter with death. This confrontation is the core event in the rites of passage of temple initiations, mystery religions, and secret societies, as well as in various ecstatic religions. According to the descriptions in historical sources and anthropological literature, such profound experiences of symbolic death result not only in an overwhelming realization of the impermanence of biological existence but also in an illuminating insight into the transcendent and eternal spiritual nature intrinsic to human consciousness. Rituals of this kind combine two important functions: On the one hand, they mediate a deep process of transformation in the initiate who then discovers a different way of experiencing the world; on the other hand, they serve as preparation for actual physical death.

In several places specific manuals were developed to guide individuals through the encounter with death, whether experienced on a symbolic level within the framework of spiritual practices or associated with the physical destruction of the biological vehicle. The so-called *Tibetan Book of the Dead* (*Bardo Thödol*), the collection of funeral texts usually referred to as the *Egyptian Book of the Dead* (*Pert Em Hru*), and the literature from medieval Europe known as *The Art of Dying* (*Ars Moriendi*) are the best known examples of this kind.

Anthropological literature abounds in descriptions of those rites of passage conducted in various cultures at the time of important life transitions such as birth, puberty, marriage, birth of one's child, change in life, and dying. In the elaborate rituals enacted on these occasions, individuals learn to experience transitions from one stage in life to the next, to die in one role and be born and incorporated into another. In many rites of passage, with the help of psychedelic substances or powerful nondrug techniques, initiates undergo an experience of death and rebirth comparable to those occurring in ancient temple mysteries. All of the encounters with dying, death, and transcendence experienced in the rites of passage during the lifetime of an individual can be seen as profound psychological and experiential training for the ultimate transition at the time of death.

In many preliterate societies, the homogeneous, intimate, and ultimately sacred nature of the human community is the weave within which the dying individual finds him or herself. Here, the consciousness of the clan, tribe, or kingdom is more important than the distinct consciousness of the individual. It is this very factor that can make the loss of individuality experienced in dying less painful than in those cultures where ego attachment is great. On the other hand, the loss of an individual from the social fabric can have profound consequences for the living if the community is a homogeneous collective. Dying and death in the situation of *communitas* allows for both group support of the dying individual and for the expression of grief and anger on the part of the survivors, who have lost an essential person in the mystically bonded social group.

Many Westerners find that some of these approaches to death are alien to their value systems. Elaborate ritual enactments revolving around death and the emphasis on impermanence in many religious practices seem to indicate a morbid preoccupation with the macabre and are frequently interpreted in the West as manifestations of social psychopathology. A sophisticated Westerner tends to consider the belief in an afterlife and the concept of the posthumous journey of the soul as products of primitive fears of individuals who have been denied the privilege of scientific knowledge. In this context the preponderance of tribal consciousness over that of the individual appears to be a sign of psychological immaturity. However, a closer look at our own culture shows that we have moved toward the other extreme— massive denial and neglect of all the issues related to death. There are very few situations in human life that are of such paramount significance as dying and death. Every single individual has to face during his or her lifetime the deaths of close relatives and, eventually, confront the issue of his or her own impermanence and biological demise. In view of the utmost relevance of death, the avoidance and denial of the problems related to this area are truly astounding. Aging, fatal disease, and dying are not seen as a part of the life process but as the ultimate defeat and a painful reminder of the limits of our ability to master nature. With our pragmatic philosophy emphasizing achievement and success, the dying person is a loser in life's race. People in our culture are only beginning to realize that there is a lesson to be learned from an encounter with aging and dying individuals.

The contemporary medical approach to a dying person is dominated by a determined effort to conquer death and delay its advent by all means possible. In this struggle for mechanical prolongation of life at any cost, very little attention is paid to the quality of an individual's remaining days. The companions of many dying individuals are infusion bottles and tubes, oxygen tanks, electric pacemakers, artificial kidneys, and monitors of vital functions. In an effort to hide from the dying the reality of their situations, medical personnel and family members often play complicated games that obscure relevant issues and instill false hope. This further deepens the feelings of isolation and despair experienced by the dying, many of whom intuitively sense the dishonesty surrounding them.

Religion, which can be of great help for the dying, has lost much of its significance for the average Westerner. A pragmatic life orientation and philosophical materialism have replaced religious fervor. With some exceptions Western religions have lost their function as vital forces in life. They have been reduced to formal rituals and ceremonies divested of their original meanings.

The scientific world-view based on philosophical materialism further confirms the grimness of the situation that dying individuals are facing. According to this view there is no reality outside of that occurring in the material world. To perceive reality one has to be a living organism with functioning organs of perception. Consciousness itself is seen as a product of the brain, and is thus critically dependent on its integrity and normal functioning. The physical destruction of the body and brain is the irrevocable end of human life.

There is little that our contemporary social structure, or our philosophy, religion, and medical science, has to offer at present to ease the psychological suffering of the dying. Many persons in this situation are thus facing a profound crisis that is basic and total, since it affects simultaneously biological, emotional, philosophical, and spiritual aspects of the human being. Yet psychiatrists, psychologists, and other members of the helping professions who have otherwise developed systems for crisis intervention in various difficult life situations surprisingly have not until recently identified this area as one where sensitive help is urgently needed. Since a variety of situations of relatively minor importance have in the past been seen as requiring emergency measures, it is important to consider some of the reasons that have kept professionals from realizing the urgent need for assistance in this most fundamental crisis in human life.

One of the more obvious reasons, certainly, is the basically pragmatic philosophy in our achievement-oriented society. According to this view, it appears more reasonable to help somebody who has the possibility of returning to a productive life than to aid someone who will no longer be able to contribute to society and who will physically cease to exist in the near future. Work with dying individuals and their families is unusually difficult; in addition to being very demanding and involved per se, it occurs in a basically pessimistic framework. The therapist is frequently confronted with intense and painful emotions that are triggered by the extreme circumstances of the dying person as well as relatives. In traditional psychotherapy it is essential to have something concrete to offer to motivate patients and show them that they can utilize their resources for a more satisfying existence. A therapist working in a Western framework does not have very much to offer in terms of a concrete positive alternative, either for the dying person or the survivors. This area traditionally has been the domain of the clergy. However, even they frequently have very little to offer beyond words of solace, emphasis on faith, and routine ceremonial procedures.

The most important reason for the reluctance of psychotherapists and others to get involved with dying individuals is their own unconscious fear of physical suffering, biological impermanence, and death. Intimate exposure to persons facing death tends to evoke one's own metaphysical anxiety associated with the idea of biological demise. Fear of death experienced by human beings is usually attributed to an intellectual awareness of the life trajectory. Unlike animals, humans *know* that they are mortal and that sooner or later they will have to face the end of their biological existence. Later in this book we will try to demonstrate that the roots of this fear are much deeper. Observations from psychedelic research, as well as data from history, comparative religion, and anthropology, seem to indicate that we all harbor functional matrices in our unconscious minds that contain an authentic encounter with death. Activation of these unconscious structures by psychoactive drugs, or by nondrug factors and techniques, results in a dramatic experience of death that, in terms of its intensity, is indistinguishable from actual dying. Thus human beings not only know intellectually that they will die, they also possess subliminal knowledge of what it feels like to experience death. This almost cellular awareness of the process of dying seems to be the most important reason for the pervasive denial and repression of problems related to death. In the absence of any social, psychological, philosophical, or spiritual support-systems that would help counteract it, this fear seems to be the major obstacle in the work with the dying and the most critical source of reluctance to offer effective help.

Our mass media, instead of using their enormous educational potential for spreading useful information about death and dying, have contributed to distortions in this area. In mediocre movies death is presented as either an absurd event or a situation of personal defeat. In reports of mortality statistics concerning victims of war, crashes of airplanes, hurricanes, floods, earthquakes, droughts, and mass epidemics, the scale of death is so great that one cannot relate to it on a personal level. The significance of death and its psychological, philosophical, and spiritual relevance become diluted in empty numbers. This is even more true with regard to the possibility of instant and total annihilation in a nuclear holocaust; the specific, individual significance of death is completely obscured by the apocalyptic nature, technological character, and mass scale of such an event.

Because of the lack of understanding of the problems related to death, emotional blocks in this area, and the nature of social and medical institutions, most members of our society have been deprived of the opportunity to participate in the process of dying in a meaningful way. This seems to apply equally to those who are dying and to their surviving relatives or friends.

At present we are experiencing a dramatic breakthrough in the attitudes of health professionals to dying and death. An important milestone in this situation was Herman Feifel's book, *The Meaning of Death* (1957), a compendium of articles by physicians, psychiatrists, psychologists, philosophers, and theologians focusing on the problems of the dying. The years following the publication of this book have witnessed an increasing interest on the part of professionals and a growing awareness of the urgent need for change. Much of the intense effort to facilitate the situation of the dying has come from humanistically oriented professionals. An important development was the creation of the Foundation of Thanatology in New York City in 1968 by co-founder and first president Austin Kutscher, to bring together members of the helping professions, ministers, philosophers, writers, and other individuals interested in the problems related to death and the management of the dying.

This wave of professional interest in the practical and theoretical aspects of dying culminated in the work of Elisabeth Kübler-Ross, M.D., carried out at the psychiatric department of the University of Chicago. In her pioneering book, *On Death and Dying,* she has summarized her experiences in psychotherapeutic work with severely ill individuals and in training seminars conducted with physicians, nurses, students, and ministers. Kübler-Ross has given ample evidence that many dying persons are in urgent need of genuine human contact and psychotherapeutic help. She has emphasized the importance of open and honest communication with them, and of the willingness to discuss any issues that are of psychological relevance for them. If approached this way the dying can teach the survivors important lessons not only about the final stages of life but also about the functioning of the human mind and the uniquely human aspects of our existence. In addition, those involved in this process will emerge from the experience enriched and perhaps with fewer anxieties about their own deaths.

From the theoretical point of view Kübler-Ross has outlined five consecutive stages characterized by specific emotional reactions and attitudes that the dying go through as their physical condition deteriorates. Thus a typical patient moves sequentially through the stages of denial and isolation, anger, bargaining, depression, and, finally, acceptance. In the last two years Kübler-Ross has been particularly interested in exploring subjective experiences associated with dying and the problem of consciousness after death. Her work has had a profound influence in professional circles as well as on the general public. The therapeutic experiment that has been under way since 1967 at St. Christopher's Hospice in London under the direction of Cicely Saunders, M.D., is another important innovation in the care of severely ill patients. The basic orientation of the staff of St. Christopher's is to do everything to enable patients to live fully and comfortably up until the day they die. The general regime and overall atmosphere is much more relaxed and informal than in a hospital. The rules for visiting and outings are much easier than is usually possible in a ward for the acutely ill. Patients are able to sit or go for walks whenever they feel like it. They can enjoy visits with their families and other suitable activities as long as they can and wish to. They are allowed to smoke in bed, and, early each evening, drinks are on the house. The approach at St. Christopher's Hospice combines good technical care and medical skill with compassion, warmth, and friendship. Cicely Saunders' work has a very definite religious emphasis, but rather than focusing on a single religious orientation, it is ecumenical and nondenominational in nature. In addition to its fame as a truly humane approach to the dying, this facility has gained a reputation for its achievements in the effective control of chronic pain.

The helping professions seem today to be keenly aware of the importance of the problems related to dying and of the need for far-reaching changes in current medical practices and procedures in this area. The number of articles and books on death and on the management of patients with incurable diseases is rapidly increasing, as are lectures, workshops, symposia, and conferences dealing with this topic. More and more research seems to be directed toward developing effective ways of helping the dying and gaining more insight into the psychological aspects of the processes of dying and death.

The research with LSD and other psychedelic drugs conducted over the last twenty-five years has opened up new possibilities for alleviating the emotional and physical suffering of patients dying of cancer and other chronic diseases, and has offered unexpected approaches to a deeper understanding of the experiences of dying and death. The spontaneous occurrence of chemically evoked experiences of death and rebirth in psychedelic sessions of normal subjects and psychiatric patients has made it possible to realize that the potential for such experiences is inherent in the human unconscious. The possibility of inducing the phenomena of death and rebirth under controlled circumstances and in a relatively predictable way has allowed for a detailed mapping of these experiences. This book will describe the practical significance of psychedelic therapy for dying individuals and discuss the implications of psychedelic research for a deeper understanding of the process of death.

2.

THE HISTORY OF PSYCHEDELIC THERAPY WITH THE DYING

Our experience with persons dying of incurable diseases has been closely associated with the development of psychedelic therapy, a comprehensive program of brief psychotherapy utilizing mind-altering substances such as lysergic acid diethylamide (LSD) and dipropyltryptamine (DPT). Although this treatment is a direct outgrowth of modern pharmacological and clinical research, it has close parallels in various contemporary non-Western cultures and its roots reach back to prehistory and the shamanic rituals and healing ceremonies of many ancient civilizations.

The first suggestion that psychedelic substances could be useful in the therapy of individuals dying of incurable diseases came from pediatrician Valentina Pavlovna Wasson. After many years of intensive ethnomycological studies, she and her husband, Gordon Wasson, became interested in the use of psychedelic mushrooms in pre-Columbian cultures and in contemporary Central America. They made several field trips to Mexico to explore this issue, and finally in June 1955 they became the first Westerners to be admitted to a sacred ritual conducted by the Mazatec *curandera,* or medicine woman, Maria Sabina.

The Wassons were deeply impressed by the powerful effect of the mushrooms that they ingested in this ceremony. Roger Heim, the French mycologist whose aid the Wassons sought, identified the mushrooms botanically as *Psilocybe mexicana* and its congeners; he then sent samples to the laboratories of the Swiss pharmaceutical company, Sandoz, for chemical analysis. In 1957 Valentina Pavlovna Wasson gave an interview in *This Week* magazine about the history of this discovery and her own experience after the ingestion of the Mexican sacred mushooms. She expressed the opinion that if the active agent could be isolated and a sufficient supply assured, it might become a vital tool in the study of psychic processes. She also stated that as the drug would become better known, medical uses would be found for it, perhaps in the treatment of alcoholism, narcotic addiction, mental disorders, and terminal diseases associated with severe pain. Several years later a team of researchers working in Baltimore independently tested the validity of her unusual vision. A group of psychiatrists and psychologists at the Maryland Psychiatric Research Center who were not familiar with the article in *This Week* conducted systematic studies of psychedelic therapy with LSD, a drug closely related to psilocybin, for exactly the same indications that Valentina Wasson predicted. We ourselves were surprised to discover the newspaper clipping in Gordon Wasson's library during a 1974 visit to his home.

The next stimulus for the use of psychedelics with dying individuals did not come from a physician or behavioral scientist but from the writer and philosopher, Aldous Huxley. He was profoundly interested both in the phenomenon of dying and in the religious and mystical experiences induced by psychedelic drugs. With unusual sensitivity and insight he assisted his first wife, Maria, when in 1955 she was dying of cancer. During her final hours he used a hypnotic technique to bring her into touch with the memory of ecstatic experiences that had occurred spontaneously on several occasions during her life. The explicit goal was to facilitate her experience of dying by guiding her toward these mystical states of consciousness as death was approaching. This deep personal experience has its parallel in Huxley's novel *Island,* where the character Lakshmi is dying under very similar circumstances. In a letter to Humphry Osmond, a psychiatrist and pioneer in psychedelic research who introduced him to LSD and mescaline, Huxley wrote:

> My own experience with Maria convinced me that the living can do a great deal to make the passage easier for the dying, to raise the most purely physiological act of human existence to the level of consciousness and perhaps even of spirituality.

To those who are familiar with the effects of hallucinogenic drugs and with Huxley's personal history, there is no doubt that the "soma" in *Brave New World* and the "moksha medicine" in *Island* are psychedelic substances similar in their effects to LSD, mescaline, and psilocybin. In Huxley's vision "moksha medicine" gives inhabitants of the island mystical insights that free them from the fear of death and enable them to live more fully. In another letter to Humphry Osmond written as early as February 1958, Huxley was quite explicit about his idea of seriously considering the use of LSD with dying individuals:

> . . . yet another project—the administration of LSD to terminal cancer cases, in the hope that it would make dying a more spiritual, less strictly physiological process.

According to his second wife, Laura, Aldous mentioned on several occasions that "the last rites should make one more conscious rather than less conscious, more human rather than less human." In 1963, when he was himself dying of cancer, Huxley demonstrated the seriousness of his vision. Several hours before his death he asked Laura to give him 100 micrograms of LSD to facilitate his own dying. This moving experience was later described in Laura Huxley's book, *This Timeless Moment*.

Aldous Huxley's suggestion, although reinforced by his unique personal example, for several years had no influence on medical researchers. The next contribution to this area came from a rather unexpected source and was unrelated to Huxley's thinking and efforts. In the early 1960s Eric Kast of the Chicago Medical School studied the effects of various drugs on the experience of pain in the quest for a good and reliable analgesic. He became interested in LSD as a possible candidate for such a substance because of certain peculiarities of its effect on humans. He learned that LSD tends to produce a marked distortion of the body image and alterations of body boundaries; furthermore, it seemed to interfere with the ability to concentrate and maintain selective attention on a particular physiological sensation. Thus, in individuals who are under the influence of LSD, simple visual impressions may take precedence over sensations of pain or concerns related to survival. Both the effect of LSD on the body image and its interference with selective focus on significant input seemed to be worth exploring in terms of their potential for altering the perception of physical pain.

In a paper published in 1964 Kast and Collins described the results of a study in which the hypothetical analgesic properties of LSD were compared to those of two established and potent drugs, dihydromorphinone (Dilaudid) and meperidine (Demerol). In a group of fifty individuals suffering from severe physical pain were thirty-nine patients with various types and stages of cancer, ten patients with gangrenes of feet or legs, and one with severe herpes zoster (shingles). The outcome of the statistical analysis of this comparison indicated that the analgesic effect of LSD proved to be superior to both Dilaudid and Demerol. In addition to pain relief, Kast and Collins noticed that some of these individuals showed a striking disregard for the gravity of their personal situations. They frequently talked about their impending death with an emotional attitude that would be considered atypical in our culture; yet it was quite obvious that this new perspective was beneficial in view of the situation they were facing.

In a later study of 128 individuals with metastatic cancer, Kast explored in more detail some of his earlier findings. This time he was interested not only in the effects of LSD on pain but also on some additional parameters: emotional changes, sleep patterns, and attitudes toward illness and death. In view of the fact that there was no psychotherapeutic emphasis and the patients were not even informed that they were being given LSD, the results were quite remarkable. A precipitous drop in pain occurred in many individuals about two to three hours after the administration of 100 micrograms of LSD and lasted an average of twelve hours; pain intensity for the whole group (not necessarily for every patient) was decreased for a period of three weeks. For about ten days after the session, Kast observed improvement of sleep and a less concerned attitude toward illness and death.

In 1966 Kast published another paper in which he paid more explicit attention to the influence of LSD on the religious and philosophical experiences and ideas of the patients. The group he studied consisted of eighty persons suffering from terminal malignant disease, with estimated life expectancies of weeks or months, each of whom had been fully informed of the diagnosis. In contrast to earlier studies, the LSD sessions were terminated by an intramuscular injection of 100 milligrams of chlorpromazine upon the appearance of fear, panic, unpleasant imagery, or the desire to rest. The beneficial influence of a single administration of 100 micrograms of LSD on physical pain, mood, and sleep patterns was similar to the preceding studies. In addition, Kast described a variety of changes in the patients that made their situation more tolerable. He noticed improved communication both between the observer and the patients and among the patients themselves; this enhanced their morale and self-respect and created a sense of cohesion and community among them. Quite significant, also, was the occurrence of "happy, oceanic feelings" lasting up to twelve days following the administration of LSD. Kast stated explicitly that a certain change in philosophical and religious attitudes in relationship to dying took place that were not reflected in his numerical data and graphs.

In spite of what to an LSD therapist might at present appear as shortcomings in Kast's studies, the historical value of his pioneering effort is unquestionable. He not only discovered the analgesic value of LSD for some patients with intractable pain, but he also brought forth the first experimental evidence for Aldous Huxley's suggestion that the administration of LSD might ease the encounter with death in persons suffering from cancer. Kast concluded the last of his studies by stating that, according to his observations, LSD is capable not only of improving the lot of dying individuals by making them more responsive to their environment and family, but it also enhances their ability to appreciate the nuances and subtleties of everyday life. It gives them aesthetic satisfaction and "creates a new will to live and a zest for experience, which, against a background of dismal darkness and preoccupying fear, produces an exciting and promising outlook."

The encouraging results of Kast's studies inspired Sidney Cohen, a prominent Los Angeles psychiatrist, friend of Aldous Huxley, and one of the pioneers in LSD research, to start a program of psychedelic therapy for individuals dying of cancer. Unfortunately the results of his study and the details of his treatment procedure have never been published. In a 1965 article Cohen expressed his feelings about the potential of psychedelic therapy for the dying, based on his pilot experiments with a small group of patients. He stated that his own work confirmed Kast's findings about the beneficial effect of LSD on severe physical pain and suggested that LSD may one day provide a technique for altering the experience of dying. Cohen saw clearly the importance of this research endeavor: "Death must become a more human experience. To preserve the dignity of death and prevent the living from abandoning or distancing themselves from the dying is one of the great dilemmas of modern medicine."

Cohen's co-worker, Gary Fisher, later published a paper in which he discussed the personal and interpersonal problems of the dying. In this context he emphasized the significance of transcendental experiences—whether spontaneous, resulting from various spiritual practices, or induced by psychedelic drugs. As a result of such experiences the individual ceases to be concerned about his or her own physical demise and begins to see it as a natural phenomenon of the cycling of the life force. This acceptance drastically alters a person's life-style; the individual no longer reacts with panic, fear, pain, and dependency to the changes that are occurring. Rather, the patient is willing and eager to share this new knowledge with close family members and friends. Fisher discussed the use of LSD therapy within the framework of a research project where this drug was compared with an experimental analgesic and only one hour was allowed for preparing patients for the session. In spite of this limitation, he observed what he described as dramatic results in terms of pain reduction, psychological aftereffects, and adjustment of the patients to their impending deaths.

Another series of observations that was later integrated into the concept of psychedelic therapy for the dying originated in the Psychiatric Research Institute in Prague, Czechoslovakia. A research team of this institute headed by Stanislav Grof (coauthor of this book) conducted experiments in the early 1960s with psychiatric patients, exploring the potential of LSD for personality diagnostics and psychotherapy. These efforts finally resulted in treatment that involved intense psychological work and a series of therapeutic sessions with LSD. Although this approach was initially based in theory and practice on psychoanalysis, in the course of years it underwent substantial modifications and became an independent therapeutic procedure combining work on psychodynamic issues with a definite emphasis on transpersonal and transcendental experiences.

In the exploratory phase of this work, all psychiatric patients from various diagnostic categories undergoing serial LSD sessions sooner or later transcended the psychoanalytic framework and spontaneously moved into experiential realms that have been described through millennia as occurring in various schools of the mystical tradition, temple mysteries, and rites of passage in many ancient and pretechnological cultures of the world. The most common as well as the most important of these phenomena were experiences of death and rebirth, followed by feelings of cosmic unity. This profound encounter with one's own impermanence and mortality was very complex and had biological, emotional, intellectual, philosophical, and metaphysical dimensions. Experiences of this kind seemed to have had very beneficial consequences for these psychiatric patients; some very dramatic improvements of various psychopathological conditions were observed immediately following the death-rebirth phenomenon and, in particular, the experiences of oneness with the universe. This suggested the existence of a powerful therapeutic mechanism as yet unknown to Western psychiatry and psychology that appeared far superior to those used in conventional psychotherapy.

Many individuals who had the experience of death and rebirth sometimes accompanied by feelings of cosmic unity independently reported that their attitudes toward dying and their concepts of death underwent dramatic changes. Fear of their own physiological demise diminished, they became open to the possibility of consciousness existing after clinical death, and tended to view the process of dying as an adventure in consciousness rather than the ultimate biological disaster. Those of us conducting this research kept witnessing, to our great surprise, a process that bore a striking similarity to mystical initiation and involved experiential sequences that resembled those described in the *Tibetan* or *Egyptian Book of the Dead*.

The claims of changes in attitudes toward death were so frequent that it seemed important to test their practical relevance. It was obvious that a deep change of consciousness of that sort could be very beneficial for dying individuals, particularly those with chronic, incurable diseases. The first author (S.G.) then had an opportunity to work with several persons diagnosed with cancer. These pilot observations indicated that the alleviation of the fear of death earlier reported as a result of LSD therapy in psychiatric patients (most of whom were young and physically healthy) can occur also in those for whom the issue of death is of immediate relevance. At this point the Prague group began seriously discussing the possibility of working systematically with dying people, and Grof designed a research program using serial LSD sessions with individuals dying of cancer. These plans were interrupted by a fellowship granted to him by the Foundation's Fund for Research in Psychiatry in New Haven, Connecticut, that took him to the United States.

After his arrival in Baltimore in March 1967, he joined the team in the Research Unit of Spring Grove State Hospital, which later became the core of the Clinical Sciences Department of the newly built Maryland Psychiatric Research Center. Here he found, to his surprise, that some time prior to his arrival this group had been interested in exploring the potential of LSD psychotherapy for alleviating the emotional and physical suffering of cancer patients. The sequence of events that spurred the interest of the research team in this problem area, briefly described, is this: Since 1963 a group of psychiatrists, psychologists, and social workers at Spring Grove had been exploring the effects of a brief course of LSD-assisted psychotherapy on the drinking behavior, psychological condition, and social adjustment of alcoholics. In a parallel study the therapeutic potential of this new treatment was tested in a group of neurotic patients. During the assessment, based on clinical interviews as well as psychological testing, the symptoms particularly responsive to psychedelic therapy appeared to be depression and anxiety.

In 1965, when the studies with alcoholics and neurotics were well under way, the Spring Grove research team first focused its attention on the needs of dying cancer patients in an unforeseen and tragic manner. A professional member of the research team, Gloria, a woman in her early forties, developed a carcinoma of the breast. She had undergone a radical mastectomy; subsequent surgery had revealed inoperable metastases of the liver. Although still ambulatory, she was in severe physical and emotional distress. She was fully aware of her condition and her prognosis and shared her feelings of despair with staff members. On the basis of the relief of depression and anxiety frequently observed in psychiatric patients following LSD-assisted psychotherapy, Sidney Wolf, a psychologist and member of the therapeutic team, suggested that the psychedelic treatment procedure might prove helpful to his colleague. It seemed possible that her depression and anxiety, although reactive in nature and well substantiated by a painful life situation, might respond favorably to LSD therapy, as was the case in other conditions of a psychogenic nature.

After discussions with her husband, her physician, and with the approval of all concerned, a course of psychedelic therapy was initiated, with Sidney Wolf in the role of "sitter." In the treatment plan at Spring Grove the primary objective was to facilitate the occurrence of a psychedelic peak experience in the context of brief but intensive psychotherapy. The preparation for the session lasted somewhat over a week; the focus was on the issue of personal identity and on current interpersonal relationships. When most of the important areas involved were satisfactorily clarified, a 200-microgram LSD session was conducted under conditions quite similar to those used for psychiatric patients. The outcome of this pioneering experiment was quite remarkable: After careful preparation and several subsequent drug-free interviews a single LSD experience seemed to have changed the quality of Gloria's remaining days. Shortly after the LSD session she went on vacation with her husband and children. Upon her return, two weeks after the session, she completed the following retrospective report:

"The day prior to LSD, I was fearful and anxious. I would at that point have gratefully withdrawn. By the end of the preparatory session practically all anxiety was gone; the instructions were understood and the procedure clear. The night was spent quietly at home; close friends visited and we looked at photograph albums and remembered happy family times. Sleep was deep and peaceful. I awakened refreshed, and with practically no fear. I felt ready and eager. The morning was lovely—cool and with a freshness in the air. I arrived at the LSD building with the therapist. Members of the department were around to wish me well. It was a good feeling.

"In the treatment room was a beautiful happiness rosebud, deep red and dewy, but disappointingly not as fragrant as other varieties. A bowl of fruit, moist, succulent, also reposed on the table. I was immediately given the first dose and sat looking at pictures from my family album. Gradually, my movements became fuzzy and I felt awkward. I was made to recline with earphones and eyeshades. At some point the second LSD dose was given to me. This phase was generally associated with impatience. I had been given instructions lest there be pain, fear, or other difficulties. I was ready to try out my ability to face the unknown ahead of me and to triumph over my obstacles. I was ready, but except for the physical sensations of awkwardness and some drowsiness nothing was happening.

"At about this time, it seems, I fused with the music and was transported on it. So completely was I one with the sound that when the particular melody or record stopped, however momentarily, I was alive to the pause, eagerly awaiting the next lap of the journey. A delightful game was being played. What was coming next? Would it be powerful, tender, dancing, or somber? I felt at these times as though I were being teased, but so nicely, so gently. I wanted to laugh in sheer appreciation of these responses, regardless of where I had just been, how sad or awed. And as soon as the music began, I was off again. Nor do I remember all the explorations.

"Mainly I remember two experiences. I was alone in a timeless world with no boundaries. There was no atmosphere; there was no color, no imagery, but there may have been light. Suddenly I recognized that I was a moment in time, created by those before me and in turn the creator of others. This was my moment, and my major function had been completed. By being born, I had given meaning to my parents' existence.

"Again in the void, alone without the time-space boundaries. Life reduced itself over and over again to the least common denominator. I cannot remember the logic of the experience, but I became poignantly aware that the core of life is love. At this moment I felt that I was reaching out to the world—to all people—but especially to those closest to me. I wept long for the wasted years, the search for identity in false places, the neglected opportunities, the emotional energy lost in basically meaningless pursuits.

"Many times, after respites, I went back, but always to variations on the same themes. The music carried and sustained me. Occasionally, during rests, I was aware of the smell of peaches. The rose was nothing to the fruit. The fruit was nectar and ambrosia (life); the rose was only a beautiful flower. When I finally was given a nectarine it was the epitome of subtle, succulent flavor.

"As I began to emerge, I was taken to a fresh windswept world. Members of the department welcomed me and I felt not only joy for myself, but for having been able to use the experience these people who cared for me wanted me to have. I felt very close to a large group of people. Later, as members of my family came, there was a closeness that seemed new. That night, at home, my parents came, too. All noticed a change in me. I was radiant, and I seemed at peace, they said. I felt that way too. What has changed for me? I am living now, and being. I can take it as it comes. Some of my physical symptoms are gone. The excessive fatigue, some of the pains. I still get irritated occasionally and yell. I am still me, but more at peace. My family senses this and we are closer. All who know me well say that this has been a good experience.''

Five weeks after the date of the session, Gloria suddenly developed ascites (accumulation of serous fluid in the abdominal cavity) and had to be rehospitalized; she died quietly three days later.

The result of Sidney Wolf's endeavor was so encouraging that the Spring Grove staff decided to explore further the potential of psychedelic therapy for alleviating the suffering of those dying of cancer. A group of open-minded surgeons at Baltimore's Sinai Hospital expressed interest in this procedure, offered their cooperation, and agreed to refer patients for LSD therapy. Three more persons were treated at this time by Sanford Unger, a psychologist who had played an important role in launching the Spring Grove studies of alcoholics and neurotics.

The next important step in this direction was made in late 1967, when Walter N. Pahnke joined the Spring Grove team. He was instrumental in changing the intial interest of the staff into a systematic pilot exploration and eventually a research project. Pahnke's background made him ideally suited for this type of work. He was a graduate of Harvard Medical School, and in addition had a doctoral degree in comparative religion and a degree in divinity.

It is hard to imagine a more useful way to combine medicine, psychology, and religion than psychedelic therapy with dying individuals. With unusual energy, enthusiasm, and devotion, Pahnke assumed the role of principal investigator in the cancer study. After pilot experimentation he was able to obtain financial support from the Mary Reynolds Babcock Foundation. He started a research program exploring the value of psychedelic therapy utilizing LSD. Later he initiated a similar project in which a short-acting psychedelic, dipropyltryptamine (DPT), was used in lieu of LSD.

Walter Pahnke's life and work were drastically terminated in a tragic accident on July 10, 1971. While vacationing in his summer cabin in Maine, he did not return from one of his scuba-diving expeditions. His body and diving equipment were never recovered and the nature of the accident has remained a mystery. Walter's demise was a great loss for the Spring Grove team, from the personal as well as professional point of view. After Walter's death the first author (S.G.) assumed medical responsibility for the cancer study as his primary research activity and interest. His objective was not only to complete the research projects and accumulate enough data but also to formulate a theoretical framework that would account for some of the dramatic changes occurring as a result of LSD therapy. It seemed important at this point to carefully analyze the data from LSD sessions of normal volunteers, psychiatric patients, and dying individuals, and to formulate a comprehensive theory of LSD therapy based on a new model of the unconscious.

A new dimension was added to these endeavors when in 1972, Joan Halifax, the second author, joined the team as co-therapist and anthropological consultant. We could now combine our backgrounds in experimental psychiatry and medical anthropology and view the data from a broad cross-cultural perspective. It was in this process of interdisciplinary cross-fertilization, when we were working as a therapeutic dyad, sharing observations and exchanging data, that the ideas expressed in this book started to crystallize into their present form.

3.

THE SPRING GROVE PROGRAM

By 1974 more than one hundred persons dying of cancer were part of the Spring Grove program of psychedelic therapy. These individuals can be divided into four groups: the early patients, who received LSD psychotherapy in the period of pilot experimentation prior to the introduction of the rating system; those who volunteered for a systematic study of psychedelic therapy utilizing LSD; persons in whom dipropyltrytramine (DPT), a short-acting psychedelic substance, was used as an adjunct to psychotherapy in lieu of LSD; and out-of-town patients, self-referred or referred by physicians from various parts of the country, who could not be included in the main LSD or DPT study because of unavailability for the follow-up team.

Most of the people in the LSD or DPT cancer study were in- and out-patients from Sinai Hospital in Baltimore. The psychiatrist-in-charge (Walter Pahnke and, later, Stanislav Grof) spent one day a week in the oncology unit at Sinai, participating in the examinations in the out-patient clinic, attending staff conferences, and making rounds on the oncology ward. During these procedures those dying individuals who might benefit from psychedelic psychotherapy were recommended for the experimental treatment program. The primary criteria for acceptance into the program were: some degree of physical pain, depression, tension, anxiety, or psychological isolation associated with the patient's malignancy; a life expectancy of at least three months (since we were interested not only in the immediate treatment outcome but also in the duration of the results); no major cardiovascular problems, such as cardiac failure, history of myocardial infarction, high degree of arteriosclerosis, or brain hemorrhage (not because of any direct pharmacological danger from psychedelic drugs, but because they elicit powerful emotions that can be extremely dangerous for such individuals); no gross psychopathology preceding the onset of malignancy or prepsychotic condition at the time psychedelic treatment was being considered. In the later stages of research we required that there be no evidence of brain metastases or serious organic brain disease. This was based on poor results with several people treated in the early years who had brain neoplasms. A history of epileptic seizures is generally considered to be another contraindication; in persons with epileptic disposition psychedelics can occasionally trigger a rapid sequence of seizures (status epilepticus) which are very difficult to control.

If the cancer patient met these criteria, the psychiatrist and the attending physician suggested that he or she consider participating in a program of psychedelic therapy. In a special interview we explained the nature of this treatment and discussed openly with the dying individual and the family the benefits and risks inherent in this experimental form of psychotherapy. If we reached an agreement, the patient was asked to sign a consent form and was accepted into the program.

After the dying person had the initial interviews, he or she was introduced to one of the therapists at the center and the therapeutic work began. The course of psychedelic therapy consisted of three phases. The first was the preparatory period; it involved a series of interactions in which we explored the patient's past history and present situation and established a relationship of trust with the dying individual and the family. The second phase was the drug session itself; during the treatment day the patient spent many hours in a special suite assisted by a therapist and a co-therapist, always a male-female dyad. The third phase involved several interviews in the postsession period, in order to facilitate the integration of the psychedelic experiences into the dying individual's life.

The preparation phase usually lasted six to twelve hours, extending in most cases over a period of two or three weeks. Since a good relationship and an atmosphere of basic trust are the most important variables in successful psychedelic therapy, we made a great effort during the preparatory period to establish close rapport with the dying individual and to facilitate a situation of trust. The actual psychotherapeutic work focused primarily on unresolved issues between the dying individual and important persons in his or her life; problems of confronting and accepting diagnosis, prognosis, and death; and significant intrapsychic conflicts that became evident as the therapeutic relationship developed. Although the problems of dying and death were usually discussed in great detail, our emphasis was not upon death but upon living in as full a manner as possible.

In no case was psychedelic therapy presented as a potential cure for cancer. If we were asked about this issue, we talked about the importance of psychological factors in determining the course of the pathological process and the ability of the organism to defend itself against the disease. On occasion we discussed some of the hypotheses implicating psychogenic factors in the etiology of cancer. This left open the possibility of exploring the psychosomatic aspects of cancer if these emerged in the sessions, but at the same time saved patients from disappointment in the event of limited success in their endeavors to heal themselves.

Many of the discussions we had with dying individuals focused on philosophical, religious, and metaphysical issues. There are several reasons why such discussions are important in the context of psychedelic therapy with the dying. The confrontation with one's own physical impermanence can create or accentuate interest in the spiritual and philosophical dimensions of existence. The concept of death, the attitude toward dying, and the quality of a dying person's remaining days are profoundly influenced by the individual's personal philosophy and religious beliefs. Moreover, psychedelic experiences frequently have important religious or mystical dimensions, and exploring this area during the preparatory period can save much confusion during the session itself.

It is essential to discuss openly the basic conflicts that the dying can have in relation to their religious programming in childhood, church affiliation, and everyday religious practice. Clarification is frequently required regarding the patient's understanding of the role of religion and spirituality in human life and confusion regarding conflict between various creeds. For those who have strongly negative feelings about the religious aspects of psychedelic therapy, it is helpful to emphasize that spiritual experiences in psychedelic sessions usually do not take an orthodox religious form. More frequently, they resemble what Einstein referred to as cosmic religion. This form of spirituality does not involve a personified godhead, a pantheon of intermediary saints, and formalized ritual procedures. The focus is on the awe and wonder one experiences when confronted with the creative forces of nature and the many mysteries of the universal design. Spiritual feelings are associated with the dilemma of time and space, origin of matter, life and consciousness, dimensions and complexity of the universe and human existence, and the ultimate purpose underlying the process of creation. If the psychedelic experience follows one of the formally established sacred frameworks, it is usually congruent with the teachings of the mystical branches of various religions rather than their orthodox mainstream. It is thus closer to Christian mysticism than traditional Christianity, to Kabbalah or Hassidism rather than orthodox Judaism, or to Sufism rather than the Muslim faith. Frequently the psychedelic experience involves elements totally alien to an individual's own religious tradition, or is experienced in the framework of a different cultural area. Thus a Christian or a Muslim can discover the law of karma and generate a belief in the cycles of reincarnation, or a rabbi may experience a conversion to Zen Buddhism.

Prior to the drug session we had to investigate the dying individual's current interpersonal relationships, especially those with family members and hospital staff. In many instances even a superficial exploration of the person's immediate social network reveals an astounding amount of distortion and confusion in interpersonal communication with relatives, friends, attending physicians, and nurses. Denial, avoidance, projection, mechanical playing of roles, instilling of false hope, and well-meant hypocrisy can reach destructive dimensions. We frequently encountered the situation in which the staff and family members, as well as the patient, knew the diagnosis and prognosis, and yet continued playing hide-and-seek in order to "protect" each other. The death of a patient under such circumstances usually left the relatives and often the hospital staff with feelings of frustration and guilt.

An important task of the therapist was to explore the social network and identify major blocks in communication. It was not uncommon that unbelievably jangled and distorted interpersonal interactions could be simplified and made direct and open by several simple, catalyzing interventions. No one technique exists for working with the family, since each situation has its own characteristics. Depending on the nature of the problems involved, we saw family members in various combinations, both with and without the dying person. Relatives were given a chance to discuss their own feelings about the patient, the patient's disease, and the fact of imminent death. Much effort was spent in facilitating open and honest interaction, resolving interpersonal conflicts, and reaching agreement on important issues. We encouraged family members to increase their interaction on as many levels as possible, in order to decrease the psychological isolation so frequently experienced by dying individuals. With communication pathways thus opened, family members often discovered their own fear of death, which was masked by evasive maneuvers in approaching their dying relative. Similar distortions in communication were frequently found in the interaction between the medical staff, the dying individual, and family members. On most occasions medical personnel were relieved after they were told that the patient knew and accepted the diagnosis.

It was our usual practice not to confront dying individuals indiscriminately with the nature of their disease and the probable fatal outcome, though it was important for us to be willing to talk about these issues openly when a patient asked for information or was ready for such discussions. During this work it became clear that our own emotional reactions were an important factor. A therapist's fear of death or unfamiliarity with it can severely inhibit the communication process and create a situation of fearful alienation for the dying individual. We feel that our own personal experiences of death and rebirth in psychedelic training sessions began to make it possible for us to engage in a more total and honest way with those who were facing death in the immediate future.

When we had explored the major issues with the dying individual and a relationship of trust had been established, plans were made for the actual psychedelic session. In a special interview immediately preceding the drug session, the patient received specific information concerning the nature of the psychedelic experience, the range of unusual states of consciousness that can be induced by LSD or DPT, and the ways of working with the various aspects of the psychedelic state. Other important issues discussed in this interview were the modes of communicating with us during the drug's period of action and various other technical aspects of the session.

Psychedelic drugs were presented as unspecific amplifiers or catalysts that make it possible for a person to explore otherwise inaccessible areas of the unconscious and make a journey into one's own mind. In describing the LSD or DPT state, it proved very helpful to use metaphors, especially that of a "waking dream" or a vivid intrapsychic movie. We asked the patient to remain in a reclining position during the session, with the eyes covered by eyeshades, and listening to music. We encouraged the individual to face everything that emerged in the session, experience it fully, and express it; special emphasis was put on the fact that a productive session usually involved total psychological surrender to the experience.

At least one week prior to the drug session, all phenothiazine medication (tranquilizing agents) was discontinued so that it would not interfere with the effect of the psychedelic. There was no interruption of narcotic, antibiotic, cytostatic, or hormonal medication. The day before the session the patient was transferred into a private room. We tried to make this setting as comfortable and warm as a hospital environment could be. Relatives were encouraged to bring in fresh flowers, fruit, photographs, or works of art that had special meaning to the dying individual. Stereophonic equipment was set up so that the patient could become accustomed to headphones and eyeshades, both of which would be used during the hours of drug action on the following day. Usually we met with the dying individual's family to help them understand the rationale, procedure, and goals of the LSD treatment. Generally we asked that any family members who wished to be with the patient on the evening following the session be present for this preparatory meeting.

On the morning of the session day, the hospital staff gave the patient the necessary routine care earlier than usual so that the session could begin as soon as we arrived. After a short discussion with the patient, focusing on his or her emotional condition and feelings about the session, we administered the drug. If the psychedelic used in the session was DPT, it was always given intramuscularly, since this drug is ineffective when ingested. The dosages ranged between 90 and 150 milligrams, depending on the patient's physical condition, psychological defensiveness, and body weight. Since the onset of the DPT effect is almost instant and frequently dramatic, the DPT patients were asked immediately after the injection to lie down and put on eyeshades and headphones.

LSD can generally be given orally, but in the cancer study we preferred intramuscular administration in some of the patients when we were concerned about inadequate resorption or incidence of nausea and vomiting. The dosage of LSD ranged from 200 to 600 micrograms, which was similar to the range of the amount of DPT. In LSD sessions there is a latency period of twenty to forty minutes between the administration of the drug and the onset of its effect. We usually spent this time in relaxing discussions or looking at pictures and listening to quiet music. As the patient began to feel the effect of the drug, he or she was encouraged to lie down and keep the eyes covered with eyeshades. This helped the individual focus on the internal phenomena that were beginning to unfold and to prevent external distractions.

Then headphones were put in place and music was played throughout most of the session day. From this moment on, there was no difference between the approach to the LSD patients and those who were given DPT.

The choice of the session music was made in consultation with Helen Bonny, a music therapist at the research center who had much experience with psychedelic therapy. The internalization of the session by the use of the reclining position, eyeshades, and headphones intensifies and deepens the LSD experience considerably.* Music has several important functions and adds new dimensions to the psychedelic experience. It activates a variety of deep emotions, helps individuals let go of psychological defenses, and provides an enhanced sense of continuity during the various states of consciousness that occur in the session. Frequently it is possible to influence the content and course of the experience by a specific choice of music. The function of music in psychedelic sessions has been discussed in a special paper by two members of our staff, Helen Bonny and Walter Pahnke.

Nonverbal support was used whenever possible, from simple touching or holding hands to cradling, caressing, and rocking. Verbal interaction at this time was usually kept to a minimum; it took the form of encouraging the individual to confront whatever material was emerging and to express everything he or she was feeling. At intervals during the session we removed the headphones and eyeshades and briefly made verbal contact with the patient, who was given an opportunity to communicate any insights or feelings he or she cared to. In general, however, the emphasis was on experiencing and feeling; discussions of the encountered phenomena were postponed until the evening or the following day. Occasionally, especially in the later hours of the session, we used family photographs to help elicit feelings and

---

* Internalized LSD sessions conducted in a simplified and protective setting are very different from "tripping out." For the person who takes LSD in a complex social situation, the external stimuli and the emerging unconscious material form an inextricable amalgam. The resulting LSD experience tends to become, under such circumstances, an incomprehensible mixture of external perception and experiences of one's inner world; as a result of this, such situations are usually not conducive to deep self-exploration.

memories about specific persons and events that had emerged as relevant during the session.

The effect of DPT lasts for a considerably shorter time than that of LSD; after four or five hours the DPT sessions usually terminated with a relatively fast return to a usual state of consciousness. The major effects of LSD lasted in most instances between eight and twelve hours; on occasion we stayed with an individual fourteen or more hours during a session day. As the patient was returning to a usual state of consciousness, family members or good friends were invited into the treatment room for a "reunion." The patient's special condition frequently facilitated more open and honest communication and led to unusually rewarding interaction. After the visiting period drew to a natural close, we spent some more time in interaction with the patient alone. On the following day and during the next week, we helped the patient integrate the experience encountered during the session and bring these new insights into a perspective of everyday living. The basis for our work in this phase was the patient's detailed written or verbal account of the session.

When the outcome of the psychedelic session was successful, no additional drug experiences were scheduled. If the result was not satisfactory, or if at a later date the patient's emotional condition began to worsen again as the disease progressed, the psychedelic session was repeated. The decision about continuation of treatment was always made by agreement of both the patient and the therapist.

What we have described up to this point is the psychedelic treatment procedure practiced in the systematic LSD and DPT study, where the therapists had to follow the requirements of the research design. Clinical work with those cancer patients who were self-referred differed considerably from the therapeutic situation in the early pilot study and in the LSD and DPT research projects. In the pilot study the major objective of therapeutic experimentation was to collect the first clinical impressions about the potential of psychedelic therapy for cancer patients. By the time we worked with the people in the self-referred group, we already had considerable clinical experience with this treatment procedure, and the goal of exploration was to learn what psychedelic therapy has to offer under conditions unrestricted by rigid methodology. In other words, we were trying to find out in what way this therapy could best be developed in order to reach its maximum potential.

There were several important differences between the therapeutic work in this category and the two main studies. In the latter, dying individuals were referred by surgeons and other physicians from Sinai Hospital. Most of these patients came into the program in the last stages of their illness, usually after all conventional medical approaches had been tried and had failed. Most of the patients in the self-referred category bypassed this routine selection process altogether. They were usually from places other than Baltimore and contacted us after the first results of the Spring Grove program had been presented at conferences, published in scientific journals, and discussed in the media. Several of these individuals were in much earlier stages of their illness, and the work with them was generally easier and more rewarding. The rest of the patients in the self-referred category came through the usual channels. They had originally been included in the DPT study but were assigned to the control group that did not receive the drug treatment. After the time required for the follow-up, they were given the option of having a psychedelic session outside the research framework.

In the main studies the time spent with the dying individual and family members was restricted by the research design. In the self-referred group it was up to us how much time we spent with the dying individual and family in the preparation process and in the interviews after the psychedelic session. Furthermore, the two of us worked as a therapeutic dyad from the first contact with the dying individual and the family until the last meeting. This differed considerably from the situation in the LSD and DPT research projects, where the co-therapist (or nurse) usually entered the treatment process a day or two before the psychedelic session.

The drug-free interviews as well as the psychedelic sessions took place in one of two special treatment suites at the Maryland Psychiatric Research Center. When the dying individual was from Baltimore, we tried to do most of the work in the comfortable and familiar setting of the home. In the later stage of our work, we were lucky enough to get permission to run psychedelic sessions in the home. The therapeutic work in this situation was a much deeper personal experience for us as well as for the patient and his or her family, and became an invaluable source of in-depth learning about the psychology and metapsychology of dying and the value of the psychedelic experience in the encounter with death.

The changes that occur in cancer patients following psychedelic therapy are extremely varied, complex, and multidimensional. Some of them are of a familiar nature, such as alleviation of depression, tension, anxiety, sleep disturbance, and psychological withdrawal. Others involve phenomena that are quite new in Western psychiatry and psychology; especially specific changes in basic life philosophy, spiritual orientation, and the hierarchy of values. In addition to their influence on the emotional, philosophical, and spiritual aspects of existence, both LSD and DPT can also deeply modify the experience of physical pain in many different ways. Because of the complexity of these changes and the lack of specific and sensitive psychological instruments for some of them, objective assessment and quantification of results is a difficult task. This is further complicated by the physical and emotional condition of many cancer patients and their frequently negative attitude toward psychological procedures in general, which limits the use of existing instruments. During the Spring Grove studies we experimented with different methods of evaluation and did not find a satisfactory solution to the problems involved.

A study of LSD psychotherapy that included thirty-one cancer patients can be used here as an example of these endeavors.* According to the original research design, each patient was expected to complete several psychological tests before and after treatment. However, this turned out to be a rather unrealistic expectation; these tests require a degree of concentration and perseverance that for many of these se-

---

* In this section we will only briefly outline the method of assessing the therapeutic outcome and of the approach to data analysis. The interested reader will find a detailed discussion of the research methodology, quantitative data, itemized tables, and results of the statistical analysis in the original papers.

verely ill individuals was not possible, due to physical pain and exhaustion. Because of this incompleteness of test data, primary emphasis had to be placed on rating by external observers. Pahnke and Richards developed for this purpose a special instrument: the Emotional Condition Rating Scale (ECRS). This scale makes it possible to obtain values ranging from -6 to $+6$, which reflect the degree of the patient's depression, psychological isolation, anxiety, difficulty in management, fear of death, and preoccupation with pain and physical suffering. Ratings with the use of this instrument were made one day before and three days after treatment by attending physicians, nurses, family members, LSD therapists and co-therapists, and in later stages by a psychiatric social worker who functioned as an independent rater. In addition, the amount of narcotics required in the management of the patient was used as a criterion for assessing the amount of physical pain.

The effectiveness of the psychedelic treatment program was evaluated by performing tests of statistical significance on before- and after-session ratings of the clinical condition. The computations were done separately for each of the individual subscales (depression, psychological isolation, anxiety, difficulty in medical management, fear of death, preoccupation with pain and physical suffering) and also for the representatives of each of the six categories of raters (LSD therapist, co-therapist, attending physician, nurse, closest family member, independent rater).

In addition, a *composite index* was obtained for each of the categories of distress by pooling the ratings of all the raters. Therapeutic results in each of the categories were then assessed by comparing the individual composite indexes from before treatment to indexes made after treatment. For gross assessment of the degree of improvement, one *global index* of the overall clinical condition was obtained for each patient by collapsing the data from all individual raters for all the clinical categories measured. This procedure made it possible to describe the condition of the patient with a single numerical index. Although this approach obscured the specifics of the clinical problems, as well as the often surprising differences of opinion among individual raters, it was useful for comparing the results in individual patients and expressing the degree of improvement in terms of percentages of the entire group.

The clinical impressions of the often dramatic effects of LSD psychotherapy on the emotional condition of cancer patients were supported by the results of the ratings. The most pronounced therapeutic changes were observed in the areas of depression, anxiety, and pain, closely followed by those related to fear of death. The results were least dramatic in the area of medical management.

"Dramatic improvement" was defined arbitrarily as an increase of the global index of four or more points and "moderate improvement" as a gain of two to four points. Patients who showed an increase of less than two points or an equivalent decrease were considered "essentially unchanged." According to this definition nine of the patients (29%) showed dramatic improvement following LSD psychotherapy, thirteen patients (42%) were moderately improved, and the remaining nine (29%) were essentially unchanged. Only two patients had a lower global index in the posttreatment period than before treatment; in both of them the decrease was negligible (-0.21 and -0.51 points respectively).

As far as the demand for narcotics was concerned, the mean daily dose for the whole group showed a definite positive trend; however, the decrease did not reach a sufficient degree to be statistically significant. As this finding appears to be in conflict with the ratings which indicate a highly significant decrease of pain, it will be analyzed in a later chapter.

The results of the DPT study have been described and evaluated by William A. Richards,* a psychologist and therapist at the Maryland Psychiatric Research Center, who has participated in the cancer program since 1967. This project involved forty-five patients assigned randomly to the experimental or control group. Two independent raters evaluated the patients and family members, using psychological

---

* Detailed analysis of the data and discussion of the results of the Spring Grove DPT study can be found in W. A. Richards's doctoral dissertation (see Bibliography).

scales. Although in individual cases DPT psychotherapy brought quite dramatic positive results, the clinical outcome for the entire experimental group did not show a sufficient degree of statistical significance. Significant results and important trends were found in regard to certain individual scales, but in general this study did not bring evidence that DPT could successfully replace LSD in psychedelic therapy of cancer patients. This seems to agree with the clinical impressions and feelings of psychedelic therapists at the Maryland Psychiatric Research Center, who almost unanimously preferred to work with LSD if asked about it or given the option.

More interesting than the overall results of the study was Richards's effort to detect the therapeutic value of the psychedelic peak experience. In this part of the study the occurrence of these experiences was measured by the Psychedelic Experience Questionnaire (PEQ) developed by Pahnke and Richards. The emphasis in this questionnaire is on the basic categories of the peak experience as described by the authors: unity, transcendence of time and space, objectivity and reality, feelings of sacredness, deeply felt positive mood, and ineffability. Items of the questionnaire relating to each of these categories are measured on a zero-to-five scale of intensity. Another source of data was the therapist's assessment of the patients' psychedelic experience. According to Richards, the data collected in the DPT study show better therapeutic results in patients who had a psychedelic peak experience than those who did not.

One important aspect of this work will necessarily elude even the most sophisticated methodology in all similar studies conducted in the future. It is the depth of the personal experience of those who are privileged to share the situation of dying with another human being and see the psychological crisis so frequently accompanying the encounter with death alleviated or even completely reversed as a result of a psychedelic experience. Repeated participation in this special event is more convincing than numerical data, and leaves no doubt in the mind of the psychedelic therapist that this work with the dying is worth pursuing.

4.

DIMENSIONS OF CONSCIOUSNESS: A CARTOGRAPHY OF THE HUMAN MIND

To understand the profound impact that psychedelic psychotherapy can have on dying individuals, we must take into consideration the nature and specific characteristics of the experiences induced by LSD. Clinical studies of LSD conducted in the last two decades have shown us that this drug amplifies mental processes, making it possible for a person to explore various domains of the unconscious not normally accessible. An LSD session thus represents an individual's journey into the hidden recesses of the mind. Descriptions of various types of LSD experiences can then be seen as maps of the psyche or "cartographies of inner space." The patterns and sequences that characterize the emergence of unconscious material in LSD sessions are determined by a variety of external factors, such as one's present life situation, the personality of the therapist, the nature of the therapeutic relationship, and elements of the set and setting.

The content of LSD sessions entails simultaneous perception of many dimensions and levels of symbolic meaning. Although any attempt to describe such a holographic complex in linear terms involves a certain degree of oversimplification, we can distinguish four major realms or types of LSD experiences: (a) abstract and aesthetic experiences; (b) psychodynamic experiences; (c) perinatal experiences; * and (d) transpersonal experiences. In the subsequent text we will describe each of these categories and their relevance for the dying individual.†

Abstract and Aesthetic Experiences in LSD Sessions

The experiences belonging to this category are very common in LSD sessions utilizing low or medium dosages. In high-dose sessions of psychedelic therapy they are usually limited to the early stages of the sessions, before the LSD effect reaches its culmination. Only rarely do abstract phenomena occur for long periods or dominate the entire course of high-dose LSD sessions. Abstract and aesthetic experiences are characterized by dramatic perceptual changes with minimal or no psychodynamic content. The most salient aspect of these phenomena is the involvement of the optical system. Changes in the perception of forms and colors are so rich and dramatic that they have been referred to as "orgies of vision" or a "retinal circus." Sometimes there may be little actual perceptual distortion of the environment, but the environment is emotionally interpreted in an unusual way. It can appear incredibly beautiful, sensual, or comical; frequently it is described as having a magical or fairy-tale quality.

Aesthetic experiences seem to represent the most superficial aspect of the LSD state. They do not convey important psychological insights, nor do they reveal deep levels of an individual's unconscious. The most important aspects of these phenomena can be explained in physiological terms, as a result of chemical stimulation of the sensory

* *Perinatal experience* is a new psychiatric term coined by the first author (S.G.). Etymologically, the term *perinatal* is a Greek-Latin composite word; the prefix *peri-* is Greek, meaning "around" or "near," the root *natal* is derived from the Latin *natalis*, or "pertaining to birth." The term *perinatal* reflects the fact that the phenomena belonging to this category seem to be closely related to the events immediately preceding, accompanying, and following biological birth.

† For more detailed and complete discussion of the experiential categories see *Realms of the Human Unconscious: Observations from LSD Research*, by Stanislav Grof (New York: Dutton, 1976).

organs, reflecting their inner structure and functional characteristics. Similar changes can be evoked by a variety of means such as pressure on the eyeball, stroboscopic light, reduced intake of oxygen, inhalation of carbon dioxide, or electrical stimulation of the optical nerve.

Most of the dying individuals in whose LSD sessions aesthetic experiences played an important part did not feel any profound changes as a result of this event. They were usually fascinated by the extraordinary beauty of the aesthetic sequences and felt grateful for this distraction in the monotony of their days of emotional and physical agony. Only rarely have such experiences had a lasting beneficial effect. On a few occasions, however, we did observe an unexpected alleviation of severe physical pain after a predominantly aesthetic session.

Psychodynamic Experiences in LSD Sessions

The experiences in this category are derived from biographical material reflecting emotionally relevant situations in a person's past and present life. They originate in various realms of the individual unconscious and in those areas of the personality that are accessible in usual states of consciousness. The least complicated psychodynamic experiences take the form of actual reliving of highly relevant emotional events; they seem to be vivid reenactments of traumatic or unusually pleasant memories from infancy, childhood, or later periods of life. More complicated phenomena in this group represent pictorial concretization of fantasies, dramatizations of wishful daydreams, screen memories, and complex mixtures of fantasy and reality.

Psychodynamic sessions can have very important therapeutic consequences. The individual can relive and integrate various traumatic experiences from the formative period of life that have had a decisive influence on the development of the personality. The opportunity to vividly experience specific memories from different periods of one's life makes it possible to see their interrelations and discover chains of unconscious neurotic patterns underlying specific emotional problems. This can be an important transforming experience that results in profound changes in the personality structure, emotional dynamics, and behavior of the individual.

Psychodynamic experiences are quite common in psychedelic sessions of the dying. Although they do not usually mediate a profound philosophical and spiritual reevaluation of the concept of death itself, they can help dying persons reach a meaningful synthesis of earlier parts of their lives and face impending death with more equanimity. In these sessions patients can reexperience painful events and attain reconciliation and forgiveness. They can reenact past conflicts, work them through, and find emotional resolution. Where the painful awareness of unfinished projects, unfulfilled dreams, and frustrated ambitions has disturbed a patient's peace of mind and created bitterness and resentment, the individual can reach psychological closure or relinquish the need to pursue past ambitions. It is not uncommon under these circumstances for the dying to experience a condensed replay of their entire lives, with a positive evaluation preceding the final emotional detachment from the life process.* The DPT experience of Sylvia, a seventy-one-year-old woman who was dying of breast cancer with multiple metastases, can be used here as an example of a psychedelic session with a predominance of psychodynamic material of an autobiographical nature.

On the day of her session Sylvia was given 105 milligrams of DPT intramuscularly in the early afternoon hours; her experience started several minutes after the injection. Although she was lying quietly and motionlessly on the bed, with her eyes covered by sleepshades, her inner world was very rich and dramatic. When she was asked to describe what was happening, she complained of fatigue, and her body shivered; she then described a series of vivid images from her childhood that were passing in front of her eyes.

Thirty minutes later we asked for some more sharing. Although Syl-

---

* Such a complete life review can occur within a very short period of objective session time; sometimes it is a matter of several minutes or even seconds. This phenomenon bears a striking similarity to the subjective experiences accompanying accidents and other situations of vital danger, as well as those associated with clinical death.

via was still physically uncomfortable, she showed much excitement about the childhood experiences that continued to flow in front of her eyes at a rapid rate; they were now experienced against the background of a sharp awareness of death. "It has been so much, I cannot pull it all together . . . I was happy then, now I am sick and dying . . . I want to die, I want to die tonight . . . Please, God, take me . . . I do not care if I die, I want it so badly . . . Why am I suffering? I have been good in life . . . I thought only bad people suffer . . . I have been good to my children, to my husband. . . ." In this context Sylvia relived the birth of her children and reviewed their lives, including her relationship with them. At one point she suddenly saw a beautiful angel who was singing a soprano part in a choir. "I see an angel . . . A Jew is not supposed to see an angel, it is against my religion, but it is very, very beautiful . . . Oh, it's O.K., it's not an angel, it's Carol Burnett! . . ." All of us burst into laughter as she shared this last with us; this was so typical of Sylvia, whose earthy humor permeated all of our interactions.

By six o'clock the effect of the drug started wearing off, but the sequences of memories continued to unfold. "Everything that has been my life is being shown to me . . . Memories, thousands of memories . . . Periods of sadness and periods of nice happy feelings . . . With the beautiful memories, everything gets very sunny, there is lots of light everywhere; with the sad ones, all gets darker . . . I do not know why I am coming up with all these things—some of them are fifty, sixty years old . . . It is interesting, all my pain is gone, I am not thinking about pain at all. . . ." Shortly afterward Sylvia went through a period of trembling and described her feelings and experiences: "I want to shake, and I don't know why. I did not know I had tensions. I must have had them unconsciously. I guess we all go through life with some tensions . . . It was such a beautiful life; no one would believe what a beautiful life I have had. . . ."

After this episode Sylvia returned quite rapidly to her usual consciousness. Her final feeling about the session was that she had had a very special opportunity to review her life, and she said that she was content now. The experience made it easier for her to face death, since she was able to recognize and appreciate how full and rewarding her life had been. Also, the deep realization that she was leaving a beautiful host of children and grandchildren who would carry on the process of life helped her to accept her own departure.

The last time we saw her before she died, she winked her eye and said, "I'll see you later out there somewhere."

Although exploring childhood traumatizations and deep psychological conflicts is not uncommon in the course of LSD sessions of individuals dying of cancer, the emphasis in the psychodynamic experiences of these persons is usually on the urgent aspects of their present difficult situation. Frequently, long sequences in psychodynamic sessions focus on such issues as accepting the impending separation from children, spouses, and other family members; facing the inevitable weakness and subsequent dependency; coping with physical pain, loss of weight, and sometimes the gross disfiguration associated with cancer or resulting from life-saving surgery. Another frequent problem of this kind is reconciliation with one's progressive loss of libido and decreasing sexual attractiveness. In individuals who prior to their disease had a great emotional investment in their professional activities, loss of productivity and drastic termination of a career can be another area of painful conflict that has to be worked through in the psychodynamic parts of the sessions. Occasionally cancer patients who prior to the LSD session had not been explicitly aware of their diagnosis and prognosis, or had not faced and accepted it, synthesized in their sessions various partial data and observations regarding their disease and formed a realistic picture of their situation.

Quite frequent are memories involving severe physical traumas; they represent a transition between psychodynamic experiences and the perinatal realm. Typically such memories deal with threats to survival or body integrity; they cover a wide range from serious operations, painful and dangerous injuries, severe diseases, and instances of near-drowning to episodes of cruel physical abuse. Reliving of such memories is a very frequent occurrence in the sessions of dying individuals. They often confront the issue of their diagnosis, prognosis, pain, and agony as well as their impending death in the framework of past physical suffering and serious threats to life.

Episodes of a psychodynamic nature experienced in psychedelic therapy with people suffering from cancer can have a very beneficial effect on various emotional symptoms associated with this disease. Temporary or lasting improvement after such sessions involves alleviation of depression, tension, free-floating anxiety, insomnia, and psychological withdrawal. Severe physical pain that had not responded to heavy narcotic medication was occasionally mitigated or even disappeared as a result of a predominantly psychodynamic session.

Perinatal Experiences in LSD Sessions

The most important common denominator of perinatal experiences is their focus on the problems of biological birth, physical pain and agony, disease, decrepitude, aging, dying, and death. The encounter with suffering and death on the perinatal level takes the form of a profound firsthand experience of terminal agony. The awareness of death in this situation is not mediated by symbolic means alone. Specific eschatological thoughts and visions of dying people, decaying cadavers, coffins, cemeteries, hearses, and funeral corteges occur as characteristic concomitants of the death experience. Its very basis, however, is an extremely realistic feeling of the ultimate biological crisis that frequently gets confused with real dying. It is not uncommon in this situation for the individual to lose the insight that a psychedelic session is a symbolic experience and to develop the conviction that death is imminent. Death-rebirth experiences on the perinatal level are very complex and have biological, emotional, and intellectual as well as philosophical and spiritual facets.

The shattering encounter with these critical aspects of the human experience and the deep realization of the vulnerability and impermanence of the human being as a biological creature have two important consequences. The first of these is a profound existential crisis that forces the individual to question seriously the meaning of existence and any values in life. One comes to realize through these experiences that no matter what one does in life, there is no escape from physical death; all human beings will have to leave this world bereft of everything that they have achieved or accumulated. This ontological crisis is usually associated with a crystallization of basic values. Worldly ambition, competitive drive, and craving for status, power, fame, prestige, and possessions tend to fade away when viewed against the background of the ending of each human drama in biological annihilation.

The other important consequence of the often painful emotional and physical encounter with the phenomenon of death is the opening up of religious and spiritual areas that appear to be an intrinsic part of the human personality and are independent of the individual's cultural and religious background. The only way to overcome this existential dilemma is through transcendence; the crisis is resolved when people find referential points beyond the narrow boundaries of the physical organism and limitations of their own life spans. It seems that everyone who *experientially* reaches these levels also develops convincing insights into the total relevance of the spiritual dimension to the universal scheme of things.

In a way that is not quite clear at the present stage of research, the above experiences seem to be related to the circumstances of biological birth. LSD subjects frequently refer to the sequences of agony, death, and birth (or rebirth) that are so characteristic for this area as a reliving of their actual biological birth traumas. Others do not make this explicit link and conceptualize their encounter with death and the death-rebirth experience in purely philosophical and spiritual terms. Even in this latter group perinatal experiences are quite regularly accompanied by a complex of physical symptoms that can best be interpreted as related to biological birth. It involves a variety of physical pains in different parts of the body, feelings of pressure, suffocation, drastic changes in skin color, tremors, seizurelike muscular discharges, cardiac distress and irregularities, profuse sweating, hypersecretion of mucus and saliva, and nausea. LSD subjects also assume postures and move in sequences that bear a striking similarity to those of a child during various stages of delivery. In addition, they frequently report images of or identification with fetuses and newborn children. Equally common are various neonatal feelings and behavior, as well as visions of female genitals and breasts.

The rich and complex material originating on the perinatal level of the unconscious appears in LSD sessions in several typical clusters, matrices, or experiential patterns. It has proven very useful for didactic purposes, theoretical speculations, and the practice of LSD psychotherapy to relate these categories of phenomena to the consecutive stages of the biological birth process and to the experiences of the child in the perinatal period. These experiences will be briefly described in the sequence in which the corresponding phases of delivery follow during actual childbirth. In psychedelic sessions this chronological order is not necessarily followed, and individual matrices can occur in many different sequential patterns.

The Experience of Cosmic Unity

This important perinatal experience seems to be related to the primal union with mother, to the original state of intrauterine existence during which the child and mother form a symbiotic unity. When no noxious stimuli interfere the conditions for the fetus are close to ideal—involving protection, security, and continuous satisfaction of all needs. The basic characteristics of this experience are transcendence of the subject-object dichotomy, an exceptionally strong positive affect (peace, tranquility, serenity, bliss), feelings of sacredness, transcendence of time and space, ineffability, and richness of insights of cosmic relevance.

The Experience of Cosmic Engulfment

LSD subjects confronted with this experiential pattern frequently relate it to the very onset of biological delivery, when the original equilibrium of intrauterine existence is disturbed by chemical signals and later by muscular contractions. The experience of cosmic engulfment is usually initiated by an overwhelming feeling of increasing anxiety and an awareness of imminent vital threat. The source of this approaching danger cannot be clearly identified, and the individual has a tendency to interpret the immediate environment or the whole world in paranoid terms. Not infrequently individuals in this state report experiencing evil influences coming from members of secret organizations, inhabitants of other planets, evil sorcerers, and mechanical gadgets emanating noxious radiation. A further intensification of anxiety usually results in the experience of a maelstrom sucking the individual and his or her entire world relentlessly toward its center. A frequent variation of such a universal engulfment is that of being swallowed and incorporated by a terrifying monster. Another form of the same experience seems to be the theme of descent into the underworld and an encounter with various dangerous creatures or entities.

The Experience of "No Exit"

This experience is related to the first clinical stage of delivery, when uterine contractions encroach on the fetus and cause its total constriction. In this stage the uterine cervix is still closed, and the way out is not yet available. In LSD sessions this experience is characterized by striking darkness of the visual field. Individuals feel caged, trapped in a claustrophobic world, and experience incredible psychological and physical tortures. Existence in this world appears to be completely meaningless; individuals are blinded to any positive aspects of life. The symbolism that most frequently accompanies this experiential pattern involves images of hell from various cultural frameworks. The most important characteristic that differentiates this pattern from the following one is the unique emphasis on the role of the victim, and the fact that the situation is inescapable and eternal—there appears to be no way out either in space or in time.

The Experience of the Death-Rebirth Struggle

Many aspects of this pattern can be understood if we relate it to the second clinical stage of delivery. In this phase uterine contractions continue, but the cervix stands wide open; it is the time of gradual propulsion through the birth canal, mechanical crushing pressures, struggle for survival, and often a high degree of suffocation. In the terminal phases of delivery the fetus can experience immediate contact with a variety of biological material, such as blood, mucus, fetal liquid, urine, and even feces. From the experiential point of view this pattern is rather complex and has several important facets: the atmosphere of a titanic fight, sadomasochistic sequences, a high degree of sexual arousal, scatological involvement, and the element of fire.

LSD subjects in this state experience powerful currents of energy streaming through their bodies and accumulation of enormous tension alternating with explosive discharges. This is typically accompanied by images of raging elements of nature, apocalyptic war scenes, and displays of frightening technological gadgets. An enormous amount of aggressive energy is being discharged and consumed in vivid destructive and self-destructive experiences. These involve bestial murders, tortures of all kinds, mutilations, executions, rapes, and bloody sacrifices.

Sexual arousal can reach an unusually high degree and be expressed in scenes of orgies, sexual perversions, or rhythmic sensual dances. Many LSD subjects at this stage have discovered a psychophysiological link between aggression and agony on the one hand, and sexual ecstasy on the other. They have realized that intense orgiastic arousal can border on suffering, and mitigated agony can be experienced as sexual pleasure.

The scatological facet of the death-rebirth struggle involves an intimate encounter with repulsive materials. Subjects can experience themselves as wallowing in excrement, drowning in cesspools, crawling in offal, eating feces, choking on phlegm, and drinking blood or urine. This is often followed by an experience of passing through a purifying fire; its flames destroy whatever is corrupt in the individual, preparing him or her for the experience of spiritual rebirth.

Several important characteristics of this experiential pattern distinguish it from the previously described no-exit constellation. The situation here does not seem hopeless, and the subject is not helpless. The individual is actively involved and has the feeling that his or her suffering has a definite direction and goal. In religious terms this situation would be closer to the concept of purgatory than hell. In addition, subjects do not exclusively play the role of helpless victims. They are observers and can identify with both sides at the same time to the point that they can hardly distinguish whether they are the aggressors or the victims. While the no-exit situation involves sheer suffering, the experience of the death-rebirth struggle represents the borderline between agony and ecstasy and the fusion of both.

The Death-Rebirth Experience

This experiential pattern is related to the third clinical stage of delivery. The agonizing process of the birth struggle culminates, the propulsion through the birth canal is completed and is followed by explosive relief and relaxation. After the umbilical cord is cut physical separation from the mother has been completed, and the child starts its new existence as an anatomically independent individual.

The death-rebirth experience represents the termination and resolution of the death-rebirth struggle. Suffering and agony culminate in an experience of total annihilation on all levels—physical, emotional, intellectual, moral, and transcendental. This is usually referred to as an "ego death"; it seems to involve instantaneous destruction of all the previous reference points of the individual. The experience of total annihilation is often followed by visions of blinding white or golden light and a sense of liberating decompression and expansion. The universe is perceived as indescribably beautiful and radiant; individuals feel cleansed and purged, and talk about redemption, salvation, or union with God.

Perinatal experiences play a very important role in psychedelic therapy with dying individuals. Typically, death-rebirth sequences occur during the hours when high-dose sessions culminate. Only exceptionally under these circumstances does one see sessions without any perinatal elements, where the entire LSD experience unfolds in the psychodynamic area or consists exclusively of transpersonal phenomena.

The confrontation with the death-rebirth experience in a psychedelic session has a very profound influence on the individual's concept of death and dying. This experience is usually so realistic that it is perceived as experientially identical with actual biological demise. Individuals come back from perinatal sessions with great certainty that they have confronted the ultimate crisis and attained deep insight into the nature of dying and death. This experience is then used as a new model for their actual encounter with death in the future. They have discovered in their psychedelic experiences the importance of accepting, surrendering, and relinquishing. Since the experience of ego death is always followed by feelings of rebirth, any resistance against the natural unfolding of this experience necessarily means prolonging the suffering. At the same time, individuals who have suffered through the death-rebirth phenomenon in their psychedelic sessions usually become open to the possibility that consciousness might be independent of the physical body and continue beyond the moment of clinical death. This insight can be quite different from or even contrary to previous religious and philosophical beliefs. Those who were previously convinced that death was the ultimate defeat and meant the end of any form of existence discovered various alternatives to this materialistic and pragmatic point of view. They came to realize how little conclusive evidence there is for any authoritative opinion in this matter and often began seeing death and dying as a cosmic voyage into the unknown.

The characteristic change in the hierarchy of values and in time-orientation resulting from the death-rebirth sequence and from the experience of cosmic unity can also become an important factor for change in the life of the dying individual. It is not difficult to understand how disregard for worldly achievements and possessions can benefit somebody whose plans and ambitions have been drastically interrupted by a fatal disease. Similarly, increased awareness of the here and now and deemphasis on the past and future make it possible for dying individuals to live each of their remaining days as fully as possible in relative freedom from concerns about unfinished business and from anxious anticipation of things to come.

Excerpts from an LSD session of Gabrielle, a forty-two-year-old social worker suffering from an inoperable gynecological cancer of enormous proportions, can be used as an example of a psychedelic experience with a predominance of perinatal phenomena. Gabrielle had a long history of severe neurotic and borderline psychotic symptoms, and had been in intensive psychotherapy with a psychoanalytically trained hypnotherapist for several years. Her analyst brought Gabrielle to the Maryland Psychiatric Research Center primarily because of her reaction to the cancer that she had developed while in therapy. There was, however, an additional problem—lack of progress in therapy itself and difficulties in the transference relationship.

In the morning before her session Gabrielle was experiencing great anxiety and apprehension. About thirty minutes after the ingestion of 300 micrograms of LSD, she started having powerful sexual feelings all over her body and began to move gently to the rhythm of the Oriental music playing at that time. She had a strong desire to touch herself and proceeded to caress various parts of her body. As her sensuous feelings increased, her body movements became more and more serpentine until she finally identified with a large python swaying slowly with the music. When the music became more and more ethereal, the death motif entered her experience and gradually dominated it. Gabrielle saw numerous images of sick and dying people, funeral rites and processions, and cemeteries. She became painfully aware of the presence of death in human life and broke into convulsive crying. The face of her analyst then appeared in front of her eyes; distorted and grotesque, this image slowly transformed into the face of Gabrielle's mother.

As this was happening Gabrielle started feeling intense labor pains; she drew up her knees and began to push as if in birth. Feelings of agony and death became intimately linked with the struggle to be born and to give birth. At one point this effort to deliver and to be delivered appeared to be associated with her illness; Gabrielle felt that she was expelling the tumor from her body. It seemed to her that completing the birth process would actually have a healing influence on her cancer.

Then Gabrielle realized that she had been born; but the situation was far from satisfactory. She found herself lying between two large female thighs, covered with foul-smelling slime. For a long period of time she experienced herself as wallowing in feces and made repeated attempts to clean her mouth, which seemed to her to be full of excrement. She had feelings of overwhelming nausea and desperately tried to vomit. The struggle to give in and let go continued; it was expressed in a desperate need to urinate and defecate and a conflict about it. Then Gabrielle experienced violent war scenes mixed with birth sequences. She felt powerful streams of aggression coursing through her; at one point she grabbed onto Stan, who was trying to assist her, and tore the shirt off his shoulders.

The following day she felt weary and physically uncomfortable. It was not until the third day after the session that she reached a state of peace and calmness and had a positive feeling about the experience: "At times it was difficult and horrible, but it was worth it; I learned a lot about myself. I do not feel particularly joyful or exultant, but I seem to have a new sense of peace. Whatever happened in the session, I feel it was very much part of me."

In view of the serious emotional problems that had predated the onset of her cancer, Gabrielle's progress was not as dramatic as in some other patients. She had a total of six LSD sessions within a period of several months. The difficulties in the relationship with her analyst were successfully overcome and many of her neurotic symptoms were considerably alleviated. Yet, in general, her clinical condition and attitude toward death were far from ideal. Although for some time her enormous tumor seemed to be shrinking, Gabrielle died several months later, after she had developed an obstruction of the intestine from a fecal impaction.

Transpersonal Experiences in LSD Sessions

The common denominator of this otherwise rich and ramified group is the individual's feeling that his or her consciousness has expanded beyond the usual ego boundaries and has transcended the limitations of time and space. In "normal" or usual state of consciousness, individuals experience themselves as existing within the boundaries of the physical body (the body image), and their perception of the environment is restricted by the physically determined range of the exteroceptors. Both internal perception (interoception) and perception of the environment (exteroception) are confined within the usual space-time boundaries. Under ordinary circumstances individuals vividly perceive their present situation and their immediate environment; they recall past events and anticipate the future or fantasize about it. In transpersonal experiences occurring in psychedelic sessions, one or several of the above limitations appear to be transcended. In some instances individuals experience loosening of their usual ego boundaries; their consciousness and self-awareness seem to expand to include and encompass other people as well as elements of the external world. They can also continue experiencing their own identities, but at a different time, in a different place, or in a different context. In yet other cases people can experience a complete loss of their own ego identities and feel full identification with the consciousness of some other individual, animal, or even inanimate object. Finally, in a rather large group of transpersonal experiences, consciousness can appear to encompass elements that do not have any continuity with their usual ego identities and cannot be considered simple derivatives of experiences in the three-dimensional world.

Many experiences belonging to this category can be interpreted as regressions in historical time and explorations of one's own biological or spiritual past. It is not infrequent in psychedelic sessions to experience quite concrete and realistic episodes that are identified as fetal and embryonal memories. Many subjects reported vivid sequences experienced on the level of cellular consciousness that seemed to reflect their existence in the form of the sperm or ovum at the moment of conception. Sometimes the regression appears to go even further, and the individual has a convincing feeling of reliving memories from the life of his or her ancestors, or even of drawing on the racial and collective unconscious. On occasion, LSD subjects reported experiences in which they identified with various animals in the evolutionary pedigree or had distinct feelings of reliving memories of their existence in a previous incarnation.

Some other transpersonal phenomena involve transcendence of spatial rather than temporal barriers. The experience of the consciousness of another person (dual unity), group of persons, or of all mankind belongs here. In a similar way, one can transcend the limits of the specifically human experience and tune into what appears to be the consciousness of animals, plants, or even inanimate objects. In the extremes, it is possible to experience consciousness of all creation, of the whole planet, or of the entire material universe.

Another phenomenon related to the transcendence of usual spatial limitations is consciousness of certain parts of the body, such as various organs and tissues, or even individual cells. An important category of transpersonal experiences involving transcendence of time and/or space are various ESP phenomena such as out-of-body experiences, telepathy, precognition, clairvoyance and clairaudience, and space or time travel.

In a large group of transpersonal experiences, the extension of consciousness seems to go beyond the phenomenal world and the time-space continuum as we normally perceive it. Quite common, for example, are experiences of encounters with spirits of deceased human beings or suprahuman spiritual entities. LSD subjects report numerous visions of archetypal forms, individual deities and demons, or even complex mythological sequences. Intuitive understanding of universal symbols or the arousal of Kundalini and activation of various *chakras* are additional examples from this category. In the extreme form the individual consciousness seems to encompass the totality of existence and identify with that of the universal mind. The ultimate of all experiences appears to be the Void, the mysterious primordial emptiness and nothingness that contains all existence in a germinal form.

Activation and opening of the transpersonal area in the unconscious of dying individuals can have far-reaching consequences for their concepts of death, their attitudes toward the situation they are facing, and their abilities to accept physical mortality. Different types of transpersonal experiences have specific relevance for the individual encountering death. When transpersonal experiences reach the level of conscious awareness and are integrated into the individual's psyche, there is generally a dramatic redefinition of his or her concepts regarding the dimensions of the human mind, the basic characteristics of consciousness, and the nature of man. Those who see themselves as an insignificant and impermanent speck of dust in an immense universe become open to the possibility that the dimensions of their own beings are commensurate with the macrocosm and microcosm. Consciousness here appears as a primary characteristic of existence, preceding matter and supraordinated to it, rather than being a product of physiological processes in the brain. It seems to be quite plausible that consciousness and awareness are essentially independent of the gross matter of the body and brain, and will continue beyond the point of physical demise. This alternative is experienced in a way that is at least as complex, vivid, and self-evident as the perception of reality in usual states of consciousness. The transcendental impact of these experiences is usually stronger in those individuals who, prior to entering the transpersonal realms, went through the experience of ego death and rebirth. The memory that consciousness emerged intact from this seemingly final annihilation constitutes a powerful emotional and cognitive model for understanding the process of actual death.

The possibility of full conscious reenactment of episodes from the lives of remote human and even animal ancestors, as well as the vivid reliving of complex racial and collective memories, can convey a strong feeling that time is a relative and arbitrary concept that can be transcended. The existence of the experiences of dual unity and group consciousness, as well as plant and animal identification, or consciousness of inorganic matter, suggests that the spatial limitations restricting individuals within the boundaries of their physical bodies do not operate in the realm of spirit. In psychedelic sessions all of the elements in the universe in its present form and throughout its history can be consciously experienced by the individual.

It is not surprising that, on the basis of such observations, LSD subjects often arrive at the conclusion that no real boundaries exist between themselves and the rest of the universe. Everything appears to be part of a unified field of cosmic energy, and the boundaries of the individual are identical with the boundaries of existence itself. From this perspective the distinction between the ordinary and the sacred disappears, and the individual—who essentially *is* the universe—

becomes sacralized. The universe is seen as an ever-unfolding drama of endless adventures in consciousness, very much in the sense of the Hindu *lila,* or divine play. Against the background of this infinitely complex and eternal cosmic drama, the fact of impending individual destruction seems to lose its tragic significance.

In this situation death as we frequently see it—the end of everything, the ultimate catastrophe—ceases to exist. It is now understood as a transition in consciousness, a shift to another level or form of existence. For those who have experienced the Supracosmic and Metacosmic Void, existence itself can become relative. As in Buddhism, they can see form as empty and emptiness as form. They can watch the unfolding of their personal dramas with deep involvement as well as philosophical and spiritual nonattachment. This attitude toward events in the phenomenal world has been compared by LSD subjects to being in an extraordinary play or watching a film. Such an approach makes it possible for the individual to participate fully in all the experiential qualities of the life drama, with its infinite nuances. However, when the emotional impact of the situation becomes too overwhelming, it is possible to resort to the "as if" framework, to a higher level of abstraction, in which the sequences and elements of events are not ultimately real. Striking parallels exist between this approach to the phenomenal world as we know it in everyday life and the Hindu concept of *Maya,* according to which objective reality is a special form of metaphysical illusion or even delusion.

Another category of transpersonal insight that is of utmost relevance for the dying is the opening of the karmic realm and the area of past incarnation experiences. This can sometimes happen in a very general form, where individuals see the evolution of life in terms of endless cycles of deaths and rebirths governed by the law of karma. On other occasions these experiences are more specific and depict the continuity of sequential incarnations. Individuals can see the possibility that they have existed many times prior to the present lifetime, and also that their karma will require further incarnations in the future. Sometimes both of these alternatives can be combined into one complex, multidimensional experience, and individuals can see the unfolding of their own karmic monad within the much broader framework of the death-rebirth cycles.

No matter what concrete form the insights into incarnation and karma take, they seem to have a profound impact on the dying person. They usually do not result in an irrefutable conviction about the existence of the law of karma and the fact of reincarnation, but rather in the acceptance of this possibility as a very plausible alternative to nihilistic and pessimistic Western concepts. Even from this point of view, the perspective of the continuation of life in another form has a very liberating effect on the individual and can considerably alleviate despair and the fear of death.

One more experience described in the transpersonal section deserves notice in this context. The phenomena of leaving one's body and out-of-body travel can contribute considerably to the subject's feeling that consciousness can exist independently of the physical body and continue beyond the point of physical death. In addition, such experiences can be of great practical significance for the dying. On several occasions patients who had psychedelic sessions later experienced brief episodes of deep agony and coma, or even clinical death, and were resuscitated. They not only described definite parallels between the experience of actual dying and their LSD sessions, but reported that the lesson in letting go and leaving their bodies, which they had learned under the influence of LSD, proved invaluable in this situation and made the experience much more tolerable.

The incidence of transpersonal phenomena in LSD sessions increased with the number of exposures to the drug. During psycholytic therapy in Prague, where we used repeated administrations of the drug, it was quite common to observe sessions that were purely transpersonal in nature. In the Spring Grove cancer program the number of sessions was small; although transpersonal sequences occurred regularly, they were usually combined with psychodynamic and perinatal elements. The following excerpts are from an LSD session of Catherine, a sixty-year-old businesswoman suffering from breast cancer and carcinoma of the intestines with metastases in the liver. The dosage used was 400 micrograms.

Catherine started feeling intense nausea, but the sensation did not seem to have a physical quality; it had a distinctly spiritual undertone. Then things quieted down and, after a brief period of calmness, Catherine started seeing beautiful emeralds and opals in soft green and bluish colors, spinning and cascading from a height. A magnificent beam of light was illuminating them; it was brilliant and seemed to be coming from inside her. The precious stones and jewels appeared to have a much deeper meaning than being just things of beauty. The green light emanating from them was of a spiritual nature and was relieving her from her sorrow and physical pain.

Then all the beauty disappeared and Catherine began reviewing various aspects of her life. Tears were pouring down her cheeks as she relived the frustrations of her childhood, confusions of her sexual history, failures of her marriage, and the humiliation she had experienced as a Jew. Through this cleansing and purging life-review much of her caustic self-hatred was transformed into biting humor. She even started experiencing, for the first time in her life, what she felt were genuine feelings of love.

Later in the session the music sounded louder and louder, like a cyclone spinning at incredible speed, like a tornado tearing her gut. The music was building up and getting very wild and angry. It scooped her up and threatened to throw her out into space, where nothing would be left of her. She was fighting the sucking force of this whirlpool and felt that if she would let herself be drawn into the middle of this vortex she would be stripped of flesh, bones, everything, so that there would be nothing of her left. Then it seemed that a vicious battle was going on, fought with very primitive weapons such as swords, daggers, halperds, and crossbows. Catherine was deeply involved in this primitive warfare; she was fiercely hacking away and being hacked in turn. As this was happening she felt she was being carried upward and held by the music. Two wheels of music were lifting her up and thrusting her forward; the pressure was unbearable, and she was afraid she might burst and explode any moment. It seemed like a gigantic A-bomb would go off any second, much larger than anything known on earth, one that would destroy the whole universe, not just one area. She felt that her face was very brittle, like the finest china, and could hear tiny bones breaking in her cheeks and her head. It seemed that her skull cracked, and blood was rushing out from the place where it had been shattered into a thousand pieces and was flooding her face. She felt like a little helpless baby struggling to be born and choking on something in the process of delivery. The experience seemed to have what Catherine called "shimmering coming togetherness." It culminated in a vision of a gigantic wheel reaching into infinity. Along the edge of the wheel, on its infinite rim, were all the religions of the world, radiating toward the center and outward. They were represented by various symbols and cryptic inscriptions. Catherine was standing in the middle of this wheel, caught right in the center, attracted, lured, and pulled apart by all these religions. All the religions wanted her and competed for her, putting forward the best they had to offer. Every time Catherine was ready to succumb to one of them or another, she found their flaws and weaknesses and changed her mind. Then the wheel was rotating faster and faster until Catherine could not discriminate any more. She was totally immobilized, completely still in the center of time and space, and the wheel that contained many creeds finally fused into one. Everything was flooded by warm and soft golden light; she floated and bathed in it, feeling cradled and comforted. This unified divine vision seemed to be what she had been craving and waiting for her whole life. She remained just one little step from a total fusion and oneness; just before she was able to merge with the divine light, she realized that the Godhead is always male, and she could not surrender and join completely.

Nothing dramatic happened in the session after this climax. Catherine felt immersed in a warm, golden glow and experienced herself as loving and being loved. When we gave her strawberries with fresh whipped cream, it was a thoroughly ecstatic experience for her: "This was the most fantastic meal I have ever had in my whole life. It was sensuous and the tastes were unbelievably distinct. Joan, sometimes I cannot tell if you are my mother, my sister, or my daughter. You are so many things to me."

Later in the evening she felt enormous gratitude for her experience and the cosmic insights; she saw them as a special grace and privilege. It seemed to be connected with two experiences that had the quality of past incarnation memories. In one of them she identified with a Greek scholar in bondage to a wealthy Roman and a tutor to his children. Although he knew he was subjugated, he felt above the situation and free in his mind. In the second, she was herself with a shaved head and dressed in saffron robes, like an Oriental monk.

Catherine saw the session as a very important event in her life. Prior to her experience she had been severely depressed and had made serious attempts to procure an effective poison for herself. Her preoccupation with suicide now disappeared completely. She felt as if she had begun a completely new chapter: "I have been *existing* all these years; I started to *live* this past Friday. I honestly feel that I am a new person, with a completely new mind. Even my body feels different; I am pain-free."

5.

THE HUMAN ENCOUNTER WITH DEATH: PSYCHEDELIC BIOGRAPHIES

In the preceding chapters we described the principles of psychedelic therapy with the dying and summarized our observations in this area. It seems important to complement this generalized information with individual histories which will offer more concrete and intimate insights into the nature of the psychedelic procedure. We have selected individuals with whom therapy was fully or at least partially successful; each of their stories illustrates certain important aspects of psychedelic therapy with cancer patients.

Matthew's situation required only minimal work with the family; being a physician, he was fully aware of the problems he was facing and so were his close relatives. Communication in the family was open and honest. It was a pragmatic and atheistic orientation that was his major problem in facing and accepting death. His experiences illustrate that elements of mystical consciousness can occur in psychedelic sessions of well-educated, skeptical, and scientifically oriented individuals.

Ted was in many respects on the opposite side of the spectrum. His education was very limited and he was fairly open to a religious world-view. Communication in his family was disoriented and complicated, and required much psychological work.

Jesse was an almost illiterate person who in his psychedelic session discovered and adopted a complex metaphysical system that involved belief in reincarnation. The psychological power of his new spiritual vision was so great that it helped him overcome his excessive fear of death and give up his desperate clinging to life.

Susanne benefited from psychedelic therapy in many important ways, but her main problem—excruciating pain—was not alleviated. She was, however, able to work through her fear of palliative surgery, which brought her the sought-for relief. John, on the contrary, can be used as an example of the capricious effect of psychedelic therapy on pain. After what seemed at first to be an unsuccessful session, his agonizing pain disappeared completely for several months.

Joan's history is an example of the potential of psychedelic therapy at its best. As a result of her three LSD sessions, she underwent a profound spiritual transformation that totally changed the quality of her remaining days. The way she handled everyday situations as well as the practical circumstances of her death was a constant source of awe and wonder among her relatives and friends. In addition, her husband, who was a professional, was able to have psychedelic sessions within the framework of our LSD training program. This helped him not only to understand better the process of Joan's dying but also to work through some of his own feelings concerning cancer and death.

MATTHEW

Matthew was a forty-two-year-old internist suffering from inoperable cancer of the pancreas. He was well acquainted with our program; several years earlier he had referred one of his cancer patients to us for psychedelic therapy, which had proven very successful. Since Matthew's wife described his condition on the telephone as critical, we responded to their request for LSD therapy immediately and went to their home the same day.

We found Matthew extremely weak, anxious, and full of despair.

He had many unpleasant physical symptoms, such as pain, nausea, feelings of fullness, belching, flatulence, and progressive loss of appetite and weight. Matthew was fully aware of his condition, not only in terms of diagnosis and prognosis but also with regard to the stage and progress of his malignancy. He regularly received his laboratory findings and followed his own case, assessing the progressive deterioration of his physiological functions. He had even diagnosed a minor pulmonary embolism that his attending physician had overlooked.

Matthew seemed completely overwhelmed by what was happening to him. His health had always been perfect and his life rewarding and successful. When the disease struck him he had a beautiful wife, a good marriage, three children, and a well-established medical practice. He was unprepared emotionally, philosophically, and spiritually for this unexpected turn of destiny. Religion had never meant much to him, and his whole approach to life had been highly rational and pragmatic.

As Matthew's suffering increased he wondered about the absurdity of his disease, asking why and how this had happened to him. His attitude toward the disease had been much better until about two weeks prior to our first visit, when he was surprised by an episode of severe pain that lasted several days. Although the pain had finally been controlled by morphine, the severe depression and anxiety that had been precipitated by the pain continued. An attempt to tranquilize him with chlorpromazine was highly unsuccessful; if anything, the medication made him feel more depressed, defeated, and hopeless. The degree of Matthew's physical and emotional distress was such that he experienced every day as an unbearable torture. He begged us to shorten the preparation to the absolute minimum and run the session as soon as possible. We decided to condense the preparatory work into two days; during each of these days we spent many hours talking with Matthew and his wife, children, and parents. Although this time was relatively short, we had the good fortune to establish a close relationship with all the persons involved, and we obtained the necessary information about Matthew's past and present situation.

In spite of Matthew's serious condition the interaction between him and his wife was very good; it was one of the rare examples of honest and open communication that we encountered in our work. The only complication the couple was facing at the time we met them was related to Matthew's problem with intimacy. Deborah's impulse was to move toward him and be physically close and loving. Because of lack of contact in his childhood, Matthew was not comfortable with this approach. He considered physical intimacy a prelude to sexual intercourse. As a result of his severe somatic condition, he could not perform sexually any more; he experienced Deborah's closeness as a painful reminder of his inadequacy and tended to withdraw. Furthermore, he believed that he had to cope with his situation by himself, and saw this kind of support as infantilizing and not dignified for an adult. Matthew's most important solace under these circumstances was music. He was a musician himself and in the past had made attempts at composing. While listening to classical music he could occasionally get so absorbed that he forgot about his serious condition.

In spite of our relatively brief contact, we felt so clear about our relationship with Matthew and the situation in his family that we decided to conduct the session without delay. At Matthew's request we obtained special permission to run his session at home instead of in the hospital ward. As we were discussing the range of experiences that can occur in LSD sessions, Matthew showed great curiosity but was incredulous and skeptical about the religious dimensions of the procedure. We suggested that he approach the session as a scientific experiment, try to be as open as possible, and draw his own conclusions after the experience was over.

On the day of his session Matthew received 200 micrograms of LSD; the drug was given intramuscularly because we were concerned about the quality of resorption from his gastrointestinal system. The latency period seemed to be longer than usual. For over an hour Matthew appeared to be completely normal; later his behavior became unusual, but he was still denying that anything was happening. He was lying on the mattress with headphones on, listening to classical music; occasionally he would toss and turn, and had episodes of difficult breathing. The fact that the visual dimension was almost entirely absent from his session made it more difficult for Matthew to identify clearly the onset of the LSD experience. Soon there was no doubt, however, that he was in an altered state of consciousness. He became ecstatic about the quality of the music; he kept asking us to listen carefully and tell him whether we had ever heard anything so fantastic. The music sounded divine; he was losing his boundaries and merging with its flow.

Quite early in the session Matthew felt an intense need for warmth and reached for Joan (the second author). She responded immediately and held and cradled him for more than four hours. He continued listening to the music in this way with an ecstatic expression on his face; his features showed an unusual mixture of infantile bliss and mystical rapture. He was uttering seemingly disconnected sentences that sounded alternately like excerpts from Buddhist texts and accounts of Jewish and Christian mystics: "One world and one universe . . . all is one . . . nothing and everything . . . everything and nothing . . . nothing is everything . . . let it go when it's time . . . it does not make any difference . . . disease . . . injury . . . it is either the real thing or it is not . . . lower forms and higher forms . . . the glittering extremities of his majesty's possession . . . so I am immortal . . . it is true! . . ."

Deborah, who occasionally came to the door of the living room where the session was taking place, could not believe that these statements were coming from her pragmatic husband. On the sixth hour she came in and took Joan's place in cradling Matthew; he was still in the eyeshades and headphones and barely noticed the shift. They spent a long time in a quiet embrace. Then Matthew took off his eyeshades and enjoyed a glass of orange juice. His eyes on Deborah, he felt overwhelmed by feelings of great love and closeness.

While he was coming down from the session, Matthew encountered intense physical discomfort. He felt constipated and made desperate efforts to move his bowels. He felt that this was the only obstacle that he had to overcome to return to a blissful state. He believed that if he could empty his bowels, he would "reach the whole world." The constipation was, however, so severe that he had to be relieved by an enema. Later that day Matthew wanted to take a bath. He sat in the bathtub for almost an hour, listening to music and enjoying himself as he was bathed. He then spent the evening again listening to music, discovering entirely new dimensions in pieces that he knew quite well. Feelings of intestinal pain were the only discomfort in his otherwise pleasant condition.

To our surprise, Matthew did not seem to be able to reconstruct the sequences of his LSD experience and did not remember much of its content. The degree of his memory lapse was quite extraordinary; most people clearly remember the major events of their sessions. All Matthew could communicate was his global feeling about the day. He felt that the experience was unbelievably beautiful; he had never experienced anything like that in his whole life. It was "being in a warm cocoon, surrounded by unending love; feeling helpless, but happy and safe." The most powerful experience was lying on the mattress with Deborah, embracing her, and feeling that he was melting into her. As Matthew recounted this they were both very moved and cried together. Before we left that evening Matthew summmarized his feelings about the session: "Whether this helps or not, I want you to know that I am very grateful for what happened today. It was truly the most beautiful and fulfilling day of my life. I can't see how this could do any harm. . . ."

Two days after the session Matthew had to be rehospitalized because of a complete intestinal obstruction. This was a harsh reminder of the rapid progress of his disease, and Matthew started slipping back into his depression. Since he had a private room in the hospital, we installed a phonograph to make it possible for him to benefit from the effect of music. We also brought the records that were played during his session; it had been our experience that the music that was associated with unusual states of consciousness has a special propensity to reactivate the same state of mind. In a special session Joan used a relaxation technique combined with suggestion. She reminded him that he had the option to focus on his disease and physical suffering or to reconnect with the experience from his LSD session. After about twenty minutes Matthew moved into a peaceful state of mind; with the help of

Deborah and the music, he was able to maintain it for his several remaining days. Deborah stayed with him for many hours each day; Matthew's block against intimacy seemed to have been lifted permanently through his LSD session, and he enjoyed physical closeness enormously. Matthew and Deborah both told us independently that this was the most meaningful period in their marriage.

We had planned to go to Hartford for two days, and before leaving Baltimore we visited Matthew in the hospital. His physical condition was deteriorating rapidly and we felt that this might be the last time we would see him. He evidently shared our feelings. At the end of our visit he told us: "It makes no sense to fight it any longer, if it is time to leave. . . . Do not worry, it is all right. . . ." While we were staying in a downtown Hartford hotel, Joan woke up at three o'clock in the morning from a dream about Matthew, in which he appeared to her smiling and repeating his last words: "It is all right." She had the distinct feeling that Matthew had just died. When we called the hospital the next morning, the attending physician told us that Matthew died at three A.M. that day.

We attended Matthew's funeral and the *Minyan* service for him, and stayed in touch with the family during their mourning period. The recovery was surprisingly easy, considering the close bonds existing in the family. This suggested to us that the severity of loss is not necessarily the most important factor determining the nature of grief. What we had witnessed clearly indicated that the feeling of meaningful participation in the process of dying can take away much of the despair of the survivors.

TED

Ted was a twenty-six-year-old Afro-American suffering from an inoperable cancer of the colon; he was married and had three children. Our research team contacted him late in 1971 in the Out-Patient Clinic of Sinai Hospital as a potential candidate for the DPT study. At that time his major complaint was almost constant intolerable pain in the abdomen. In addition, he was severely depressed, irritable, and anxious, and had considerable difficulties in his interpersonal relationships, particularly his marriage. The interaction between him and his wife, Lilly, was very unsatisfactory and complicated. There was a deep sense of alienation between the spouses; periods of stubborn silence alternated with angry encounters in which they accused each other of various things, most frequently lack of interest and affection.

Six years earlier, when Ted's disease was first diagnosed and he had to undergo a colostomy, Lilly was told by the attending physician that his condition was very serious and that he had only several weeks to live. She was strongly advised not to disclose his diagnosis and prognosis to him, since he might have a desperate reaction and perhaps even commit suicide. Ted's will to live and his physical resistance were enormous, and the time of his survival surpassed all expectations. During the months and years when he was defying his disease, Lilly anxiously avoided any allusions to his diagnosis and prognosis. As a result of this their interaction became mechanical, superficial, distorted, and increasingly painful. Lilly had extramarital relationships, became pregnant by another man, and had to have an abortion. Ted, in spite of his severe clinical condition and the handicap imposed on him by his colostomy, had an affair with another woman, who became pregnant.

After a brief interview Ted was accepted into the program, but as a result of the random assignment in the research design, he was referred into the control group. After the follow-up period was over the patients in the control group had the option of having psychedelic therapy outside the framework of the study. Ted and Lilly expressed interest in a course of psychotherapy including high-dose LSD sessions. In a private interview Lilly stated her condition for giving her consent. She insisted that the diagnosis and prognosis not be disclosed to Ted or discussed with him in the procedure. Our experience had been that sometimes the patients with whom the situation could not be openly discussed discovered the truth themselves in the course of psychedelic therapy. In view of Lilly's strong feelings on the subject, we decided to accept Ted with this restriction and started therapeutic work.

In the preparation we briefly reviewed Ted's stormy personal history. His entire childhood was characterized by severe emotional deprivation and outright physical abuse. He lost both parents at the age of three and spent several years in various orphanages. Finally he ended up in the house of his uncle and aunt, who became his foster parents. In their home he suffered much rejection and cruel emotional and physical abuse. During his childhood and adolescence Ted was involved in minor antisocial activities, had frequent fistfights with individuals in the framework of street-gang skirmishes, and liked rough entertainment. Later he enjoyed his involvement in the war, where his aggressive tendencies found a socially approved channel. In marriage, he was extremely jealous of Lilly, but had strong tendencies toward extramarital affairs himself.

First LSD Session

On the day of the session Ted was given 300 micrograms of LSD. At the very onset of the drug action he became confused. Since this was his first session he was not familiar with the effects of the drug. He felt he was losing reference points and did not know what was happening; he compared it to floating on a cloud. He started thinking about his family and present life, and saw before his eyes the faces of his three children. Then the scene changed, and Ted and Lilly were participating in a television show, something like "This Is Your Life"; the children were in it, too. Later the experience deepened and Ted found himself in an atmosphere of a big hospital; he was lying in an operating room, surrounded by surgical instruments, infusion bottles, syringes, life-maintaining gadgetry, X-ray machines, orderlies, and nurses. He was a patient being operated on by a surgical team; he was not sure whether this was a reliving of one of his real operations or a situation that he was just imagining. He felt he was close to death and saw many people in similar situations—soldiers dying in wars, adults and children perishing in epidemics, and various persons killed in accidents. Somehow he could, however, see beyond death; nobody involved in these situations really died; it was merely a transition into a different kind of existence. He saw eternal cycles of life and death unfolding in front of his eyes. Nothing really got destroyed; everything was in eternal flux and transformation.

He then felt transported into his childhood and started reliving various episodes of physical and psychological abuse that he had experienced in his aunt and uncle's house. The feeling was so deep and real that he lost the critical insight of being in an LSD session. Stan (the first author) was transformed into his uncle and Ilse (the cotherapist) into his aunt. Ted felt deep mistrust toward both of them and experienced himself as trapped, cornered, and suffocating. In a state of fear and panic, he made several attempts to get up and leave the room, some of them quite assertive and aggressive. Ilse was in the second half of her pregnancy at the time of the session, and her condition seemed to attract Ted like a magnet; much of his aggression was focusing on Ilse's full abdomen. On several occasions he tried to send her out of the room: "Lady, you better get out of here, it is too dangerous for you here." Ilse, who approximately a year prior to this session had lost a baby in the sixth month of her pregnancy, was naturally sensitive to these threats and moved into the corner of the treatment room. Ted's mistrust was increasing to a critical level. As we later discovered, two more factors were involved in this experience. Memories of Ted's indiscriminate killing during the war were coming to the surface, and he felt we were brainwashing him to confess. On the deepest level, he perceived Stan as the devil, who was tempting him and trying to steal his soul. In the most critical moment of the session, when Ted's paranoia was culminating, a penetrating and shrill siren went off; it sounded for three entire minutes, announcing a fire drill. The fire inspector and his helper appeared at the door, asking resolutely that we evacuate immediately. Keeping one eye on Ted, whose mistrust was further nourished by this strange scene, and the other one on Ilse, whose safety was endangered, Stan tried to explain to the two men determined to carry out their duty the exceptional nature of the situation. This was by far the most difficult episode that we have experienced during our psychedelic work, and, for a while, Ted's session appeared to be a total failure. To our surprise, however, in the termination period all of the problems were resolved and integrated. Ted was able to move into an ecstatic, free-floating, and painless state. He felt that he had gotten rid of much material that had been bothering him for years. His enthusiasm about the LSD experience was without end, and before the session was over he talked about having another one. The outcome of the first session was, however, so good that it did not seem necessary or desirable to run another in the near future. Ted's pain was reduced to the point that he stopped taking analgesics and narcotics. Although previous to it he was bedridden, he now took on a voluntary job and was able to keep it for several months. In addition, he was doing all kinds of minor things around the house.

Ted's clinical situation started deteriorating rapidly around Thanksgiving, five months after the first LSD session. He was getting depressed and progressively weaker; his pain returned and was reaching an intolerable level. Lilly contacted us by telephone and asked for help. Ilse, who was the co-therapist in the first session, had discontinued her work in the center; she had delivered in the meantime and was staying home to take care of her baby. Joan agreed to take her place in working with Ted. We had several long meetings as a preparation for the second session; in addition, there was much telephone contact among Joan, Lilly, and Ted. We spent a great deal of time exploring the recent situation, Ted's condition, and the patterns of interaction between him and the other members of the family; during these talks Lilly's love and genuine concern for Ted soon became obvious. Yet there was a considerable degree of alienation between them. It seemed that their stunted and chaotic interaction was a direct derivative of their inability to communicate about Ted's disease, diagnosis, and prognosis. At this time, however, Lilly was accepting the idea that this situation should be clarified; playing the hide-and-seek game had become an almost unbearable burden for her.

In a private talk with Ted we found out that he had suspected his diagnosis from the very beginning, since he had overheard two interns discussing it outside the door of his hospital room. Later he had confirmed his suspicion by finding in a medical book that the only indication for one of the drugs he was taking was cancer. Since Lilly did not discuss the diagnosis with him, he presumed that she had not been told. He decided to conceal the truth from her, being convinced that she would leave him if she knew he had cancer, saying to us, ''Who wants to live with a man who has cancer?'' In a rather stormy episode we catalyzed the exchange of the ''secret'' between the spouses. After an initial aggressive outburst and mutual accusations of dishonesty, both Lilly and Ted were extremely happy about the new, open situation: Lilly because she did not have to lie and pretend any more, Ted because he discovered, to his surprise, that Lilly had stayed with him for six years in spite of the fact that she knew he had cancer.

Another important area of our discussion was the intimate and sexual interaction between the spouses. For the last several months Ted had not been able to have sexual intercourse, and he felt discouraged and humiliated by this fact. At one point he complained bitterly: ''What am I good for? I cannot move around, go to work, provide money for the family, or satisfy Lilly sexually.'' Since the time of his sexual failure he had been avoiding any physical closeness. We discussed his impotence as a natural consequence of the disease process that does not have any bearing on his value as a man or as a human being. We also encouraged nongenital intimate physical expression of the affection that they felt for each other.

Some time was spent with the children, working through blocks in Ted's interaction with them. Ted wanted to be a father who was strong, independent, and supportive of his children. Being helpless and dependent on them was painful and unacceptable for him. He did not want to have them around and frequently chased them out of the room whenever they appeared. We tried to show Ted the importance of the present situation for his children's future concept of death and their attitude toward it. He finally understood that there was an invaluable lesson to be learned from a person who is dying and that he could function as a teacher for his children, communicating a very unique message. He also was able to accept their help without feeling humiliated, and saw this as an important opportunity for them to achieve a sense of mastery.

Shortly before the second LSD session we discussed several issues with Ted that we considered to be of crucial significance; in particular, the necessity to stay with the experience no matter what it is, and the problems related to trust. The latter was especially important in view of his paranoid episode in the first session.

Second LSD Session

In this session we used the same dose as in the first session: 300 micrograms of LSD. This experience was extremely smooth, almost the opposite of the first one. Ted was able to use the eyeshades and headphones all through the session and had very few difficult experiences. In general, he enjoyed this session much more, but he remembered the sequences less vividly. One of the possible reasons was that there was less concrete visual content in this session and more emphasis on emotional states and thought processes.

The first effects of the drug occurred about twenty-five minutes after its administration. We spent this time in the presence of Lilly, listening to a tape that Ted had recorded the evening before the session. The first experience in the session was the image of crossing a river that appeared to have some deeper symbolic meaning, like travel to another world. For a brief period thereafter Ted enjoyed music and experienced himself as playing a vibraphone in the orchestra. Then things got much more dramatic; he again became aware of the life cycles that repeat themselves, as he had seen them in his first session. This time, however, the major emphasis was on people helping each other. Ted again saw sequences of dying, some of them in human situations, others in the world of animals, such as the interior of a slaughterhouse with hundreds of hogs being killed. There were allusions and links to his disease; he became aware of his body on a tissue and cellular level and felt that it was rotting inside and dying. At one point he saw his family as beautiful apples in a basket; he was the only rotten one among these perfect specimens.

In this context Ted started seeing visions of scenes from a great variety of nations, races, and creeds. For some time he was annoyed, because he desperately searched for God, and this endless variety of the world appeared to be distracting and misleading. As it continued, however, it began coming together, and he started realizing the underlying unity of it all. He became convinced that he had died, and God appeared to him as a brilliant source of light telling him not to fear and assuring him that everything would be all right. He was overwhelmed at the realization that behind the seeming chaos and complexity of creation there is only one God. He was questioning the meaning of his disease and of his suffering. Why did God inflict this seemingly senseless and absurd agony on him? He felt at one point that he had almost reached an understanding.

The rest of the session was spent in beautiful experiences. Ted had visions of crystals, diamonds, jewels, ornate goblets and chalices in beautiful colors, and supernatural radiance. He sensed an upsurge of loving feelings toward Lilly and his children, but also for the two of us. At one point he envisioned a scene in which the four of us (including Lilly, who was actually absent at that time) were sitting near a fireplace in friendly communion, enjoying delicious food and having a good time. There were no more dramatic sequences. Ted had feelings of warmth and wholeness; he was relaxed, and experienced himself as floating. His pain seemed to have disappeared and the mobility and control of his legs increased considerably. Also his appetite was enhanced, and he enjoyed a substantial dinner in Lilly's company. He did not sleep until about four o'clock in the morning, reviewing all his experiences and impressions of the day.

The changes in Ted after this session were so dramatic that Lilly found it baffling. He was very peaceful, serene, centered, and in good spirits. Lilly commented on the new situation: "I can't understand it; he is the one who is dying, and I am having all the problems. It is as if he has settled something and accepted the situation. . . . As if he has found the answer, but I did not; for me it is still as difficult and painful as before." Ted himself summarized his feelings after the session: "Something has changed . . . I feel more peace inside . . . I feel like I might come to heaven if I die . . . I was there. . . ."

Although Ted's mental state was relatively stable, his physical condition deteriorated relentlessly. Because of his problems with urination, an indwelling catheter had to be induced into his bladder with a little plastic bag attached to his thigh, adding to the inconvenience that he had with his colostomy and further complicating his everyday life. He spent most of his time in bed and found the visits to the hospital more and more fatiguing. Although the session helped the pain, it did not relieve it completely; physical movement especially precipitated episodes of painful sensations.

Another of Ted's problems was loneliness and boredom. When Lilly was at work and the children at school, he spent many hours at home alone; at this time he was particularly aware of the meaninglessness of his life. We asked him to use a small Sony tape recorder and record for us his ideas, feelings, and reflections. Ted very much enjoyed this activity and continued giving us tapes with messages he had recorded for Lilly, his children, and both of us. At this point he was aware and proud of the fact that because of his special situation there was much he could teach others about a dimension of life that is of basic importance. He also knew that he was one of few dying people involved in a new experimental program, and that his data were of great significance for us.

At this time we were contacted by the British Broadcasting Company (BBC), who wanted to film the process of psychedelic therapy with a cancer patient. They heard about our research and wanted to include a report on it in a special program on the problems of dying and death. Because of very bad experiences with the media in the past we were reluctant to cooperate. During the negotiations with the BBC team, however, we developed the feeling that because of the people involved the situation would be handled with tact and dignity. With some hesitation we contacted Ted, who seemed to be the logical candidate, and told him about the offer. He was full of excitement and enthusiasm, and saw this as an opportunity to give meaning to his otherwise hopeless situation. It had such an enlivening effect on him that when the film crew arrived at his house expecting him to be bedridden, they found him in the backyard, fully dressed and polishing his car.

We tried to arrange Ted's third session in a way that would be least obtrusive. Only the presence of the cameraman and special lamps and cables installed in the treatment room distinguished this session from the others. With the help of closed-circuit TV monitoring, the audio taping and all the other operations could be controlled from outside the room. Our agreement with the crew was that Ted's well-being was of primary importance, and that if the filming would seriously interfere with the course of the session at any point, it would be discontinued without regard to the economic losses involved.

Third LSD Session

Under these circumstances Ted received his third dose of LSD. The nature of this session combined the elements of his first and second experiences. At the very beginning he had a powerful religious experience of being in a large cathedral with beautiful stained-glass windows. The presence of God filled this church, and Ted had an experience of communicating with Him. He was again seeing life as an endless sequence of cycles in which becoming, being, and perishing were just chapters in the same great book. It was not merely a repetition of what he had experienced in his first two sessions; he was able to recognize new dimensions and certain aspects that had previously remained unexpressed. Then the element of mistrust began to dominate his experience—not unlike in his first session, although in a much more mitigated form. He relived a number of his negative experiences with women and expressed much hostility toward the females in his life—his aunt, a number of girl friends, and particularly Lilly. As the memories of Lilly's extramarital affairs and pregnancy, as well as her dishonesty about his disease, were reenacted in his mind, he felt much bitterness, resentment, and aggression. He took off his eyeshades, and as he was looking at Joan she first became transformed into Lilly and later into an epitome and personification of all female deception. As this was happening Ted had the opportunity to ventilate much of his deep-rooted anger in this transference. After this dramatic episode, when the trust bond between us was reestablished, he was able to reconnect with the positive feelings that characterized the first part of his session. When Lilly later joined us Ted actually felt that after the emotional outburst directed toward her which he had experienced, his feelings for her were much deeper than ever before. He felt that his mistrust and insecurity in the relationship were fading away, and sensed an upsurge of warm, loving feelings. We concluded the day with a family dinner; Ted was coming down from the session in very good condition and enjoyed the meal enormously. After dinner we drove Ted and Lilly home and spent some time by Ted's bed, discussing his LSD experience and the events of the day.

The third session further reinforced Ted's spiritual orientation toward life, his disease, and death. His tapes were full of statements resembling Buddhist philosophy and Hindu cosmology. He talked about cycles of death and rebirth, causes of suffering, and need for detachment; his fear of death diminished greatly in spite of his rapidly deteriorating condition.

Shortly after the third session the ureter of Ted's remaining kidney became obstructed and he developed symptoms of uremia. Although this condition was relieved by a palliative operation (see page 181 for detailed description of this episode), Ted's body, consumed by his chronic disease and further weakened by prolonged intoxication from his own waste products, showed signs of profound toxic deterioration. He was losing weight at a fast rate and wasting away in front of our eyes.

We left Baltimore a month after Ted's session. Before our departure we visited him, all of us knowing that this was the last time we would see each other. Toward the end of this visit we spent a few minutes in silence, looking at each other. Ted interrupted the silence: "My body has had it, my body is all shot with cancer, it is time for me to go. . . . But my mind is all right. . . . I am beyond fear now. . . . I am going to make it. . . . Thank you for all your help. . . ."

We found later that Ted had died several weeks after our last visit. The tube draining his ureter had become clogged and he had had to be rehospitalized. Lilly was spending much time with him in his hospital room. On the last day of his life Ted sent Lilly home, insisting that she bring him clean pajamas. Lilly left the hospital to do what he requested; a nurse who entered Ted's room several minutes later found him quietly resting on his pillow; when she came closer, she discovered that he showed no signs of life.

JESSE

Jesse was referred to our program in a severe physical and emotional condition. At the age of thirty-two he had had a partial resection of his upper lip because of a squamous cell carcinoma. Now, thirteen years later, he returned to the hospital because of an uncontrollable spread of cancer of the same type. Large, visible, tumorous masses were located on the left side of his neck, the right side of his face, and around his forehead. He complained of severe pain, excessive weakness and fatigue, coughing, and difficulties with swallowing. This was associated with deep depression, emotional instability, frequent crying spells, bouts of anxiety, disturbances of sleep, feelings of impending death, and anxious clinging to life. Jesse was also preoccupied with the aesthetic aspects of his disease—the disfiguration of his face and neck and the odor of the bandages soaked with tissue-fluid leaking from his skin ulcerations. The malignant process was proceeding rather rapidly, in spite of external radiation and chemotherapy. Since nothing more could be done to arrest the neoplastic process, Jesse was accepted into the DPT program with the goal of alleviating his emotional suffering and physical pain.

During the preparation for a psychedelic session, Jesse shared with us his complicated life history. He was one of sixteen siblings who had become orphaned after their parents had died in a car accident. Jesse was five years old when this happened; he was raised in an orphanage until the age of fourteen, when he started working and became independent. He changed jobs several times, and because of his limited education did not reach a high position in any of them. His first job was as an unskilled laborer on a farm; later he moved to Baltimore and worked successively as a carpenter, plumber, and roofer.

Jesse had always had difficulty relating successfully to women. After several superficial relationships he married a woman with a strict

Catholic background who had just started the process of liberating herself from her restricting past. The marriage was short-lived and ended after about a year, when his wife became involved with another man. Jesse learned about it and had a fistfight with his rival. His wife walked out on him, and he never saw her again.

During the fifteen years prior to our meeting with him, he had been having a rather steady relationship with a widowed woman considerably older than himself. The friendship between them had been a sexual one, but that had ceased years before Jesse's DPT treatment. She and her sister were taking care of Jesse in a most remarkable way, sharing their small apartment with him and functioning literally as full-time nurses. Jesse, as a convinced Catholic, had deep guilt feelings about this relationship; he believed that marriage in the Church represents an eternal bond that cannot be dissolved even by physical death; certainly not by separation. As far as he was concerned, his obligations to his wife remained unchanged by her departure.

During the preparation for his DPT session, Jesse expressed his overwhelming fear of death. When he thought about dying he saw two alternatives, and each of them was frightening in its own way. According to the first one death was the absolute end of everything, a step into nothingness and darkness, where one loses everything there is. The second possibility available to him was the Christian concept he was introduced to in his strict Catholic upbringing: When one dies existence and consciousness continue for eternity, and the quality of this afterlife depends on one's conduct on earth. Jesse did not find this alternative comforting. On the one hand, it was not quite convincing; on the other, if it was true, he saw himself forever condemned, assigned to the tortures of hell for having lived his life in sin. As a result of this Jesse's clinging to life was desperate and fraught with profound anxiety.

On the day of the session Jesse manifested an almost childlike fear and was very apprehensive about what might happen. He was given 90 milligrams of DPT intramuscularly, and much effort had to be exerted to persuade him that he should put on the eyeshades and headphones. The beginning of the session was marked by an intense fight against the effect of the drug; he seemed to hold onto reality with the same anxious determination with which he was clinging to life in his everyday struggle. This fight against the experience was marked by strong physical distress: coughing and nausea that finally culminated in repeated vomiting. Jesse was overwhelmed by the impact of the material that was pouring out of his own mind; the music sounded rough, loud, and distorted, and he experienced it as an assault. He felt that he would die if he surrendered to the experience. On several occasions Jesse voiced his deep regret for having taken the drug.

During this heroic struggle an unbelievable number of images and scenes were passing in front of his eyes. He was the observer, but also a participant in all of them. His nausea was accompanied by visions of gigantic, frightening creatures of various forms that were attacking him, trying to destroy him. He envisioned thousands of war scenes full of aggression and destruction, and other situations in which "people were dying and disposing of themselves." There was a long episode during which Jesse saw numerous scenes of junkyards strewn with corpses, carcasses, skeletons, rotting offal, and trash cans spreading foul odors. His own body lay there, wrapped in stinking bandages, eaten by cancer, its skin cracking, leaking, and covered with cancerous ulcerations. Then a gigantic ball of fire appeared suddenly out of nowhere and all of this mess and garbage was dumped into its purifying flames and consumed. Jesse's flesh and bones were destroyed in this fire, yet his soul survived the procedure. He found himself in a Last Judgment scene where God ("Jehovah") was weighing his good and evil deeds. Numerous memories from his life were passing through his mind in what felt like a final reckoning. The positive aspects of his life were found stronger than his sins and transgressions. It felt as if a prison had opened up and he was set free. At this point he heard sounds of celestial music and angelic singing, and started to understand the meaning of his experience. The following message was coming to him through some supernatural, nonverbal channels and was permeating his whole being: "When you die, your body will be destroyed, but you will be saved; your soul will be with you all the time. You will come back to earth, you will be living again, but you do not know what you will be on the next earth."

As a result of this experience Jesse's pain was alleviated and his depression and anxiety disappeared. He emerged from the session with a deep belief in the possibility of reincarnation, a concept alien to his own religious tradition and which his mind had created under these unusual circumstances. It was very moving to see Jesse struggling with the limitations of his educational background to communicate the nature and scope of his experience. He did not know that in talking about reincarnation, he was describing a concept that is a cornerstone of Eastern religious and philosophical thinking and part of many other cultural traditions. He was tentative and apologetic in sharing his new conviction, afraid that his challenge to accepted Christian beliefs might be considered a symptom of mental illness.

It appeared as though Jesse developed a new acceptance of his situation and a new attitude toward his impending death. The perspective of another incarnation freed him from clinging to his body, which was now destroyed by cancer. He saw it as a burden and an unfair complication in the lives of his loyal friend and her sister, who had accepted the duty of its maintenance. Jesse died peacefully five days later, perhaps a little earlier than he would have otherwise surrendered in his struggle against inevitable death, almost as if hurrying to get a new body on the "next earth."

SUSANNE

Susanne was sent to us by her attending physician from the Department of Gynecology at Sinai Hospital. She was an attractive, sensitive, and intelligent woman, a divorced mother of three children. At the time of our first encounter, she was thirty-two years old and was involved in the study of psychology. She was hospitalized because of advanced gynecological cancer that had spread all through her pelvis in spite of a radical hysterectomy and a subsequent course of intensive radiation. The neoplastic process had invaded the nerve plexuses along her spine, causing excruciating pain that responded only poorly to morphine medication. Her surgeon had suggested a cordotomy—an operation of the spinal cord consisting of selective severing of the neuronal tracts which conduct pain stimuli. Susanne was facing a serious conflict; she desperately desired alleviation of her pain but was unable to face the possible risks of this procedure, namely paralysis of the legs and incontinence. She became deeply depressed, to the point of seriously considering suicide; she felt completely exhausted and lacked interest and initiative in anything. Susanne welcomed the offer of psychedelic therapy, especially when she learned that in some instances it had helped to alleviate intractable pain associated with cancer.

During the preparation period we became acquainted with Susanne's moving life story, particularly her severely deprived childhood. Her mother was an attractive but emotionally unstable person who was very promiscuous and at times was involved in prostitution; she had had five marriages and many boy friends. Susanne spent her childhood mostly alone; her mother's neglect concerned even basic aspects of her existence. She remembered that on numerous occasions she was starving, sometimes sitting on the neighbor's doorstep to get a meal, sometimes eating leftovers from trash cans. Susanne's resentment toward her mother was quite obvious; she described her as deceptive, destructive, and domineering. Even the confining and restrictive regime of a boarding school she was sent to seemed a definite improvement over the home situation. Episodes of deep depression with suicidal fantasies, panic fear of darkness, and terrible nightmares complete the picture of Susanne's emotional struggles in childhood.

Susanne's adolescence and adulthood were also fraught with problems and conflicts. She had had only a few superficial relationships before she met her husband. Their relationship, which was initially quite exciting and fulfilling, deteriorated quickly after they got married. Susanne was subjected to emotional and, later, even physical abuse by her husband, and at the time of their divorce had to be hospitalized in a psychiatric institution. As a result of her emotional problems, her husband was awarded the children. Following the divorce suit Susanne saw them only rarely and missed them very much.

Shortly after her divorce Susanne started living with Michael, an unemployed artist. The couple was financially supported by Susanne's mother, who, according to Susanne, was now appeasing her guilt from all the earlier neglect and also using the money issue to manipulate and control them. Susanne spent much effort trying to free herself from the strong ambivalent bond with her mother and "cut the umbilical cord."

Susanne's gynecological problems started during a trip to Mexico; she had fallen ill with dysentery and developed vaginal bleeding. Upon her return she had a Pap test and cervical biopsy that came out positive. She responded to this situation with fear and depression, and cried bitterly for many days. Occasionally she had episodes of anger, feeling that life had played a dirty trick on her. Her suicidal tendencies were very strong; the only stabilizing factor was her sense that all this was happening for a reason and had some deeper meaning that was escaping her. Susanne related the origin of this feeling to an unusual religious experience which occurred spontaneously after her hysterectomy. She felt that she had left her body and was floating above the city of San Francisco, which was illumined by thousands of lights. All of her emotional and physical pain had disappeared and she was experiencing ecstasy and transcendental bliss. For about a week after this episode, she could leave her body at will and have similar experiences, but was too frightened to experiment further in the area.

First DPT Session

Susanne's first session was very dramatic and difficult. Shortly after the injection of 120 milligrams of DPT, she felt that everything began to spin, and she became involved in a vicious struggle that was overwhelming and totally incomprehensible to her. She felt enormously constrained and was panting and gasping for breath. Her whole body was shaking and her thighs trembled violently. The prevailing feeling was of intense pain and sickness. She tried to stop the experience, but her efforts seemed hopeless. Waves of nausea permeated her whole being and culminated in explosive vomiting that had a powerful purging quality.

During this period we tried to give Susanne support, but contact with her was very limited; she was totally absorbed in her experience. Later she described to us her efforts to fight her way through a large triangular mass of shiny black material that looked like a mountain of anthracite coal with ragged edges. She felt that she was biting and chewing her way through, and was tearing the black mass with her fingers. When she finally made it through she envisioned flowing forms in pink and gold colors; she felt that pink symbolized pain and gold goodness. Then the experience opened into a world of millions of colors and, eventually, into images of swirling galaxies. Later Susanne identified the black mountain from which she was liberated as a symbol of death.

As a result of this session Susanne's emotional condition improved considerably. Her depression totally disappeared, her fears were alleviated, and she felt an upsurge of energy and initiative. The improvement did not occur, however, in the area where we all wanted to see it most—her agonizing pain. Since the only alternative was neurosurgery, we scheduled a second DPT session shortly after the first one to give Susanne another chance.

Second DPT Session

In the second session we used the same dose of DPT, 120 milligrams, intramuscularly. Several minutes after the injection Susanne started feeling nauseous. This time, however, she clearly associated it with pregnancy; she experienced herself as the pregnant mother, but simultaneously identified with the baby in the womb. She was hypersalivating and experiencing the water in her mouth as amniotic fluid. Suddenly a patch of spattered blood appeared in her visual field; in a moment everything appeared to be flooded with bloody splashes. She started experiencing sequences of dying and being born in many variations, a strange mixture of the agony of dying and the ecstasy of birth. She oscillated between feelings of being trapped and desperate attempts to escape and free herself, between the tortures of metaphysical loneliness and striving for reunion, between anger and murderous rage and feelings of passionate love. She felt a deep identification with all of the mothers who have ever given birth and all children who have ever been born; then she subjectively became all of them. Through birth and death, she appeared to be connected with all of suffering humanity, millions and millions of people crying in pain. She was crying with them and at the same time *was* them, experiencing the ecstasy of this union in agony. Several times she flashed on something that felt like sequences from previous lifetimes. In one of them she became an African native running with her fellow tribespeople on plains scorched by the sun. At the end of this episode she was killed by a spear that hit her back,and penetrated deep inside. She lost consciousness and died. In another sequence she gave birth to a baby in medieval England. Later in the session she became a bird flying through the skies; she was shot by an arrow and fell to earth with a broken wing. Finally all of these sequences of dying and being born seemed to converge into a powerful synthesizing image; she became the mother of all the men who have ever been killed in all the wars in human history. As she became all these mothers and all these children, she felt that she was growing inside of herself and trying to give birth to herself. In a final sequence of being born and dying, her adult ego died while a new, baby self was born. Then she became a tiny speck in space, in an infinite universe filled with beautiful stars.

Later in the session, as she was coming down, Susanne remembered different periods of her life. She experienced herself crying in the crib, relived her childhood nightmares for which she had had to sleep with a light on, and saw her mother and father fighting. It was possible for her to relive these episodes and reevaluate them against the background of her new universal insights. Then she felt deep love for Michael and the need for him to join us in the session.

The second DPT session was a disappointment in terms of its influence on Susanne's pain; in the following days her physical suffering was as excruciating as ever. In every other respect, however, she benefited from the experience. Her depression had completely disappeared and she radiated energy and determination. Susanne decided to continue her psychological studies as intensely as her disease would allow her. She also solved the problem of the impending cordotomy and decided to risk paralysis and incontinence in order to get rid of pain: "I do not care if I am crippled from my neck down and pee all over Baltimore; I want my consciousness clear and not absorbed by this pain." The operation was performed shortly after the session, and its outcome was stunning. Susanne's pain completely disappeared, and the surgeon managed to sever only the sensitive tracts without the slightest impairment to the motor neurons.

The most striking consequence of the session was the change in Susanne's concept of death and her attitude toward it. She became open to the possibility that after death part of the energy that constitutes the human being continues to exist in a conscious form. Instead of seeing death as absolute blackness, nothingness, emptiness, as she did originally, she started thinking in terms of cycles and transitions. The concept of reincarnation became quite plausible for her in this context.

She was able to continue her life without thinking about her cancer, taking one day at a time, focusing on the problems of each day as it unfolded. "That is actually what we all should do whether we are healthy or sick; none of us knows the day and the hour when death will come." For some time it seemed that Susanne's new attitude would conquer her disease. An exploratory laparotomy conducted a few weeks after her cordotomy actually showed that the tumor was shrinking. That confirmed Susanne's optimism and for several months she lived as if she had never had cancer: "I don't think about it at all." During this time she applied for a fellowship and was determined to complete her psychological studies. The tentative title of her thesis was "The Effect of Psychedelic Therapy on Persons Suffering from Cancer."

Then her pain returned, at first gradually, but later it increased suddenly and became excruciating. It originated in the residual tumor and radiated into her pelvis and legs. Another surgical intervention brought only temporary relief. Susanne continued losing weight and developed severe side effects to chemotherapy, which had only minimal effect. The tumor spread into her kidneys and caused damage incompatible with life. All through this painful downhill course Susanne was able to maintain the insight from her DPT sessions that there might be some form of existence beyond physical death, that "there is light on the other side of that anthracite mountain."

JOHN

When we first met John during rounds in the oncology unit, he was deeply depressed and totally absorbed in his pain. He had been bedridden for several weeks, incapable of getting up even to go to the toilet. He rarely ate his meals, would not listen to the radio, read a book or newspaper, and was not interested in watching the new color television set that his father-in-law had bought especially for him. The only thing he seemed to be interested in enough to discuss was the nature and intensity of his suffering and physical distress. He complained that no matter what position he assumed, he had intolerable pain, and this pain was getting worse with every moment. He was afraid of even minor changes of position, passive or active, and felt literally immobilized by a physical agony that had captured and absorbed all of his attention.

A year earlier the physicians at Sinai had discovered that John had a malignant tumor of his right kidney originating in the adrenal gland (hypernephroma). A nephrectomy (radical surgical removal of the kidney) was ordered and performed without delay. It was, however, too late; the tumor had already metastasized, and in the following months John developed progressive symptoms from the secondary growths. At the time when we first met him, the tumor had spread to his spinal column and was causing severe neurological disturbances.

John was thirty-six years old, married, and the father of three children. Both spouses considered their marriage to be better than average. They had occasional arguments about the upbringing of their children, but basically there was a sense of deep loyalty, cooperation, and warmth in the family. John's wife, Martha, came to the hospital every day around ten o'clock in the morning and stayed until the evening. She was doing this in spite of the fact that at this time her husband communicated very little with her and was not showing any interest in family affairs. He either complained about his agonizing pain or was heavily medicated and was dozing off as a result of pain-allaying narcotics. Martha always brought some kind of work with her to the hospital; she would sit quietly in an armchair and was available whenever John needed something.

Martha had been told her husband's diagnosis shortly after it was made and seemed to be facing this problem with considerable courage. She hid the diagnosis and prognosis from John for many months, until she finally could not bear it any longer. Shortly before we met him she had decided to tell him the truth. John now knew that he had cancer, but was oscillating between pessimism and optimism about his future. On several occasions he mentioned death and even instructed Martha to arrange a simple funeral to save money for the children. On another occasion he talked about long-term plans for his job and a vacation abroad that they all would take in the future when he got well. Shortly after Martha told John she decided to discuss his situation openly with his mother. She decided, however, not to tell John that she had told his mother, because "John would get upset knowing how much this information would disturb his mother."

John appeared to be a rather problematic patient for psychedelic therapy, where psychological preparation and cooperation are considered essential for a successful outcome. It was extremely difficult to establish contact with him and engage him in conversation. He was either so preoccupied with his disease and pain or so mentally altered by narcotics and sleep medication that any focused discussion with him was essentially impossible. He did not want to talk about his life situation, past history, or the psychological aspects of psychedelic therapy, since he did not see any direct and immediate link between these topics and his physical pain. Thus the preparation had to be shortened to a bare minumum, and some of the basic data were obtained from his wife.

We were quite reluctant to run the session under these circumstances, not feeling that there was enough of the rapport, trust, and understanding which we consider important for successful therapy. Finally, under the influence of Martha's demands and John's desperate insistence that we give him the promised treatment if there was any chance of it alleviating his pain, we decided to proceed in spite of our mixed feelings.

In the morning of the session day, John was given 60 milligrams of DPT intramuscularly. When the drug started to take effect, he was encouraged to put on the eyeshades and headphones. He complied after some reluctance, when he emphasized several times that all he could bear was soft, gentle, and unobtrusive music. This was an attitude that was obvious even before the session; John preferred to rest in darkness and in absolute silence. Visual, acoustic, and tactile stimuli of any kind seemed to increase his pain. In the early stages of the session, John kept complaining about his discomfort, feelings of heat, and dislike of the music. He was nauseated and vomited several times. In general, his experiences seemed quite uninteresting and uneventful. He spent much time fighting the effects of the drug and exerting great effort to maintain control. It was extremely difficult for him to let go of his defenses and to face the emerging unconscious material.

The content of the DPT session appeared to be relatively superficial and mostly of a psychodynamic nature. John remembered various periods of his life and relived several traumatic events. One of them was the memory of a railroad accident that he witnessed as a young boy; another one was the recollection of an injury that his three-year-old sister suffered when her sled hit a tree and she broke her leg. There was an episode of aggressive war scenes that opened into the reliving of some of John's memories from his military service. At another point in the session John saw visions of a stormy ocean, sinking ships, and drowning people. Following this, he got in touch with a memory of a dangerous event on the Chesapeake Bay, when he and some of his close relatives went cruising on a boat that almost collided with a Japanese freighter. In the second half of the session, John grew progressively more tired and finally insisted on taking off the eyeshades and headphones. There was no major resolution or breakthrough; the drug wore off and we all had feelings of disappointment and failure.

The only redeeming aspect of the session for John was the memory of a brief episode in which he saw a large bowl or pitcher filled with iced tea that appeared to be of great relevance and was related to some important situation or problem from his childhood. He returned to this image again and again in our discussions following the session. Although he never understood the meaning of this vision, the memory of it filled him with excitement. When we saw John in the hospital on the day following the session, he was in bed, weak and extremely tired, almost incommunicative. This only confirmed our previous feeling that the session was unproductive and, in general, a failure. This situation, however, changed radically on the second day after the session. John's condition improved in a dramatic way; his mood got better, he was smiling at people, and started communicating with his family and the staff. When he talked with his wife he showed interest in the children and the family, something he had not done for months. He asked for a radio and was listening to soft music. The new color television set was now on for many hours a day.

To everyone's amazement John's pain had completely disappeared; he was able to get to the toilet without assistance and even to take short walks in the hospital corridor. He stopped talking about his disease and his suffering and enjoyed discussions about political, social, and family issues. According to Martha, John appeared totally transformed, was a "completely different person." It was not uncommon to see him laugh and joke and show interest in many things. He discontinued all medication and was completely free of pain until more than two months later, shortly before his death. An interesting additional insight occurred about ten days after John's session, when we were analyzing his answers on the Psychedelic Experience Questionnaire. We discovered that he responded positively to the item "Visions of religious personages (Jesus, Buddha, Mohammed, Sri Ramana Maharishi, etc.)" and rated it 5 on a 0–5 scale. This was surprising, since we had asked him explicitly after his session whether there were any religious elements in his experience and he had denied it. When we asked him to clarify this discrepancy for us, he answered: "At one point I saw large bronze and golden statues of these Oriental . . . how do they call them . . . Buddhas. There were some inscriptions under them, but they were all in Latin. I don't read Latin and could not figure them out. That's why I didn't tell you about them."

This was the most dramatic effect of psychedelic therapy on intractable pain that we saw in the course of our study. The incongruence between the content and course of the session and the therapeutic outcome is a good illustration of the unpredictability of the effect of psychedelic therapy on pain.

JOAN

At the time Joan volunteered for our LSD program, she was a forty-year-old housewife and mother of four children. Two of these children, a seventeen-year-old daughter and an eight-year-old son, were from her first marriage; she was also taking care of an adopted boy of nine and a nine-year-old boy from her husband's first marriage. In addition, she was involved in a number of activities, including encounter groups and a ballet school. Her cancer was diagnosed in August 1971, after a long period of superficial and transitional gastrointestinal disturbances. The physician whom she consulted first discovered a gastric ulcer, and when this failed to heal over a period of six weeks, he recommended surgical intervention. The surgeon found tumorous changes in the stomach and conducted a high subtotal gastrectomy. He noted aggressive regional invasion but no generalized metastases. Microscopic examination of the resected gastric tissue revealed infiltrating, highly anaplastic carcinoma.

Joan was told about her diagnosis in several stages. First she learned that she had a gastric ulcer and later got the information that it was a tumor, but without specification about its nature. Then her doctor told her that the tumor was malignant, and finally disclosed to her the most disquieting fact: that the malignant tissue reached all the way to the point of resection. She thus had some time to gradually adjust to the diagnosis, with all of its prognostic implications. She reacted at first with deep depression and anxiety; later her feelings of hopelessness and helplessness were replaced by detachment and withdrawal. At the same time, she decided that she did not want to spend the rest of her life awaiting death but wanted to do something about her disease and to contribute somehow to the therapeutic process, no matter how little hope there might be in this endeavor. After the physicians had stated that nothing more could be done for her along medical lines, Joan spent some time looking for faith healers and other unorthodox help. During this time she heard about the Spring Grove program for persons suffering from cancer and made an appointment with us to see the place, meet the people involved in the project, and get more specific information about the treatment program. We explained to her the nature of psychedelic therapy, describing both its therapeutic potential and its limitations. We mentioned that, according to our experience, this therapy can have a very beneficial effect on physical pain and on the emotional distress accompanying the disease. We also talked briefly about the changes of the concept of death and the attitude toward it that we have seen following successful LSD sessions. We made clear to her that we had no conclusive data as to what effect psychedelic therapy might have on the cancer process itself. We did not, however, explicitly exclude the possibility that a favorable change in the patient's condition can influence the cancer process itself. Joan came for the first interview accompanied by her husband, Dick. As an educator he was naturally quite concerned about the possible adverse effects of LSD. We had to spend some time explaining that in the judicious use of LSD the ratio between benefits and risks is drastically different from that in unsupervised self-experimentation. After this issue had been clarified, both Joan and Dick enthusiastically participated in the LSD program.

The preparation for Joan's first LSD session consisted of several drug-free interviews with her alone and one meeting with her and Dick. During this time Joan was depressed and anxious. She felt a drastic decrease of zest and lack of interest in subjects and activities that prior to her disease used to bring her much joy. In the course of her illness she became very tense and irritable; her frustration tolerance was "an all-time low." During our preliminary discussions her physical suffering was still tolerable; she had undifferentiated gastrointestinal discomfort, but her pain had not reached an intensity that in and of itself would make her life unbearable. She felt that, by and large, her problem at that time was preoccupation with and fear of things that will come rather than suffering from things that are. Joan was fully aware of the situation she was facing in regard to diagnosis and prognosis. She was able to discuss her disease quite openly when asked explicitly. In everyday life, however, there seemed to be a considerable degree of denial, with an underlying fear of death and preoccupation with her final fate. Joan's major concern was to reach a decent and honest closure in the relationship with Dick and all the children. She wanted to leave them resolved and with good feelings, without guilt, anger, bitterness, or pathological grief, in a situation where they could continue to live their own lives without having to carry the psychological burden of her death.

Joan understood that it was necessary for her to explore her personal history before the LSD session and to reach as much clarity and comprehension of the patterns and conflicts underlying her life trajectory from birth to the present time as was possible. She worked on this task with an unusual interest and degree of motivation. She wrote a detailed autobiography that was used as a basis for our further discussions about the most important aspects of her life.

Joan's childhood was very strongly influenced by her emotionally unstable mother, who suffered from severe depressions and was treated by electroshocks during her numerous psychiatric hospitalizations. Joan's relationship with her lacked any intimacy and was erratic and confusing. Joan felt much closer to her father, who was able to express warm feelings toward her and give her support. In later years, however, she became aware of a sensual element in their interaction; this became a source of fear and guilt in the context of a strong Catholic emphasis in her upbringing with explicit taboos regarding sexuality. The relationship between her parents was disharmonious, with constant fights and quarrels, and finally terminated in a divorce.

Joan described herself in her early years as "a moderately with-drawn child with a rich fantasy world." She had only a few friends and interacted little with her peers outside this close circle. Of her four siblings, she had a close bond and coalition with her younger brother and felt intense rivalry toward her sister. At the time of her LSD treatment, she felt extremely alienated from the rest of her siblings.

Attendance at a parochial school run exclusively by nuns reinforced the puritanical elements in Joan's background. This contributed to the complications in her sexual development. During adolescence she had difficulty relating to people in general because of her anxieties, insecurity, and feelings of inadequacy. All these problems were much more intense in regard to potential sexual partners. Joan's world of rich romantic fantasies was in sharp contrast with her real life. Her several relationships were short-lived and superficial; she did not have any sexual experiences until her first marriage. Her marriage was plagued by many problems and conflicts, particularly by strong jealousy and possessiveness on the part of both spouses. Later, her husband, who initially had had strict opinions about premarital sex and monogamy, became interested in other women and had a series of extramarital affairs. His involvement with one of his pupils resulted in pregnancy and expedited separation and divorce.

Shortly after she had divorced her first husband, Joan married Dick. The second marriage was much better than the first, but was not free of problems. In a joint interview with both partners, we tried to identify the sources of difficult interaction and facilitate the communication between them. Joan, when asked what she considered the most disturbing aspect of their marriage, pointed to Dick's tendency to impulsive reactions and to his possessiveness. Dick had a feeling that Joan did not have a sufficiently deep commitment to and emotional investment in their relationship and family life. He found her high degree of independence very disquieting and threatening. As we explored various vicious circles in Joan and Dick's everyday interaction, they both found interesting precedents and possible causes for their fears, insecurities, and specific idiosyncrasies in their childhood experiences. The result of this interview was a joint decision that they would seek new channels of more effective exchange on various levels. They came to the conclusion that they would try to live fully each of Joan's remaining days, one at a time, without letting past programs and concerns about the future contaminate their everyday interaction. We all felt that the situation was ready for Joan's first psychedelic session.

First LSD Session

At nine o'clock in the morning Joan was given 300 micrograms of LSD intramuscularly because there were uncertainties about the quality of resorption in her gastrointestinal system, which was so heavily afflicted by gastrectomy and the cancer process. She started the session with considerable apprehension and held onto our hands. About twenty minutes after the injection she started having floating and vibrating sensations. As she was listening to Brahms's second piano concerto, she experienced herself standing in the gigantic hall of a futuristic, supersonic airport, waiting for her flight. The hall was crowded with passengers clad in an extremely modern fashion; a strange feeling of excitement and expectation seemed to permeate this unusual crowd. Suddenly she heard a loud voice through a system of airport speakers: "The event that you are going to experience is Yourself. . . . With some of you—as you may notice—it is already happening." . . . As she looked around at her fellow travelers, she saw strange changes in their faces; their bodies were twitching and assuming unusual postures as they began the journeys into their inner worlds. At that point Joan noticed an intense humming sound of a comforting and soothing quality, like a radio signal, guiding her through the experience and reassuring her. It seemed as if her brain were being burned very slowly, revealing its content in one picture after another. Her father's image appeared with great clarity, and the nature of their relationship was analyzed and explored with the precision of a surgical operation. Joan perceived his need for her to be something or someone that she could not be; she realized that she has to be herself even if it disappoints him. She became aware of a whole network of other people's needs—her husband's, children's, friends': "I just cannot be all those things to all those people—I *have* to be myself." More specifically, Joan realized that the needs of other people made it more difficult for her to accept the reality of her impending death and to surrender to the process.

Then the inward journey deepened and Joan was encountering various terrifying monsters—demons and "lean, hungry, surrealistic creatures in weird colors like dayglow green.'' It was as if a whole panoply of demons appearing in Asian art were evoked and performed a wild dance in her head. Whenever she moved toward them and into them, they would get more and more vague, and the picture would change to something else, usually quite pleasant. At one point, when she was looking at some slimy, evil creatures, she said to herself, "Un huh, that's me too—all right.'' The encounter with demons was accompanied by an intense struggle for breath; on several occasions Joan made the comment: "I wish I could still breathe.'' This difficult part was of relatively brief duration; after she had transcended the fights with demons, Joan felt she "became electric with fantastic energy'' going through her. It was so much energy that no single individual could contain it and handle it effectively; it was commensurate with the entire universe. It became clear to her that she contained so much energy that in everyday life she had to deny it, misuse it, and project it on other people in a disowning fashion. She had a flash of herself in various stages of her life, trying on different roles—daughter, lover, young wife, mother, artist—and realized that they could not work since they were inadequate containers for her energy. The most important aspect of these experiences was their relevance for the understanding of death. Joan saw the magnificent unfolding of the cosmic design in all its infinite nuances and ramifications. Each individual represented a thread in the beautiful warp of life and was playing a specific role. All these roles were equally necessary for the central energy core of the universe; none of them was more important than others. After death the life energy underwent a transformation and the roles were recast. Joan saw her role in this life to be a cancer patient and was able to accept it. She envisioned the dynamics of reincarnation represented symbolically as a view of the earth with many paths leading in all directions that looked like ant tunnels. "There have been many lives before this one and many others will follow; the purpose is to experience and explore whatever is assigned to you in the cosmic screenplay. Death is just one episode, one transitional experience within this magnificent perennial drama.''

As a result of these insights Joan seemed to have developed an affirmative attitude toward the totality of existence and a general acceptance of whatever happens in life as being ultimately all right. She made many enthusiastic comments about the incredible cosmic wit and humor built into the scheme of existence.

Throughout her session Joan had visions of pictures, sculptures, handicraft, and architecture of a number of different cultures: ancient Egypt, Greece, Rome, and Persia, various Amerindian tribes, as well as pre-Columbian Peru and Central America. This was accompanied by many insights into the nature of human existence. Through the richness of her experience Joan discovered that the dimensions of her being were greater than she thought: ''There is a lot to me, much more than I have ever suspected; there are forms, colors, and textures—indescribable, indescribable. . . .'' Whatever she perceived the world doing—inventing hostile countries, internecine wars, racial hatred and riots, corrupted political schemes, or polluting technology—she saw herself doing it and projecting on other people the things she denied in herself. She got in touch with what she felt was pure being and realized that it cannot be comprehended and does not need any justification. With this came an awareness that her only task is to get the energy going and flowing and not to ''sit on it'' as she used to do. The flow of life was symbolized by many beautiful images of fish and plants in water moving with the stream, and delightful dancing scenes, some majestic and ethereal, others down to earth. When this was happening Joan felt alive, genitally and generally; her entire body was vibrating with excitement and delight. Experiencing these sequences, she curled into a comfortable fetal position.

About five hours into the session Joan decided to take off her eyeshades, sit up, and connect with the environment. She sat on the couch in deep peace and relaxation, listening to Zen meditation music and watching the rosebud on the table. Occasionally she closed her eyes and returned to her inner world; her face was radiant and had the expression of quiet bliss found in Buddhist sculptures. She envisioned a single eye that persisted in her visual field for a long time and took on many different forms: suffering Jew, Persian emperor, starved Pakistani refugee, a little boy peeping through a simple wooden fence. For a long period of time she experienced nothing but a beautiful warm, nourishing golden glow, like a transcendental rain of liquid gold. The grapes on the table tasted like ambrosia and the grape stems looked so beautiful that Joan decided to take some of them home as a souvenir.

Later in the afternoon Dick joined us in the session room. Immediately after his arrival he and Joan fell into each other's arms and stayed in a close embrace for a period of about twenty minutes. Dick was sensing an enormous amount of energy radiating from Joan, and mentioned that he was aware of an almost tangible energy field surrounding her body. They were given about two hours of privacy, during which Joan shared her experiences with Dick. One of Joan's best memories from the session was the shower they took together; Joan felt unusually tuned into Dick's body and suddenly discovered how to massage him. Later we all shared a Chinese meal; although the food was brought from a carry-out restaurant, and was of average quality, Joan considered it the best she had ever tasted. She could not recall ever enjoying food, or herself, more.

The rest of the evening the couple shared a quiet time together, lying on the couch and listening to stereophonic music. Dick was very impressed by Joan's wisdom and openness. He was convinced that she was tapping genuine levels of cosmic wisdom that were closed to him. He admired the consistency in her reporting and the spontaneous confidence and authority with which she spoke about her experience. Dick's conclusion was that Joan was just pure pleasure to be with. She showed a high level of elation, a radiant mood, and an absolute freedom from anxiety. Her ability to enjoy music, tastes, colors, and the shower was greatly enhanced. This was such a contagious experience that Dick himself felt a desire to have a psychedelic session.

He decided to explore the possibility of participating in the LSD training program for professionals in our center.*

Although she felt very good and quite sleepy, Joan stayed up a long time and awoke several times during the night. She had one dream about working in a library and hearing others say: "This Zen stuff does not make any sense." She smiled to herself, knowing it was too simple to make sense to them.

Joan's feelings during the days following the session are reflected in her account: "The next morning I felt refreshed, relaxed, and very in tune with the world. Dick put Bach's Brandenburg Concerto on the record player and it seemed absolutely perfect. The outside appeared clear, serene, and beautiful. I saw things I have never seen on the road going home. The trees, grass, colors, sky—all were a real delight to behold."

For about two months after the first LSD session Joan felt relaxed, elated, and optimistic; the psychedelic experience also seemed to have opened new realms of mystical and cosmic feelings within her. The religious elements that she experienced in her session transcended the narrow boundaries of the traditional Catholic religion she had been brought up with. She was now precipitating toward the more universal approaches found within Hinduism and Buddhism.

During the weeks following the session Joan felt so much overflowing energy that it baffled her attending physicians. They found her energetic resources quite incongruent with her serious clinical condition, and explicitly expressed their surprise that she was still able to move around on her own and to drive a car. They also voiced their doubt that she would be able to spend her vacation the next summer in Cali-

* Important parts of Dick's LSD training sessions dealt with his problems regarding cancer and death. Joan was the third important woman in Dick's life dying of cancer; in the past he had witnessed the slow deaths of his mother and first wife. He realized that his unconscious feelings toward these women ranged from anger ("I need you and depend on you, how can you do this to me?") to guilt and responsibility for their disease ("I am the common denominator in the lives of these three women; am I the cause of their disease?"). The LSD sessions proved very beneficial for resolving those deep conflicts.

fornia, as the family was planning. Joan herself felt very confident and believed that this would be possible. The later course of events justified her feelings when the vacation in California proved to be a very meaningful and rewarding time for the whole family.

This rather positive development was drastically interrupted in mid-January, when Joan saw her physician because of continued belching and retching; he discovered a new mass in the area of the spleen, which he identified as metastatic growth. Joan was very disappointed when, in spite of this finding, no concrete medical procedure was suggested; she felt that the doctors had given up on her. Both Joan and Dick felt very strongly at this point that another psychedelic session should be conducted. Joan felt very optimistic about the possibility of the session influencing her emotional condition and deepening her philosophical and spiritual insights; she was also toying with the idea that she might be able to influence the psychosomatic component that she suspected in the etiology of her cancer. Dick was confident that this time he would be able to handle the influence that Joan's session might have on his own emotional condition much more adequately.

Second LSD Session

The second LSD session took place in February 1972. Since the dosage of 300 micrograms had had a powerful effect the first time, we injected the same quantity in this session. The following is Joan's account of her experience, which summarizes the most important events of the session:

"This session was a grim one for me. It contrasted with my first in almost every way; black and white rather than color; personal rather than cosmic; sad, not joyous. There was a short time at the beginning when I felt myself in a universal place or space where I knew again that the whole universe was in each of us and that there was a meaning to our lives and deaths. After that the experience narrowed and became much more personal. Death was the subject of my trip. I experienced several funeral scenes in ornate or traditional church surroundings, sometimes at the cemetery, sometimes inside a church with a choir of many people. I cried often in the course of the several hours. I also asked many questions and answered them; they would lead to ultimate unanswerable problems and then it would seem funny. Early on I remember thinking: 'All that ugliness is really beauty.' In the course of the day other polarities came to my mind—good and evil, victory and defeat, wisdom and ignorance, life and death.

"I feel that I experienced my childhood, but not any specific scenes, just a feeling tone, a very sad one. Much of it had to do with very early feelings of frustration and deprivation, hunger and starvation. It flashed through my mind whether there might have been a connection between these experiences and my peptic ulcer that turned into cancer. I remember once just the feeling of being out in the rain for what seemed like a long time. I recall being with my brothers and being turned away from a show or circus by the man in charge, and feeling very sad as we walked away, not too sure where we were going. The hidden allusion to my present situation is obvious—being denied further participation in the show of life and facing the uncertainty of death.

"For what seemed like a fairly long time, I experienced my present family in terms of preparing them for my death. There was a scene in which I finally told them, after preparing myself for some time. In a sequence of scenes I was able to say good-bye to my children, my husband, my father, and other relatives, as well as friends and acquaintances. I did it in a very individualized way, with regard to the personality and special sensitivity of each of them. Tears followed, but after a time there was warmth and cheer; at the end they all gathered around me to take care of me. I recall their fixing warm and sweet things to eat. After this I spent some good bit of time saying good-bye to them and to my husband—in turn—and realizing that there were caring people who were going to look after them. I said good-bye to them, too, and felt that something of me would live on in them.

"There was a happy, warm scene toward the end of my trip—which I felt I was observing, not part of, but really enjoyed. It was a scene with adults and children playing outside in the snow. I felt it was in some very northern place. All were bundled up and staying warm in spite of the cold and the snow. The children were being enjoyed and cared for by the grown-ups, and there was laughter and play and general good cheer. Then I remember seeing a whole row of boots, knowing that children's feet were in them and were warm.

"In the evening after the session I felt good in some ways—quite responsive and pleased to see Dick, but I found myself crying off and on for the rest of the evening. I felt that I saw myself and my situation realistically, that I could handle it better now, but still felt very sad. I also felt unfinished—that I could have gone on for a few more hours and might have gone on from the grimness to joy."

The second session proved to be very beneficial for Joan. She became reconciled to her situation and decided to spend her remaining days in a spiritual quest. After a vacation that the family spent on the west coast, she decided to say good-bye to her husband and her children. She thought that it would save them from the painful process of watching her progressive deterioration and make it possible for them to remember her full of life and energy. In California Joan remained in close contact with her father, who was himself interested in the spiritual path; he introduced her to a Vedanta group.

In the summer Joan became interested in having another LSD experience. She wrote us a letter inquiring about the possibility of arranging the third session in California. We recommended Dr. Sidney Cohen, who had had extensive experience with psychedelic therapy of cancer patients. The following is Joan's account of her third LSD session, which she had under Dr. Cohen's auspices. The dosage was 400 micrograms.

Third LSD Session

"My first response after the drug took effect was to get cold, colder, and colder. It seemed that no amount of covers could alleviate the zero-feeling-bone-cold, angular and greenish. It was hard to believe later that so many warm blankets had been put on top of me, for nothing—at the time—seemed to alleviate the cold. I called for hot tea, which I sipped through a glass straw.

"Then, at some point, I went into a very intense experience while holding the hot cup of tea. The cup became the universe and all was vividly clear and real. The greenish, brownish color of the tea melted into a swirling vortex. No more questions; life, death, meaning—all were there. I had always been there—we all were. All was one. Fear did not exist; death, life—all the same thing. The swirling circularity of it all. The intense desire for everyone to realize the universe is in everything. The tear coming down my cheek, the cup—everything! What harmony, I felt, is there behind the seeming chaos. Wanting not to lose sight of this, wanting all to share in this experience; then there could be no discord. I was feeling that Dr. Cohen knew with me. Then my father came in and I tried to share with him what I could of the intense earlier experience, trying to express the inexpressible: that there is no fear, no question of fear. We have always been where we are going. Just *being* is sufficient. No need to worry, ask, question, reason. Just be. I told him the importance of us all in keeping things moving in the everyday world.

"I consumed my hot broth and tea, craving for nourishment and warmth. After a break I got back into myself. This time I experienced bleak and sad scenes of my very early life that I was familiar with from my previous sessions. The pictures took the form of small skeletal creatures floating about in emptiness looking for, but not finding, nourishment. Emptiness—no fulfillment. Scrawny birds looking for food in an empty nest. Some feeling of me and my brothers alone, looking, nowhere to go.

"At some point I got into my sadness. Sadness as an overriding theme running from early childhood throughout my life. I became aware of the progressive effort to disguise it—to satisfy what others seemed to want instead ('Smile'—'look alive'—'stop daydreaming').

"Later in the session I had the feeling that some are chosen to feel the sadness inherent in the universe. If I am one, fine. I thought of all the children looking for mothers who are not there. Thought of the Stations of the Cross and felt the suffering of Christ or the sadness he had to feel. I realized that others' karma is to feel the gladness, or the strength, or the beauty—whatever. Why not gladly accept the sadness?

"At another time I was on many cushions with many comforters on top of me—warm, secure. Wanting not to be reborn as a person—

perhaps as a rainbow, orangey, reddish, yellowish, soft, beautiful. At some point in the afternoon I became aware of the centrality of my stomach. So many pictures of people being comforted with food, my earlier craving for the hot tea, broth, always something coming into my stomach. I realized that I am aware of that in my day-to-day life now—always wanting the tit and substituting spoon, straw, cigarette. Never enough!

"I became aware of being a child again—dependent, but now having a mother [her father's second wife] to take care of me, who *wants to* and likes taking care of me. I found comfort and pleasure in getting what I never had as a child. There were moments to enjoy the smell and feel of the fruit—a beautiful mango, pear, peach, grapes. While looking at them I saw the cellular movement. Much later I enjoyed the rosebud—velvety, fragrant and lovely.

"Toward the end of the day I became suddenly aware that I had found a way to legitimize my lifelong sadness: to become terminally ill. The irony of this situation was that I then found happiness and felt relief in this discovery. I wanted to get into the sources of my sadness. I saw that from very early my mother had not much to give me; that, in fact, she looked to me to give *her*. I did indeed have more to give her than she me. I experienced this as a heavy burden.

"I had much discussion with my father about sadness, what is wrong with it and why it is so discouraged by others. I described to him how much energy I expended pretending to be glad or happy or to smile. I talked about the beauty in sadness—sad sweetness, sweet sadness. Allowing yourself and others to be sad when they feel it. Sadness perhaps is not in vogue, as is joy, spontaneity, or fun. These I expended great energy in acting out. Now I am just being—not being this or that, just being. Sometimes it is sad, often peaceful, sometimes angry or irritable, sometimes very warm and happy. I am not sad any longer that I am to die. I have many more loving feelings than ever before. All the pressures to be something 'other' have been taken off me. I feel relieved from sham and pretense. Much spiritual feeling permeates my everyday life."

A member of our team who visited Joan in California a short time before her death gave us a moving description of her everyday life during her remaining days. She maintained her interest in the spiritual quest and spent several hours a day in meditation. In spite of her rapidly deteriorating physical condition, she appeared to be emotionally balanced and in good spirits. Quite remarkable was her determination not to lose any opportunity to experience the world fully as long as she could. She insisted that she be served all the meals that others were eating, although the passage through her stomach was now totally obstructed and she could not swallow anything. She chewed the food slowly, savored its taste, and then spat it out into a bucket. The last evening of her life she was totally absorbed in watching the setting sun. "What a magnificent sunset," were her last words before she retired into her bedroom. That night Joan died quietly in her sleep.

After Joan's death her relatives and friends on the east coast received the invitation for a memorial get-together that she wrote personally when she was still alive. After they all assembled at the appointed time, they were surprised to be addressed by Joan's voice from a cassette tape. It was much more than an unusual and moving farewell. According to the participants, the content and tone of her speech had a powerful comforting effect on those who had come to this meeting with a sense of deepest tragedy.

6.

PSYCHEDELIC METAMORPHOSIS OF DYING

When we first began to work with dying cancer patients, we somewhat naively anticipated that, in contrast to the work with psychiatric patients, this would by and large entail the administration of LSD to relatively "normal" persons who had a severe physical illness and an understandable and fully justifiable emotional reaction to their situation. This illusion was quickly dispelled, as many persons suffering from cancer proved to have a variety of serious psychological conflicts and emotional problems that predated the onset and diagnosis of their physical illness. As a matter of fact, in quite a few instances the nature of these emotional problems was such that it almost suggested an association of a causal nature. In general, the incidence of depressive states, strong negative attitudes toward life, and even self-destructive and suicidal tendencies seemed to be higher than one would expect from a random sample of the population. Although this is based on clinical impressions and was not studied in a controlled and systematic way, we saw surprisingly frequent instances of severe guilt, feelings of self-hatred, and autopunitive tendencies that had preceded the clinical manifestation of cancer by years or decades. It was not infrequent that cancer patients in their LSD sessions saw direct links between such tendencies within themselves and their malignancies. Less frequent but also common was an inclination to interpret already existing cancer in terms of punishment. There was also a high proportion of individuals who had suffered emotional and/or physical deprivation in childhood; in some instances actual physical abuse was part of the early history. For these individuals one of the dimensions that consistently emerged in the LSD session was reliving of intensely painful sequences related to anxiety, loneliness, hunger, and abuse. In some instances dying individuals saw this early deprivation as a possible cause of their illness.*

We frequently found that the area which was affected by primary cancer had been an object of the patient's increased attention for many years prior to the development of the tumor. On occasion we were able to trace various psychosomatic symptoms in the organ afflicted later by cancer to childhood or even early infancy. We detected important psychotraumatic material associated with such an area in a significant number of people, either in the preparatory work or in the course of the psychedelic experiences. Some patients indicated that the site of the cancer had always been an area of least resistance or the weakest link in the chain of their psychosomatic processes, and that the organ or area afflicted with cancer had responded in a specific way to various emotional stresses in their lives. It was not exceptional, for example,

---

* It is interesting to mention in this connection an article by Carl and Stephanie Simonton, in which they reviewed the medical literature covering different aspects of the relationship between emotional factors and malignancy. According to them, there is general agreement in over two hundred articles which they analyzed that there is a relationship between the two; the question, thus, does not seem to be the existence or nonexistence of such a connection but its degree and practical significance. The personality characteristics of cancer patients and most plausible predisposing factors mentioned by the authors of the above articles were: (1) great tendency to hold resentment and a marked inability to forgive; (2) a tendency toward self-pity; (3) poor ability to develop and maintain meaningful long-term relationships; and (4) a very poor self-image. The Simontons suggested that a life-history pattern of basic rejection might be a possible common denominator behind all these personality characteristics. According to them, this life pattern frequently culminates in the loss of a serious love object six to eighteen months prior to the diagnosis.

to find that a history of severe sexual psychotraumatization and conflicts about sexuality in women preceded the development of gynecological cancer. Similarly, significant psychopathology related to the oral area and ingestion of food antedated the onset of stomach cancer in several individuals; in one instance peptic ulcer was an intermediary stage between gastric dysfunction of a neurotic nature and manifest carcinoma. We also saw examples of a long history of gastrointestinal discomfort preceding the development of pancreatic cancer, and important anal problems of long duration heralding malignant changes in the colon. Although these are scattered observations without a solid statistical basis, they appeared so striking during the in-depth psychological approach of LSD-assisted psychotherapy that they warrant a more systematic study in the future.

As far as the psychedelic sessions themselves were concerned, many individuals dying of cancer seemed to have had quite strong psychological defenses and considerable difficulties in letting go and accepting the experience. They were frequently reluctant to take a deep look into their own unconscious, and were generally able to relinquish their psychological resistance during their sessions only if good therapeutic rapport had been established. Although problems of surrendering to the experience were quite common, there were also, of course, significant exceptions.

The nature of the psychedelic sessions with dying cancer patients did not differ substantially from what we have observed in various categories of psychiatric patients with whom we have worked, such as neurotics, alcoholics, and narcotic addicts, or in "normal" volunteers who had sessions for training purposes. The experiences of dying individuals, like those of persons in other categories, covered a wide range, from abstract and aesthetic sequences, reliving of traumatic or positive childhood memories, and episodes of death and rebirth, to profound archetypal and transcendental forms of consciousness. In spite of this general similarity, there were certain characteristics that seemed to be specific for sessions of cancer patients and that differentiated them from those in the other groups of individuals.

As might be expected, individuals with cancer generally had a higher incidence of difficult somatic symptoms and more preoccupation with their physical beings. Various psychosomatic manifestations, such as nausea, vomiting, tremors, cardiac distress, and breathing difficulties are quite common in psychedelic therapy, without regard to the population involved. They are especially frequent during the onset of the drug's effect and in the culmination periods of sessions. Intense physical manifestations can indicate the emergence of deeply relevant unconscious material and are correlated with the individual's struggle to break through the usual resistances and defenses. In addition to these psychosomatic symptoms various physical problems would occur in the sessions of cancer patients that were directly related to their malignancy and reflected specific disturbances in their physiological functioning. The most frequent complications of this kind were nausea and vomiting in patients with gastric cancer or intestinal obstruction, and incontinence of urine and feces in patients with pelvic tumors or metastases to the spinal cord. Persons suffering from advanced cancer also seemed to find their psychedelic sessions more fatiguing than the other categories of individuals with whom we have worked. Especially after the long LSD sessions many patients felt tired not only on the evening of that same day but also during the entire day following their sessions. Because of this the beneficial effects of a session were frequently masked by various degrees of physical and emotional exhaustion and did not become noticeable to hospital personnel until the second day after the psychedelic session.

Among experiences quite specific for cancer patients were, of course, those sequences that were directly related to their malignancies. In several instances individuals with whom the issue of diagnosis and prognosis was not discussed prior to their LSD experiences because of strong resistance on the part of the patient or close relatives arrived at the correct conclusion during the session. This was based on the insightful synthesis of various clues and observations or on direct body awareness of their own tissues and cellular processes. Many persons with whom we worked had a direct experience of their disease, either by visualizing the cancer itself or intuiting the malignant process. Images of the cancer site, its anatomical and topographical characteristics, and vascular supply, were common. These insights were frequently associated with psychodynamic material that appeared to be related to the genesis of the cancer.

Individuals who became clearly aware of the cancer process occasionally made spontaneous attempts at self-healing. They usually followed their intuition as to what the specific therapeutic intervention should be. Sometimes they tried to free themselves of psychological or physical blocks in the affected parts of the body. On other occasions they became consciously aware of destructive forces allegedly underlying the malignancy and tried to discharge them. Another approach that cancer patients would try in psychedelic sessions was an attempt to create a healing energy field enveloping the diseased organ or the whole body; sometimes they would describe it in terms of color, such as a green or blue light. Some other alternatives observed in this situation were a vivid visualization of the growth and an attempt to constrict the arteries supplying it with blood, or an effort to mobilize the defenses of the organism and increase the access of antibodies to the tumor.* In view of the sensitivity of the phychedelic treatment procedure and the lack of knowledge about the nature of cancer, our approach was neither to program specifically such therapeutic experimentation nor to discourage it when it occurred spontaneously.

Certain types of experiences that occur regularly in sessions of other subjects seemed to occur more frequently in dying individuals or were experienced with more emotional involvement. So the emphasis on the experiences of death and the search for meaning in human existence was quite understandable in view of the circumstances. Another frequent theme in these sessions was the crystallization of attitudes toward various family members, close friends, and acquaintances with an effort to finish "old business" and reach a greater understanding of the meaning of these relationships. Dying persons often reviewed their entire present social fields and histories with the desire to complete

* These efforts bear a striking similarity to the therapeutic approach developed by Carl and Stephanie Simonton, who, in addition to specific anticancer treatment, conduct meditation groups where they teach cancer patients techniques of relaxation and visualization aimed at enhancing the protective mechanisms of the human body.

the pattern of their existence in view of their impending deaths. More frequently than in an average psychedelic session, the sessions of dying individuals seemed to contain the element of a condensed replay and reevaluation of their entire past history from the moment of birth on.

Another frequent experience was the sense of a vivid encounter with the spiritual essence of various deceased relatives, and a reassuring telepathic exchange with them. These experiences were unusually vivid and convincing; they often contributed considerably to the belief that there might be some form of existence beyond the point of physical demise. In several instances they helped to introduce an element of joyful expectation and familiarity into a previously terrifying concept of dying and death. In this way a psychedelic session can induce a situation that naturally occurs in many non-Western cultures, where a deep belief in the spiritual existence of ancestors can be a powerful factor in easing the transition to death.

In discussing the results of LSD-assisted psychotherapy with cancer patients, we are dealing with a complex process that combines chemical and psychological elements. It is interesting to consider the contribution of these two components to the final therapeutic outcome. Without a specifically designed control study it is difficult to determine conclusively to what extent the results can be explained in terms of the direct pharmacological effects of LSD per se, and the degree to which they may be attributed to the psychotherapy that precedes, accompanies, and follows the drug administration. In the absence of statistical data from a large-scale control study, all the conclusions presented here will be tentative and based on clinical observations and impressions. Evidence already exists of the value of both drug-free psychotherapy and LSD chemotherapy with dying cancer patients. Elisabeth Kübler-Ross, Cicely Saunders, Carl and Stephanie Simonton, and others have reported noteworthy psychotherapeutic progress with the dying without the aid of psychedelic drugs. Hospital chaplains have assisted patients and their families in the task of living as fully as possible while confronting the imminence of death. On the other hand, Eric Kast obtained positive results with a predominantly chemotherapeutic approach and minimal interpersonal interaction.*

The relative contribution of the pharmacological and psychological components in psychedelic therapy is more or less an academic question. Psychotherapeutic work and the drug's effects are interdependent; they complement and deepen each other, and create a new treatment process that is qualitatively different from any of its parts. The history of the use of psychedelics and of LSD research indicates that psychotherapeutic rapport maximizes the benefits and minimizes the risks of LSD administration. Yet that Kast obtained clearly positive results without a psychotherapeutic matrix strongly suggests that the potential analgesic and therapeutic value of the drug itself should not be underestimated.

We will now focus on the therapeutic changes observed in cancer patients as a result of psychedelic treatment and discuss the possible psychological and physiological mechanisms involved. Since these changes occurred in several different areas, they have to be discussed in separate categories. The most important results were observed in the following five areas: (1) emotional symptoms, such as depression, suicidal tendencies, tension, anxiety, insomnia, and psychological withdrawal; (2) physical pain and distress; (3) fear of death, philosophical concept of death, and attitude toward dying; (4) time orientation and basic hierarchy of values; (5) grief and mourning of the surviving family members, and their ability to integrate the loss.

Our previous clinical experiences from the work with various categories of psychiatric patients, as well as data from existing LSD

---

* It is very difficult to compare the findings of the Spring Grove group with those reported by Eric Kast because of the differences in the dosage levels, therapeutic concepts, and objectives, as well as the set and setting. Kast routinely used 100 micrograms of LSD in his experiments; he did not forewarn his patients; and he frequently terminated the sessions with chlorpromazine at the occurrence of the slightest signs of distress. In our approach LSD was administered in much higher dosages (200–600 micrograms) after careful preparation and in the framework of intensive psychotherapy. Our aim was to relieve not only the physical but also the emotional suffering and, more specifically, the individuals' fear of death. In spite of the fact that a profound positive transcendental experience was considered the most desirable objective, the patients were strongly encouraged to work through emotionally difficult experiences if these occurred in their sessions.

literature, indicated that psychedelic therapy can have a positive effect on a variety of *emotional symptoms and problems*. In fact, there has been general agreement among LSD therapists that depression, tension, and free-floating anxiety—symptoms commonly observed in people dying of cancer—are among those that most readily respond to LSD-assisted psychotherapy. The experience of the first author (S.G.) based on his early work in Europe suggests that the experience of ego death in psychedelic sessions is the most powerful remedy against suicidal tendencies. The changes in this category were not, therefore, particularly surprising for the researchers. The only piece of new information was that the above symptoms can respond to LSD therapy, even if they are of a reactive nature and appear to be an understandable response to a most difficult life situation. This aspect makes such symptoms different from those occurring in psychiatric patients, where the pathological emotions can usually be traced back to early childhood, and where the individual is frequently instrumental in complicating his or her own life.

It is not easy to explain the often dramatic changes in symptoms and personality structure which occur as a result of psychedelic therapy. The preparatory period that initiates the process of change is a matter of days, and the transformation itself occurs during the drug session, even though the final integration of such an experience can take days or weeks. It is quite clear that this process is very complex and cannot be reduced to a single common denominator. We can briefly review what we know about the underlying dynamics and outline some of the factors that are involved.

It seems that LSD-assisted psychotherapy involves a favorable combination of a number of mechanisms that operate in conventional psychotherapeutic approaches. Because of the amplifying effect of LSD, all these mechanisms are greatly intensified. The most important of the well-known therapeutic factors that play an important role in LSD psychotherapy are recall and vivid reliving of traumatic childhood memories; facilitation of emotional and intellectual insights; corrective emotional experiences; and intensification of the transference phenomena between therapist and patient

Many of the dramatic changes following psychodynamic LSD sessions can be explained in terms of shifts in the interplay of specific memory constellations, *systems of condensed experience (COEX systems)*.* Observations from LSD psychotherapy indicate that emotionally important events from the life of the individual are recorded in the memory banks in such a way that they form specific experiential clusters. The dynamic structure of these constellations is such that memories from various periods of life that involve similar elements or have an emotional charge of the same quality are stored in close association with each other. According to the nature of the emotional charge, we can distinguish *negative COEX systems* reflecting specific traumatic events and unpleasant experiences, and *positive COEX systems* involving pleasant aspects of the individual's history. Those persons who are tuned into the network of negative COEX systems perceive themselves and the world in a pessimistic way; they experience depression, anxiety, or some other form of emotional distress (depending on the nature and content of the COEX systems involved). Those who are under the influence of positive COEX systems are in a state of emotional well-being and optimal functioning, and are capable of enjoying themselves and the world. Changes in the governing function of COEX systems can occur as a result of various physiological or biochemical processes occurring inside the organism or as a reaction to a number of external influences of a psychological or organic nature. The LSD session seems to represent a deep intervention into the dynamics of COEX systems. Sudden clinical improvements occurring during LSD therapy can be explained as a shift from a psychological dominance of a negative COEX system to a state where the individual is under the influence of a positive memory constellation. Such a change does not necessarily mean that all the unconscious material underlying the pathological state has been worked through or, for that matter, that any of it has been resolved. It simply indicates an inner

* The concept of COEX systems and their dynamics has been described in detail in *Realms of the Human Unconscious; Observations from LSD Research,* by Stanislav Grof.

shift from one system to another; such a situation can be referred to as *COEX transmodulation.*

Such a systemic shift does not always mean clinical improvement. There is a possibility that a poorly resolved LSD session will result in a shift from a positive system to a negative one; this situation is characterized by the sudden occurrence of psychopathological symptoms that were not apparent prior to the session. Another possibility is a shift from one negative COEX system to another negative system with a different content; the external manifestation of this intrapsychic event is a change in psychopathology from one clinical syndrome to another.

Although the mechanisms that we have discussed above can account for many instances of important alleviation of emotional symptoms in psychedelic therapy, they certainly do not provide an adequate explanation for all sudden improvements. Most really dramatic results in this area have been observed in connection with LSD sessions that have had a very important perinatal emphasis. In those individuals who have gone through the ego death and rebirth followed by a unitive experience, the presession symptoms were frequently drastically mitigated or even completely eliminated. Such an improvement following a single LSD session can last for days, weeks, or even months, depending on many variables. It seems that this profound experience, usually referred to as the psychedelic peak experience, may constitute a new and powerful means for eliciting profound therapeutic changes and for facilitating restructuring of the personality.

The last dimension of LSD-assisted psychotherapy with dying individuals associated with therapeutic changes is of an interpersonal rather than intrapsychic nature. Certain aspects of the improvement of a dying individual's emotional condition are directly related to psychotherapeutic work with family members and the surrounding social network. Clarifying distorted communication, cutting through protective screens, and opening channels of direct and honest interaction are themselves important factors of change. This experience has a predictably beneficial influence on the feelings of hopelessness, alienation, and confusion frequently experienced by a person facing death.

The often dramatic effect of LSD or DPT psychotherapy on *severe physical pain* is more difficult to explain. A single psychedelic session has often been followed by considerable alleviation or even disappearance of excruciating pain, on occasion even in individuals who did not respond to high dosages of powerful narcotics. This potentially important phenomenon is very complex and puzzling, and poses a difficult theoretical problem. The explanation of this effect of LSD on physical pain in all its ramifications could well contribute to radical revision of our understanding of the nature of pain.

The effects of LSD on pain cannot be interpreted simply in terms of its pharmacological action. They are not sufficiently predictable and consistent to be considered a pharmacological analgesia. There also is no clear dose-response relationship; dramatic alleviation of pain occurred after some sessions with relatively low dosages, and some of the high-dose sessions did not have a detectable analgesic effect. It has happened that in cancer patients who had more than one session, this effect occurred after some sessions but not after others, although the same dosage was used in all of them. Also, in some instances relief of pain was observed for a period of weeks or even months after a single administration of the drug. All this suggests the participation of a definite psychological component in the analgesic effect.

Changes in the perception of pain following LSD sessions did not consist in all instances simply of a reduction of the intensity of pain. The transformation of pain perception followed several distinct patterns. Some individuals reported that following their LSD sessions or shortly thereafter, pain was considerably mitigated or totally disappeared. Others noticed that the pain was still there, but their attitude toward it had changed; there was suddenly a much higher pain tolerance, or the pain did not attract their attention so irresistibly, and they could focus on a variety of other things. On occasion, dying individuals have reported quite unusual changes in their perception of pain and attitude toward it. They were able to reevaluate the emotional connotation of their pain and find in it philosophical significance, transcendental experiential qualities, religious meaning, or karmic value. For one of these patients, Susanne (see p. 83ff.), the psychedelic session proved very beneficial in terms of alleviating her persistent depression and fear of death but failed to influence the excruciating pain that was consuming her total awareness. The session, however, contributed to her strong resolve to go through the palliative surgery that she had formerly regarded with overwhelming fear. Susanne's experience clearly shows the possibility of dissociation of the effect of psychedelic sessions on severe physical pain from the and on the emotional condition.

In several sessions cancer patients also discovered various attitudes and techniques that made it possible for them to overcome pain during drug sessions or when it occurred at a later time. Some of these proved so effective that we adopted and routinely taught them as part of the preparation for the session. In many instances it has proven very helpful to direct one's attention away from the pain to the flow of music, to let oneself be fully involved in the sequences of images and experiences as they unfold in the session, and be totally immersed in the here and now. Another very useful approach to the modification of pain is what could at first appear to be the exact opposite—focusing and concentrating on the pain with an accepting attitude. This usually results in a temporary amplification of the unpleasant sensations to the point that the individual briefly reaches his or her experiential limit of pain and then transcends it. Thus, paradoxically, accepting pain, yielding to it, "going into it and with it" can make it possible to move experientially beyond pain altogether. In general, the least useful approach to pain seems to be to let it occupy the center of awareness, while at the same time resisting it and fighting against it.

In postsession intervals it proved unusually helpful for patients to evoke images or entire episodes from their psychedelic sessions that were characterized by highly positive emotions and freedom from pain. This could be facilitated by listening to the same music that was played during these episodes in the psychedelic session. Sometimes an explicit suggestion made in a light hypnotic trance to move beyond the suffering and pain served a similar function.

Although the significance of the psychological component in the mechanism of pain relief induced by LSD is unquestionable, the specifics of this phenomenon are at this point still obscure. We have not been able to find any relationship between the nature of the LSD session or its content and the degree or pattern of pain relief. Changes in pain perception have sometimes been observed after otherwise unsuccessful and poorly resolved sessions that did not have a particularly beneficial effect on other aspects of the patient's clinical condition. On the other hand, in cases such as Susanne's, we saw instances of sessions that transformed an individual in every respect except the intensity of physical pain. The correlation between the level of the unconscious activated in the session and the effect on pain seems to be minimal. Pain relief has been observed after sessions of every type; yet we have worked with a number of individuals where seemingly similar sessions did not have any effect on pain. The almost capricious quality of this phenomenon can be illustrated by the story of John (see p. 89ff.). He was probably the most salient example of the dramatic effect that psychedelic drugs can have on the experience of pain, in spite of the fact that his session at first appeared to be uneventful and unsuccessful.

As emphasized in articles by Eric Kast and V. J. Collins, pathological pain is a composite phenomenon that has a neurophysiological component, represented by the pain sensation, and a psychological component, namely the pain affect. It seems that psychedelic therapy influences the pain experience primarily by modifying the psychological component—the way the actual neurophysiological stimulation is interpreted and dealt with—rather than by obliterating or reducing the neuronal impulses responsible for painful sensations. Many observations from LSD sessions seem to indicate that various physically painful experiences in the life history of an individual are recorded in the memory banks in close association with each other. The resulting memory constellations are then functionally linked with the experiences on the perinatal level. Thus, episodes of pain and physical suffering from the individual's life related to operations, injuries, diseases, and physical abuse are typically relived in LSD sessions in the context of the birth experiences. If an individual is exposed to situations that produce actual physical pain during a disease, accident, or surgical intervention, this seems to activate the specific memory constellations involving physical suffering and threat to body integrity or survival. The nature and content of past experiences involving pain will then determine and color the resulting pain perception and the individual's reaction to it. In the case of patients suffering from chronic and progressive diseases, particularly those that are considered incurable, there is also a tendency to create in fantasy a rather concrete trajectory of continuation and increase of pain in the future. It was Kast who first drew attention to the possibility that reducing this anticipation could be an important mechanism responsible for at least part of the analgesic action of LSD (in a pioneering paper, "Pain and LSD-25," published in the 1964 book *LSD-25: The Consciousness-Expanding Drug*). He has clearly pointed out that symbol formation and anticipation, so vital to survival in ordinary life, in grave situations tend to augment the agony of an individual.

The totality of the pain experience seems thus to involve not only the direct neurophysiological response to tissue damage but also the past programming of the individual regarding painful events and anticipation of suffering in the future. One of the important effects of LSD is to divest traumatic memories of their emotional charge, making it possible for individuals to free themselves from this impact and to focus more fully on the present moment. This is usually accompanied by a comparable lessening of emotional investment with regard to the future. The resulting here-and-now orientation can be an important element in changing an individual's experience of pain.

Another aspect of the analgesic action of LSD seems to be related to the powerful tyrannizing effect that physical pain usually has on the patient's field of attention. Intense pain, quite predictably, tends to absorb the individual's awareness, to the exclusion of many other sensory phenomena. Many patients in this situation find it difficult or impossible to carry on conversations, read, watch television, or pursue any of their previous hobbies that could make their situation a little more tolerable. In extreme cases they even lose interest in keeping up with important events in the lives of close family members. LSD can break this emotional barrier and sensory impoverishment as a result of its mind-expanding effects. With unusual intensity, the field of awareness is flooded with material from the individual's unconscious and from the sensory organs, particularly the optical system. Fascinating visual displays of colors and forms, sounds, and unusual sensations inundate the consciousness of the patient who was previously dominated by the excruciating monotony of pain. The LSD experience opens the way to various important memories from an individual's life, as well as from transpersonal sources within him or herself. Returning from a well-resolved LSD session, the patient can once again enjoy the richness of sensory experiences—the beauty of nature, sounds of music, taste of food, or elements of human interaction. This expansion of awareness and emotional interest can persist for days or weeks after a successful LSD session.

Sometimes after a psychedelic session the individual is capable of refocusing attention from pain and physical discomfort to another area. Several patients developed a deep interest in books on mysticism, yoga, Buddhism, or unusual states of consciousness, and pursued this interest with great enthusiasm. Through their insights in LSD sessions others discovered how they can best spend their remaining days. Thus one woman decided that her dying could become a powerful catalyst in bringing her alienated relatives closer together, and she spent the last weeks of her life working systematically on this task.

The influence of psychedelic therapy on pain associated with cancer cannot be explained in all its complexity within the framework of the traditional neurophysiological theories. Ronald Melzack, professor of psychology at McGill University in Montreal, collected many laboratory and clinical observations that represent an equally serious challenge to contemporary concepts of pain.* In his 1973 book, *The Puzzle of Pain,* Melzack suggested a radical revision of medical thinking

---

* The most important observations analyzed by Melzack are congenital insensitivity to noxious stimuli and its opposite, spontaneous psychogenic pain occurring without detectable external input; peculiar characteristics of some pain syndromes such as phantom limb and various neuralgias; high rate of failure after radical surgical operations aimed at alleviating pain, and surprising success of certain other procedures; and, above all, the analgesic and anaesthetic effect of acupuncture.

in this area. Since his work seems to throw some light on our findings in psychedelic therapy of cancer patients, we will briefly review his most important contributions. According to Melzack, it is necessary from the theoretical as well as practical point of view to distinguish three major components of pain. First is the sensory-discriminative dimension of pain; it is mediated by the specific sensory pathways (spinothalamic projection system) and involves perceptual information regarding the location, magnitude, and spatiotemporal properties of the noxious stimulus. Second is the emotional and motivational dimension actuated by the reticular system of the brainstem and by limbic structures; this contributes a distinctly unpleasant emotional quality to the pain experience and the aversive drive to escape the stimulus and seek relief from pain. Third is the cognitive and evaluative dimension of pain, which is the neocortical addition to the total experience; here belong cultural learning, the unique history of the individual, the meaning the individual gives to the pain-producing situation, the effect of suggestion, and the state of mind of the individual at that moment. These three components of pain, as well as their relative participation in the pain experience, can be selectively influenced by a variety of factors.

In 1965 Melzack and Wall formulated the so called gate control theory of pain, which seems to account for many seemingly mysterious aspects of pain. They postulated a neural mechanism in the dorsal horns of the spinal cord (probably the so-called gelatinous substance) that acts like a gate; this gating mechanism can increase or decrease the flow of nerve impulses from peripheral fibers to the central nervous system. The degree to which the gate facilitates or inhibits sensory transmission is determined by the relative activity in large-diameter and small-diameter fibers and by descending influences from the brain. Somatic inputs from all parts of the body, as well as visual and auditory inputs, are able to exert a modulating influence on the transmission of impulses through the gating mechanism. The presence or absence of pain is thus determined by the balance between the sensory and the central inputs to the gate-control system. When the amount of information that passes through the gate exceeds a critical level, it activates the neural areas responsible for the pain experience and pain response.

Melzack and Wall's theory seems to provide a plausible theoretical framework for a better understanding of and insight into the seemingly capricious effect of psychedelic therapy on the pain experience of cancer patients. The variability of results seems to reflect a dynamic interaction between the multidimensional nature of the psychedelic experience and the complexity of the neurophysiological structures and mechanisms underlying the pain phenomenon. Thus clinical observations concerning the effect of LSD and DPT on pain can be considered an important additional source of supportive evidence for the gate-control theory of pain.

We will try to account for the seeming discrepancy in the Spring Grove LSD study of the relief of pain not being reflected by an equally dramatic drop in the consumption of narcotics. At least four factors should be taken into consideration in evaluating this situation. First, no attempt was made to reduce narcotic medication. Neither the patients nor the nurses were asked to make an effort to change the pharmacological regime. The consumption of narcotics reflected the spontaneous interaction between the patients' demands and the response of the medical personnel. So one element of these paradoxical findings reflects simply an element of inertia and habitual routine on the part of the patients as well as the staff. In some cases the narcotic medication might have been continued even if the need for it decreased. Second, most of the patients received, in addition to narcotics, a variety of other psychoactive substances, such as major or minor tranquilizers, nonnarcotic analgesics, and hypnotics. The changes in consumption of these drugs were not taken into consideration or measured systematically in our study. This is especially important in the case of phenothiazine derivatives and minor tranquilizers that we routinely discontinued a week before the session in order not to interfere with the effect of LSD. Third, in many patients even heavy narcotic medication did not control pain successfully prior to the administration of LSD. As a matter of fact, lack of response to narcotic medication and persisting severe pain was one of the main reasons many of the patients were accepted into our study. In some of these patients the narcotic medication was not reduced after the LSD session, but the same amount of narcotic became effective in controlling pain and made life more tolerable. Finally, it is possible that the apparent discrepancy between the experience of pain and the demand for narcotics also reflects the element not only of habituation but actual physiological addiction in individuals who had been under heavy narcotic medication for many months prior to the session.

An important dimension of the changes following psychedelic therapy of individuals dying of cancer was the modification and frequently dramatic transformation of their *concept of death* and attitude toward the situation they were facing. In LSD treatment of psychiatric patients or normal subjects, we have frequently heard comments concerning feelings about death. Those who have gone through death and rebirth sequences in their psychedelic sessions often describe a very radical change in their attitude toward death. Deep experiences of cosmic unity and of certain other transpersonal forms of consciousness seem to render the fact of physical death irrelevant.* The fact that these experiences can have a profound transformative influence on individuals for whom the prospect of physical death is a matter of months, weeks, or days suggests that they deserve serious attention. They occur in a complex psychological, philosophical, mythological, and spiritual context, and appear to be much more than momentary self-deceptions resulting from altered brain functioning.

In discussing the changes in attitudes toward death in the previously mentioned paper, Kast suggests that some mechanism must protect

---

* Observations from psychedelic therapy with individuals dying of cancer concerning the alleviation of fear of death are indirectly supported by the findings of Charles A. Garfield. In his 1974 doctoral dissertation this investigator explored the relationship between long-term systematic experiences in consciousness alteration and the level of death-related fear in 150 selected male subjects. Using a combination of clinical interviews, psychometric testing, and psychophysiological measurements, Garfield studied the differences in conscious and unconscious fear of death among the members of five subcultures: graduate students in psychology, graduate students in religion, psychedelic drug users, Zen meditators, and American-born disciples of Tibetan Buddhism. In this study the groups who had extensive experience with altered states of consciousness (psychedelic drug users, Zen meditators, and students of Tibetan Buddhism) showed a significantly lower level of fear associated with death than the student groups.

dying patients from a devastating realization of hopelessness. According to him, however, the "desperate" situation of such individuals is only quantitatively different from that of any person who can anticipate death at any time with some probability and ultimately with certainty. Kast therefore assumes that the mechanisms that protect us daily from the realization of our own mortality operate with greater force in the dying patient. He believes that the terror experienced in the contemplation of death by "preterminal" patients, as well as by healthy persons, is based on the fear of loss of control over their bodies and their environments. The acceptance of and surrender to the inevitable loss of control during and after LSD administration are seen by Kast as indications that LSD apparently eases the blow which impending death deals to the fantasy of infantile omnipotence.

In addition, Kast emphasizes the diminution of anticipation as an important factor in relieving both the experience of pain and the fear of death. Under normal circumstances anticipation represents a very important mechanism that is useful not only for orientation but also for defense and procurement of food. According to Kast, anticipation can offer nothing to the welfare of the dying person, however, and can only accentuate feelings of helplessness. Anticipation is contingent upon the ability to use words meaningfully and to form and manipulate symbols. Kast sees the decrease in the power of words and the resulting loss of the ability to anticipate, together with the expansion of the immediate sensory life, as the most important factors modifying the attitudes of dying individuals toward death.

The above explanations, although they certainly point to important aspects of the LSD effect, do not account for all of the profound changes observed in many dying individuals undergoing psychedelic psychotherapy. Unlike the transformation of the experience of pain that can occur after any type of LSD experience, changes in feelings about dying and death seem to be associated with the specific content of the session. In our experience dramatic changes in the concept of death and attitudes toward it only took place following LSD sessions that had perinatal and transpersonal elements. Those individuals who experienced the phenomenon of ego death followed by the experience of rebirth and cosmic unity seemed to show radical and lasting changes in their fundamental understanding of human nature and its relation to the universe. Death, instead of being the ultimate end of everything, suddenly appeared as a transition into a different type of existence; the idea of the possible continuity of consciousness beyond physical death seemed to be much more plausible than the opposite. Dying persons who had transcendental experiences developed a deep belief in the ultimate unity of all creation; they often experienced themselves as integral parts of it, including their disease and the often painful situations they were facing.

The vivid experiential encounters with elements of the deep unconscious in the form of perinatal or transpersonal phenomena made it possible for the dying to relate in a very tangible and convincing manner to spiritual and psychic dimensions that were beyond their previous conceptual frameworks. As a result of their psychedelic experiences, these individuals became consciously aware of their archetypal heritage and the ancestral, racial, collective, phylogenetic, and karmic elements in their unconscious. The sharp demarcation between the ego and nonego tended to dissolve, and the usual distinction between the inner world of one's own mind and external reality became much more arbitrary. The opening of this enormous cosmic panorama provided a new referential system of such proportions that the fact of individual destruction, viewed against this background, appeared to lose its terrifying impact.

It would be a purely academic exercise at this point to debate whether the changes of consciousness occurring in psychedelic sessions have any ontological relevance through offering valid insights into the nature of human existence and the universe. Whatever the final answer to this question, the cosmic visions experienced in psychedelic sessions appear very real to individuals facing death, and they make their otherwise dismal situations much more tolerable.*

The striking changes in the subject's *hierarchy of life values* ob-

---

* It should be mentioned in this context that an increasing number of scientists seems to be finding deep parallels between the mystical world-view and the revolutionary findings of twentieth-century science, particularly modern physics. More information about this transition can be found, for example, in Fritjof Capra's *The Tao of Physics* and Bob Toben's *Space-Time and Beyond*.

served after psychedelic sessions are usually directly related to the insights associated with perinatal and transpersonal experiences. Psychological acceptance of impermanence and death results in a realization of the absurdity and futility of exaggerated ambitions, attachment to money, status, fame, and power, or pursuit of other temporal values. This makes it easier to face the termination of one's professional career and the impending loss of all worldly possessions. Time orientation is typically transformed; the past and future become less important as compared with the present moment. Psychological emphasis tends to shift from trajectories of large time periods to living "one day at a time." This is associated with an increased ability to enjoy life and to derive pleasure from simple things. There is usually a distinct increase of interest in religious matters, involving spirituality of a universal nature rather than beliefs related to any specific church affiliation. On the other hand, there were many instances where a dying individual's traditional beliefs were deepened and illumined with new dimensions of meaning.

The significance of psychedelic therapy with the dying transcends the narrow framework of help to the patient. Times of death are times of crisis in any family. Although most of the suffering is experienced by the patient, the situation of impending separation is one of profound emotional relevance for many other persons involved. Close relatives and friends frequently have strong reactions to the immediate situation; in addition, some of them are facing the possibility of long-term adverse consequences. Practicing psychiatrists are well aware of the fact that the deaths of parents and other close relatives play a very important role in the development of many emotional disorders, either as original traumata if they occurred in childhood, or as important triggers of manifest symptoms later in life.

It seems that the *nature of the grieving and bereavement period* is deeply affected by the degree and nature of the conflicts in the survivors' relationships with the dying person. Adjustment to the death of a family member may be more difficult if relatives have ambivalent feelings about the appropriateness of their behavior regarding the dying person and about the way the entire situation was managed. The absence of the opportunity to express one's compassion for the dying, to utter words of gratitude for the past, or to find a way to say good-bye leaves survivors with feelings of dissatisfaction, bitterness, and often intense guilt. If the therapist can enter the system as a catalyzing agent and help to open channels of effective emotional exchange and communication, dying and death can become an event of profound meaning for everyone involved. It can result in feelings of an encounter with the eternal forces of the universe to which we are all subject; under these circumstances very little guilt is experienced regarding human suffering and death, and the grief period seems to be considerably shortened. In addition, participation in the process that the dying person is going through can influence the concepts of death of surviving children and even adults, help them to form the model of their own deaths, and possibly influence favorably their own approaches to this ultimate transition. Adequate therapeutic intervention often gave us the opportunity to ease the agony of death for the one who died and, at the same time, to help those who went on living to absorb and integrate this trauma.

Psychedelic therapy is not chemotherapy, nor does it provide therapeutic magic. The quality of the human encounter, sensitive psychotherapeutic guidance of the dying, individual work with the family, and the optimism of the therapist are factors of crucial significance. Therapist optimism is a powerful factor in many forms of psychotherapy. Dramatic experiences in psychedelic sessions and subsequent positive changes in feelings, attitudes, and behavior are more than enough to keep the enthusiasm of the therapist at a high level, even in the face of what is frequently a grim reality.

Enthusiasm and optimism would not be enough, however, for conducting a program of LSD-assisted psychotherapy. For those who may attempt to replicate the Spring Grove LSD program for cancer patients or start their own modification thereof, a word of caution should be offered regarding the need for specialized training. According to our experience, an optimal preparation involved not only familiarization with the existing literature, watching videotape material from LSD sessions, and actual participation in sessions conducted by an experienced therapist, but also LSD training sessions for the future therapist. Thus, in the LSD training program for professionals conducted at Spring Grove, psychiatrists and psychologists had the opportunity to experience firsthand drug-induced altered states of consciousness and appreciate the dimensions of the LSD reaction. Such intimate knowledge seems to be necessary for effective and sensitive LSD psychotherapy. As has been frequently emphasized in the past, psychedelic states seem to defy adequate description, and it is impossible to gain a deep understanding about them by reading books and articles in scientific journals.

Another important dimension of the LSD training exposure is that the future sitter is given the opportunity to confront and work through his or her own fear of death and other emotional areas that will emerge in work with the dying. The equanimity and centeredness of the therapist when confronted with such material is one of the most important variables in successful LSD psychotherapy. During his work in the Psychiatric Research Institute in Prague, as well as the Maryland Psychiatric Research Center in Baltimore, the first author (S.G.) collected much evidence indicating that it is extremely helpful if nurses and other members of the professional team who come in contact or are working with individuals undergoing psychedelic therapy have the opportunity to experience the LSD state themselves.

Our clinical experience suggests that with adequate training such as we have described above, LSD-assisted psychotherapy can be a relatively safe and promising approach in an area that has thus far been most discouraging. Although members of the helping professions and the public have developed an awareness of the urgent need to help dying individuals, very few effective programs exist in this area. A majority of dying patients are still faced with a very dim picture, described by Aldous Huxley in *Island* as "increasing pain, increasing anxiety, increasing morphine, increasing demandingness, with the ultimate disintegration of personality and a loss of the opportunity to die with dignity."

7.

CONSCIOUSNESS AND THE THRESHOLD OF DEATH

Individuals who experience the encounter with death in psychedelic sessions frequently report that it feels extremely authentic and convincing, to the point of being indistinguishable from actual dying. Many descriptions of changes of consciousness in persons facing situations of vital emergency or experiencing clinical death exist in autobiographical accounts, novels, and poetry, but this area has been surprisingly neglected by psychiatrists and psychologists. There are only a few studies in which this interesting field has been systematically explored. We will briefly summarize the work that has been done, illustrate it with subjective accounts of survivors, and relate it to our observations from psychedelic research.

The first study in this area was not conducted by a psychiatrist or psychologist; the pioneering work was done in Switzerland by a Zürich geology professor, Albert Heim, who became famous for his studies of the Alps and for his book on mountain-forming processes. Having had several near-fatal accidents himself, Heim was very interested in subjective experiences of dying. Over a period of several decades he collected a number of observations and accounts from survivors of situations involving serious, vital threats. The persons who volunteered their reports were soldiers wounded in wars, masons and roofers who had fallen from heights, workers who survived disasters in mountain projects and railway accidents, and a fisherman who had nearly drowned. However, the most important part of Heim's study is based on the numerous reports made by Alpine climbers who had fallen off cliffs and were rescued, including three professional colleagues.*

Heim's conclusion in this study was that the subjective experiences of near-death in about 95% of the victims were strikingly similar and showed only slight variations. It did not seem to make much difference whether the precipitating situation was a fall from a cliff, a fall from ice or snow, or a fall into a ravine or waterfall. Even the subjective perceptions of those individuals who had been run over by a wagon, crushed by machines, shot on the battlefield, or experienced near-drowning basically followed the same pattern. In practically all persons who faced death in accidents, a similar mental state developed. There was no pain or despair, grief, or overwhelming anxiety, which tends to paralyze individuals in instances of lesser danger that do not threaten life acutely. Instead, mental activity at first became enhanced and accelerated, rising to a hundred-fold velocity and intensity. Then the individuals experienced feelings of calm and profound acceptance. The perception of events and anticipation of the outcome were unusually clear; there did not seem to be disorientation or confusion. Time became greatly expanded and individuals acted with lightning quickness and on the basis of accurate reality-testing of their situation. This was followed in many cases by a sudden review of the victim's entire past. Finally the person facing the threat of death often heard heavenly music and had an experience of transcendental beauty.

We will illustrate Heim's description of life-threatening situations

* Heim first presented his findings before the Uto Section of the Swiss Alpine Club on February 26, 1892. His paper was subsequently published under the title, "Notizen über den Tod durch Absturz" ("Remarks on Fatal Falls") in the yearbook of the Swiss Alpine Club.

with two subjective reports included in his original paper. The first is
an account of his own mountaineering accident, which occurred when
he was climbing in the Swiss Alps. He fell off a glacial sheet, dropped
about sixty-six feet, and landed on a border of snow.

As soon as I began to fall I realized that now I was going to be hurled
from the crag and I anticipated the impact that would come. With clawing
fingers I dug into the snow in an effort to brake myself. My fingertips were
bloody but I felt no pain. I heard clearly the blows on my head and back as
they hit each corner of the crag and I heard a dull thud as I struck below.
But I first felt pain some hours afterward. The earlier-mentioned flood of
thoughts began during the fall. What I felt in five to ten seconds could not
be described in ten times that length of time. All my thoughts and ideas
were coherent and very clear, and in no way susceptible, as are dreams, to
obliteration. First of all I took in the possibilities of my fate and said to
myself, "The crag point over which I will soon be thrown evidently falls
off below me as a steep wall since I have not been able to see the ground at
the base of it. It matters a great deal whether or not snow is still lying at
the base of the cliff wall. If this is the case, the snow will have melted
from the wall and formed a border around the base. If I fall on the border
of snow I may come out of this with my life, but if there is no more snow
down there, I am certain to fall on rubble and at this velocity death will be
quite inevitable. If, when I strike, I am not dead or unconscious I must in
stantly seize my small flask of spirits of vinegar and put some drops from it
on my tongue. I do not want to let go of my alpenstock; perhaps it can still
be of use to me." Hence I kept it tightly in my hand. I thought of taking
off my glasses and throwing them away so that splinters from them might
not injure my eyes, but I was so thrown and swung about that I could not
muster the power to move my hands for this purpose. A set of thoughts and
ideas then ensued concerning those left behind. I said to myself that upon
landing below I ought, indifferent to whether or not I were seriously injured, to call immediately to my companions out of affection for them to
say, "I'm all right!" Then my brother and three friends could sufficiently
recover from their shock so as to accomplish the fairly difficult descent to
me. My next thought was that I would not be able to give my beginning
university lecture that had been announced for five days later. I considered
how the news of my death would arrive for my loved ones and I consoled
them in my thoughts. Then I saw my whole past life take place in many

images, as though on a stage at some distance from me. I saw myself as the chief character in the performance. Everything was transfigured as though by a heavenly light and everything was beautiful without grief, without anxiety, and without pain. The memory of very tragic experiences I had had was clear but not saddening. I felt no conflict or strife; conflict had been transmuted into love. Elevated and harmonious thoughts dominated and united the individual images, and like magnificent music a divine calm swept through my soul. I became ever more surrounded by a splendid blue heaven with delicate roseate and violet cloudlets. I swept into it painlessly and softly and I saw that now I was falling freely through the air and that under me a snowfield lay waiting. Objective observations, thoughts, and subjective feelings were simultaneous. Then I heard a dull thud and my fall was over.

A second example from Heim's paper is, according to him, a classical presentation of subjective perceptions occurring during sudden accidental falls. It is an account of a theology student who was involved in a train disaster with the collapse of the Monschenstein Bridge in 1891.

Near the Birs Bridge, I felt a sudden strong shock that ensued from our erratic progress. But at the same moment, the train stopped in the middle of the fastest run. The shock threw the riders up to the roof. I looked backwards, unable to see what had happened. From the powerful metallic crashing that resounded up ahead, I presumed that there had been a collision. I opened the door and intended to go out. I noticed that the following car had lifted itself upwards and threatened to tumble down on me. I turned in my place and wanted to call to my neighbor at the window: "Out the window!" I closed my mouth as I bit my tongue sharply. Now there took place, in the shortest possible times, the ghastliest descent that one can imagine. I clung spasmodically to my seat. My arms and legs functioned in their usual way, as if instinctively taking care of themselves and, swift as lightning, they made reflex parries of the boards, poles, and benches that were breaking up around and upon me. During the time I had a whole flood of thoughts that went through my brain in the clearest way. The thoughts said, "The next impact will kill me." A series of pictures showed me in rapid succession everything beautiful and lovable that I had ever experienced, and between them sounded the powerful melody of a prelude I had heard in the morning: "God is almighty, Heaven and Earth rest in His hand; we must bow to His Will." With this thought in the midst of all the fearful turmoil I was overwhelmed by a feeling of undying peace. Twice more the car swung upwards; then the forward part suddenly headed perpendicularly down into the Birs, and the rear part that I was in swung sideways over the embankment and down into the Birs. The car was shattered. I lay jammed in and pressed under a heap of boards and benches and expected the near car to come crashing down on my head; but there was sudden quiet. The rumbling noise stopped. Blood dripped from my forehead, but I felt no pain. The loss of blood made me light-headed. After a short struggle I worked my way out of the heaps and fragments and through a window. Just then I formed, for the first time, a conception of the immensity of the disaster that had taken place. . . .

Heim concluded his paper by stating that death through falling is subjectively a very pleasant death. Those who have died in the mountains have, in their last moments, reviewed their individual pasts in states of transfiguration. Elevated above corporeal pain, they were under the sway of noble and profound thoughts, glorious music, and feelings of peace and reconciliation. They fell in a magnificent blue or roseate heaven, and then everything was suddenly still. According to Heim, fatal falls are much more "horrible and cruel" for the survivors than for the victims. It is incomparably more painful in both the feeling of the moment and subsequent recollection to see another person fall than to fall oneself. In many instances spectators have been deeply shattered and incapacitated by paralyzing horror and have carried a lasting trauma away from this experience while the victim, if he or she is not badly injured, comes out of this event free of anxiety and pain. Heim illustrated his point with his personal experience of seeing a cow falling, which was still painful for him, while his own misfortune was registered in his memory as a powerful and even ecstatic transfiguration—without pain and without anguish—just as it actually had been experienced.

The interest in certain specific aspects of dying shown by some researchers at the end of the nineteenth and beginning of the twentieth century had two different sources of motivation. One group of observers was interested in the subjective experiences of dying individuals from the point of view of prognostication, and were looking for psychological indicators of impending death. At this time the visions of dying persons attracted much attention, since they were considered very ominous portents. Edward Clarke's book *Visions: A Study of False Sight,* written while he was dying, became a classic in the field; it contains many accounts of near-death experiences and is an invaluable source of data for any serious researcher.

In the second group were professionals motivated primarily by their interest in parapsychology. They were studying the phenomenological aspects of dying and looking for indications of survival after physical death. With a few exceptions these psychic researchers were little concerned with the behavior and experiences of dying people themselves. Rather, their primary interest was in the extrasensory and visionary experiences of other people, especially relatives and friends, that coincided and were related to the death of a certain individual. The interest in actual experiences of the dying person was very limited and mostly revolved around the idea of "Peak in Darien" cases, originated by Miss F. P. Cobbe in 1877 and later emphasized and elaborated by James Hyslop in 1908, William Barrett in 1926, and Harnell Hart in 1929. This concept is based upon the belief that the spirits of dead relatives come to aid the dying, ease their transition, and take them away to another world. According to this view, dying patients frequently see the dead as apparitions in their sickrooms. This occurs in individuals with clear consciousness who are not delirious, disoriented, and confused, so that the apparitions cannot be explained simply in psychopathological terms. The "Peak in Darien" concept implies that dying persons see in this way only persons who are already dead. Particularly strong evidence was then seen in the situation where a patient saw an apparition of a dead person about whose death he or she was not informed.

Much more interesting for our purposes is an extensive study of the death-bed observations of physicians and nurses conducted by Karlis Osis and his co-workers, published in 1961. Instead of testing a specific narrow hypothesis, Osis decided to scan a wide range of phenomena occurring in dying individuals and to analyze the patterns in the data. The study was based on a large questionnaire survey; ten thousand questionnaires covering various aspects of death-bed observations were sent out, half of them to physicians and the other half to nurses. Detailed analyses were conducted on the 640 questionnaires that were returned. The respondents who returned these questionnaires claimed 35,540 death-bed observations.

Osis found that about 10% of dying patients appeared to be conscious in the hour preceding death. Surprisingly enough, fear was not the dominant emotion in these individuals, according to the physicians and nurses in the sample. They indicated that discomfort, pain, and even indifference were more frequent. It was estimated that about one in twenty dying persons showed signs of elation. A surprising finding in this research was the high incidence of visions with a predominantly nonhuman content. They were approximately ten times more frequent than one would expect in a comparable group of persons in normal health. Some of these visions were more or less in accordance with traditional religious concepts and represented heaven, paradise, or the Eternal City; others were secular images of indescribable beauty, such as landscapes with gorgeous vegetation and exotic birds. According to the authors, most of these visions were characterized by brilliant colors and bore a close resemblance to psychedelic experiences induced by mescaline or LSD. Less frequent were horrifying visions of devils and hell or other frightening experiences, such as being buried alive.

The main focus of this study was on hallucinations of dying individuals involving human beings. Osis was able to support Barrett's and Hyslop's hypotheses that dying individuals predominantly hallucinate phantoms representing dead persons, who often claim to aid the individual's transition into post-mortem existence. He also confirmed the apparitional nature of these hallucinations, since a large majority of patients experienced them in a state of clear consciousness. Their mental functioning was not disturbed by sedatives, other medication, or high body temperatures, and only a small proportion had a diagnosed illness which might be conducive to hallucinations, such as brain injury, cerebral disorders, mental disease, and uremia. Most dying individuals were fully conscious, with adequate awareness and responsiveness to the environment. This study also demonstrated the relative independence of the characteristics of these hallucinations from physiological, cultural, and personality variables. The roots of this type of experience seemed to go beyond the personality differences between the sexes, beyond physiological factors such as clinical diagnosis and type of illness, and beyond educational level and religious backgrounds. Hallucinations of dead people involved mostly close relatives of the dying individuals; visions of nonrelatives usually represented living persons.

Autobiographical accounts and descriptions in fiction and poetry seem to confirm that persons experiencing vital danger and those actually approaching death typically have episodes of unusual states of consciousness. These experiences are qualitatively different from our everyday consciousness and do not yield easily to verbal descriptions. It is therefore necessary to refer to accounts of individuals who are both gifted in introspection and very articulate in order to convey the flavor and dimensions of such experiences. One of the best descriptions of this kind can be found in Carl Gustav Jung's autobiography, *Memories, Dreams, Reflections*. Early in 1944 Jung broke his foot, and this accident was followed by a heart attack. While he hung on the edge of death and was getting oxygen and camphor injections, he had a series of profound visionary experiences. The following is a condensed version of his detailed account of this state:

> It seemed to me that I was high up in space. Far below I saw the globe of the earth, bathed in a gloriously blue light. I saw the deep blue sea and the continents. Far below my feet lay Ceylon, and in the distance ahead of me the subcontinent of India. My field of vision did not include the whole earth, but its global shape was plainly distinguishable and its outlines shone with a silvery gleam through that wonderful blue light. In many places the globe seemed colored, or spotted dark green like oxydized silver. Far away to the left lay a broad expanse—the reddish-yellow desert of Arabia; it was as though the silver of the earth had there assumed a reddish-gold hue.

Then came the Red Sea, and far, far back—as if in the upper left of a map—I could just make out a bit of the Mediterranean. My gaze was directed chiefly toward that. Everything else appeared indistinct. I could also see the snow-covered Himalayas, but in that direction it was foggy or cloudy. I did not look to the right at all. I knew that I was on the point of departing from the earth.

Later I discovered how high in space one would have to be to have so extensive a view—approximately a thousand miles! The sight of the earth from this height was the most glorious thing I had ever seen.

After contemplating it for a while, I turned around. I had been standing with my back to the Indian Ocean, as it were, and my face to the north. Then it seemed to me that I made a turn to the south. Something new entered my field of vision. A short distance away I saw in space a tremendous dark block of stone, like a meteorite. It was about the size of my house, or even bigger. It was floating in space, and I myself was floating in space.

I had seen similar stones on the coast of the Gulf of Bengal. They were blocks of tawny granite, and some of them had been hollowed out into temples. My stone was one such gigantic dark block. An entrance led into a small antechamber. To the right of the entrance, a black Hindu sat silently in lotus posture upon a stone bench. He wore a white gown, and I knew that he expected me. Two steps led up to this antechamber, and inside, on the left, was the gate to the temple. Innumerable tiny niches, each with a saucerlike concavity filled with coconut oil and small burning wicks, surrounded the door with a wreath of bright flames. I had once actually seen this when I visited the Temple of the Holy Tooth at Kandy in Ceylon; the gate had been framed by several rows of burning oil lamps of this sort.

As I approached the steps leading up to the entrance into the rock, a strange thing happened: I had the feeling that everything was being sloughed away; everything I aimed at or wished for or thought, the whole phantasmagoria of earthly existence, fell away or was stripped from me —an extremely painful process. Nevertheless something remained; it was as if I now carried along with me everything I had ever experienced or done, everything that had happened around me. I might also say: it was with me, and I was it. I consisted of all that, so to speak. I consisted of my own history, and I felt with great certainty: this is what I am. "I am this bundle of what has been, and what has been accomplished."

In Jung's case the visionary quality and mythical nature of his account could be interpreted as a result of his unusual personality and professional interests. The second example comes from an individual whose character and profession were very different from Jung's. The author is the German actor Curt Jurgens, who died a clinical death during a complicated surgical operation conducted in Houston, Texas, by Dr. Michael De Bakey. In order to replace the defective aorta with a plastic tube, the surgeon had to take the heart out of circulation. During this operation Curt Jurgens was dead for several minutes. The following is the account, from Jean-Baptiste Delacour's *Glimpses of the Beyond,* of his unusual experiences during this time:

> The feeling of well-being that I had shortly after the Pentothal injection did not last long. Soon a feeling that life was ebbing from me rose up from the subconscious. Today I like to say that this sensation came at the moment my heart stopped beating. Feeling my life draining away evoked powerful sensations of dread. I wanted to hold onto life more than anything, yet it was impossible for me to do so. I had been looking up into the big glass cupola over the operating room. This cupola now began to change. Suddenly it turned a glowing red. I saw twisted faces grimacing as they stared down at me. Overcome by dread, I tried to struggle upright and defend myself against these pallid ghosts, who were moving closer to me. Then, it seemed as if the glass cupola had turned into a transparent dome that was slowly sinking down over me. A fiery rain was now falling, but though the drops were enormous, none of them touched me. They splattered down around me, and out of them grew menacing tongues of flames licking up about me. I could no longer shut out the frightful truth: Beyond doubt, the faces dominating this fiery world were faces of the damned. I had a feeling of despair, of being unspeakably alone and abandoned. The sensation of horror was so great it choked me, and I had the impression I was about to suffocate.
>
> Obviously I was in Hell itself; and the glowing tongues of fire could be reaching me any minute. In this situation, the black silhouette of a human figure suddenly materialized and began to draw near. At first I saw it only indistinctly amid the flames and clouds of reddish smoke, but quickly it became clearer. It was a woman in a black veil, a slender woman with a lipless mouth and in her eyes an expression that sent icy shudders down my

back. When she was standing right face to face with me, all I could see were two black, empty holes. But out of these holes, the creature was nonetheless staring at me. The figure stretched out her arms toward me, and, pulled by an irresistible force, I followed her. An icy breath touched me, and I came into a world filled with faint sounds of lamentation, though there was not a person in sight. Then and there I asked the figure to tell me who she was. A voice answered: "I am death." I summoned all my strength and thought: "I'll not follow her any more, for I want to live." Had I betrayed this thought? In any event, she moved closer to me and put her hands on my bare breast so that I would again be under the spell of her magnetic force. I could feel her ice-cold hands on my skin, and the empty eye sockets were fixed immovably on me.

Again I concentrated all my thoughts on living, so as to escape death in this womanly guise. Before entering the operating room, I had embraced my wife. Now the phantom of my wife came to rescue me from Hell and lead me back to earthly existence.

When Simone [his wife] appeared on the scene, the woman with the black veil departed soundlessly, on her lipless face a dreadful smile. Death could avail nothing against Simone, all radiant with youth and life. I felt only freshness and tenderness as she led me back by the hand along the same way that just before had been under the dark figure's spell. Gradually, gradually we left the fearful realm of shadows behind us and approached the great light. This luminousness guided us on, and finally became so bright that it began to blind me, and I had to close my eyes.

Then suddenly a severe, dull pain set in, threatening to tear apart my chest cavity. I clutched Simone's hand harder and harder after my sudden return to consciousness. I found Simone sitting on my bed wearing a white nurse's uniform. I just had the strength to muster a weak smile. It was all I could do to utter one word: "Thanks." With this word I concluded a fearful but still fascinating journey into the afterworld, one I shall never forget as long as I live.

Additional accounts of near-death experiences and subjective concomitants of clinical death have been collected by Jess E. Weisse in a book entitled *The Vestibule.* Outstanding examples of fictional accounts are Lev Nikolaevich Tolstoy's *The Death of Ivan Ilyitch,* and his description of the death of Andrey Bolkonski in *War and Peace;*

Edgar Allan Poe's *A Descent into the Maelstrom;* Ambrose Bierce's *An Occurrence at Owl Creek Bridge;* and Caresse Crosby's *Passionate Years.*

In the past, efforts to understand the mechanism of experiences associated with death and to formulate a theoretical framework for their interpretation have been even more scarce than descriptive and phenomenological studies. Edward Clarke in *Visions: A Study of False Sight,* found a satisfactory explanation for the alteration of consciousness observed in dying individuals by relating them globally to impaired functioning of the brain. Others have made references to a more specific mechanism, cerebral anoxia, and pointed to the similarity between near-death experiences and various abnormal phenomena observed in high altitudes, during anaesthesia, in experimental subjects in hypoxic chambers, and other situations involving lack of oxygen. Karlis Osis (1961) and Russell Noyes (1971) found interesting parallels between visionary experiences of the dying and the states induced by psychedelic drugs. The latter observation, although of great theoretical significance, does not contribute to our understanding of dying. Psychedelic experiences are themselves very complex phenomena which have not yet been adequately explained and which represent a serious challenge to present theoretical thinking (we will return to this important problem in the following chapters).

All the above explanations are related at best to only one aspect of near-death phenomena: the physiological or biochemical trigger of these experiences. They do not say anything about their specific content and deeper psychological significance.

Two psychoanalytic studies have made serious attempts to apply basic psychoanalytic concepts to the study of death experiences. In the first of these papers Oskar Pfister used as a basis for his speculations the study conducted by Albert Heim that was described earlier in this chapter. In addition to Heim's observations collected during twenty-five years following his own near-fatal fall, Pfister had at his disposal a letter from Heim describing many details of his experience that were not mentioned in the original paper. The rich data obtained from Heim made it possible for Pfister to become acquainted with the general nature of near-death experiences. However, for a deeper psychodynamic assessment and interpretation of these phenomena, he needed the experient's free associations to the specific manifest content. Such analysis was made possible on the basis of information volunteered by a casual travel acquaintance. This man had been nearly killed in a wartime trench thirteen years prior to meeting Pfister. He was able to describe the fantasies he had had in that situation and to offer free associations to their content. On the basis of this material Pfister drew tentative theoretical conclusions about the psychodynamic mechanisms of the *shock thoughts* and fantasies of an individual in mortal danger.

Freud, in *Beyond the Pleasure Principle,* expressed the idea that the living organism would be annihilated by the energy-charged external world were it not equipped with a special protective apparatus that functions as a stimulus barrier. Pfister found this concept most useful for understanding the mechanism of near-death experiences. According to him, shock fantasies save the individual from excessive emotional trauma and function as a mechanism protecting him or her from losing waking consciousness and plunging into sleep or fainting. This mechanism would thus be a counterpart of the function that dreams play in protecting sleep. Where the danger is mild an individual will react with paralysis and speechlessness. Extreme danger, however, results in high activation and stimulation of thought production. Several protective mechanisms occur in this phase. One of these is the illusion that the danger can be coped with effectively; another is the ability to register all the accompanying feelings. Also, the derealization so frequently observed in this situation seems to have a protective function, because it involves a denial of the situation or its relevance. When it is not tenable any more to cope realistically with the danger, reality orientation breaks down and regressive fantasies enter in. Some of the recollections that are part of the frequently observed life review are memories of a comforting nature, allusions to dangerous situations in the past that had a happy ending, or free fantasies. Déjà vu experiences or flight into anticipation of the future can also be seen as denial of a grim reality situation. The extreme, of course, is escape into a transcendental experience of heaven or paradise that, according to psychoanalytic concepts, is a regression into the oceanic bliss of prenatal existence. Pfister thus sees near-death experiences as manifestations of "a brilliant victory of wishful thought over dreadful facts and illusion over reality." One more aspect of his work deserves special notice in this context. He himself pointed out that his concept of the protective function of shock thoughts raises interesting questions about the nature of consciousness. If consciousness contains knowledge of danger but does not let it become conscious, does this not mean that consciousness contains unconsciousness?

Another psychoanalytic study of the process of dying that has relevance for our discussion was published by R. C. Hunter, who had the unique opportunity of analyzing the content of a near-death experience of a medical nurse with whom he was working in long-term psychoanalysis. He saw her in regular analytic sessions two hours prior to her accident and twenty-two hours after it. These circumstances thus permitted the early collection of her fantasies and remembered experiences and some free associations to these. His patient was a physically healthy thirty-four-year-old woman who was the mother of three children. At the time of the accident she did not seem pathologically depressed, and there was no reason to suspect that she had suicidal impulses. She was in analysis because of interpersonal problems with her husband.

The near-fatal accident was unexpected and had an abrupt onset. Her dentist took an X ray of a tooth that was causing her pain and diagnosed an abscess forming at its root; he prescribed aspirin-codeine and penicillin. She took a tablet of the antibiotic when she was driving home with her husband in the rush-hour traffic. Twenty minutes later, as a result of penicillin allergy, she developed laryngeal and glottal edema accompanied by a high degree of suffocation and eventual unconsciousness. She was given adrenaline and taken by ambulance to a nearby hospital, where she was put on oxygen, more adrenaline, and cortical steroids. She recovered fully within a short time, and the next day she was able to talk about her experience in an analytic session. The following is Hunter's account of her report:

She had never before suffered from any allergic manifestations, nor was there a family history of allergy. Being a nurse, she was aware, however, of the occurrence of penicillin allergy, and when she took the tablet, the thought crossed her mind that she might be allergic to penicillin. In the car, when her breathing began to become difficult, she realized what was happening and she experienced frantic fear, which, however, soon passed. (She would never fear dying again, she said.) She felt intense sympathy for her husband. Then she felt guilty that she was putting him through this ordeal. She was ashamed. It felt to her now (*post hoc*) that it had been partly revenge, but really she had had no control over it. She remembered a "last violent reaction" in which she had fought desperately against it, but she was not afraid, and then she had given in, knowing she wanted it (death).

She had then witnessed, in rapid succession, a great many scenes from her life. They seemed in retrospect to start from about the age of five. She remembered the impression of vivid color. She had seen a beloved doll that she had had and was struck by how bright blue the glass eyes were. There was also a picture of herself on her bright red bicycle on the equally bright green lawn. She was confident that her whole life was not pictorially represented, only some scenes from her childhood, and she emphasized that it was all ecstatically happy.

Her next memory was of a state of "bliss" and of "ecstasy." There was a picture of the Taj Mahal in which she was deeply, idyllically engrossed. It was a picture that she must have seen on several occasions—the usual one taken from the end of the lily pond in front. It was colored, the pond and lily pads blue and green, the minarets and the dome a very lovely gold and cream. She became aware of people trying to wake her up and felt resentful and irritated. She wanted to be left alone with her beautiful dream of the Taj Mahal. Then she became aware of an oxygen mask and the fact that an intravenous was running. She reluctantly regained consciousness to find herself in the emergency out-patient department of a hospital.

Analyzing her experience, Hunter was surprised by the similarity of her account to that published by Pfister. In both of them the recognition of danger is followed by a brief fear reaction, denial of the threat, and then a review from the victim's earlier life of unusually happy or ecstatic scenes. Hunter suggests on the basis of his observations that we should differentiate between death as a state and the experience of dying. Whereas death might have many idiosyncratic meanings for different individuals, the process of suddenly and unexpectedly dying may move through certain definable and predictable stages. The content of these experiences is, however, colored by established personality patterns. Hunter sees the life review that occurred in his patient as a denial or negation of the life-threatening situation. The pleasant quality of the experience resulting from the sequence of regressive joyful memories and screen memories actually masked an unpleasant affect. In Hunter's interpretation the vision of the Taj Mahal had an idiosyncratic psychodynamic meaning for the patient. In addition to serving the purpose of negating and transcending the mortal danger, it also reflected her wishful fantasies toward her husband, as the Taj Mahal is a mausoleum built by an adoring husband for a beloved wife. On a deeper level of regression, according to Hunter, the pool and the dome were suggestive of intrauterine and breast fantasies.

The recent revival of scientific interest in the experience of dying is closely related to the work and thinking of Russell Noyes, M.D., professor of psychiatry at the University of Iowa. In a series of articles Noyes has reviewed a number of subjective accounts of individuals facing death and analyzed them from the psychiatric and psychodynamic point of view. He discovered striking uniformity, typical patterning, and characteristic experiential sequences underlying the seemingly rich and multiform content of individual accounts. According to Noyes, the descriptions of near-death and death experiences break down into three successive stages: *resistance, life-review,* and *transcendence.* Although the degree to which these individual stages are represented in a particular account can vary considerably, and despite the fact that in a particular case one of them might be missing, there is enough constancy and consistency in these phenomena to warrant such a division.

The initial stage of *resistance* involves recognition of danger, followed by fear of it or struggle against it, and finally acceptance of death. The realization that death is imminent precipitates a brief though violent struggle, often accompanied by marked anxiety. The individual oscillates between the need for active mastery and an urge for passive resignation. As long as even a slight chance of survival remains, the awareness of the dangerous situation and alertness to it are usually greatly enhanced. Under these circumstances the energy available for both physical and mental activity can be enormously increased. Disorganizing panic is delayed, but may emerge with full strength as soon as the immediate danger has passed. The remarkable acceleration of mental processes occurring in an individual facing death or serious injury often results in a fully conscious, sustained, and complex series of thoughts and even effective life-saving activity. This can be illustrated by Albert Heim's account of his accident, where such extraordinary activation of his mental resources saved him from extensive physical damage:

> In the summer of 1881, I fell between the front and rear wheels of a wagon traveling between Aosta and St. Remy and for a fleeting moment I was still able to hold onto the edge of the wagon. The following series of thoughts went through my mind: "I cannot manage to hold on until the horse comes to a stop; I must let go. If I simply let go, I will fall on my back and the wheel will travel forward over my legs. Then at least a fracture of the knee-pan or shinbone will be unavoidable; I must fall upon my stomach and the wheel will pass over the backs of my legs. If I will then tense the muscles, they will be a protective cushion for the bones. The pressure of the street will be somewhat less likely to break a bone than the pressure of the wheel. If I am able to turn myself to the left, then perhaps I can sufficiently draw back my left leg; on the other hand, turning to the right would, by the dimensions of the wagon, result in both legs being broken under it." I know quite clearly that I let myself fall only after these lightning-fast, wholly precise reflections, which seemed to imprint themselves upon my brain. Thereupon through a jerk of my arm, I turned myself to the left, swung my left leg powerfully outward, and simultaneously tensed my leg muscles to the limit of their strength. The wheel passed over my right ham, and I came out of it with a slight bruise.

Individuals undergoing the process of dying in a more gradual manner feel as though their will to live sustains them and are afraid that if they yield they will die. At the point of surrender fear subsides and the individual facing death develops a feeling of serenity and tranquility. When death becomes a certainty its advent is faced with inner calmness.

Usually the stage of *life-review* immediately follows the shift from active mastery to passive surrender. This is accompanied by a splitting of the self from its bodily representation that can give rise to out-of-body experiences. Individuals can actually see their bodies approaching death, but death as a reality is negated and they become witnesses watching this scene with detached interest. The review of life that occurs at this time usually takes the form of panoramic memories that follow in rapid succession and appear to encompass an individual's entire past. The unrolling of this life-film is sometimes retrogressive, moving from the time of the accident back into childhood; sometimes progressive, repeating the actual chronological sequence of events. This is typically accompanied by pleasant emotions, less frequently by a negative and painful affect. On occasion the life-review is of a holographic instead of sequential nature—in this case important memories from different periods of life appear simultaneously as part of a single continuum.

The stage of life-review can be illustrated by an excerpt from a letter written by Admiral Beaufort (in W. Munk's 1887 book, *Euthanasia or Medical Treatment in Aid of an Easy Death*) in which he describes his own near-drowning accident. When he was a youngster on board ship in Portsmouth harbor, he fell into the water. Being unable to swim, he soon became exhausted and temporarily sank below the surface before he was rescued.

> All hope fled, all exertion had ceased, a calm feeling of the most perfect tranquility superseded the previous tumultuous sensations—it might be called apathy, certainly not resignation, for drowning no longer appeared to be an evil. I no longer thought of being rescued, nor was I in any bodily pain. On the contrary, my sensations were now of rather a pleasurable cast, partaking of that dull but contented sort of feeling which precedes the sleep produced by fatigue. Though the senses were thus deadened, not so the mind; its activity seemed to be invigorated in a ratio which defies all

description, for thought rose after thought with a rapidity of succession that is not only indescribable, but probably inconceivable, by anyone who has not himself been in a similar situation. The course of these thoughts I can even now in a great measure retrace—the event which had just taken place, the awkwardness that had produced it, the bustle it must have occasioned, the effect it would have on a most affectionate father, and a thousand other circumstances minutely associated with home were the first series of reflection that occurred. They then took a wider range—our last cruise, a former voyage and shipwreck, my school, the progress I had made there and the time I had misspent, and even all my boyish pursuits and adventures. Thus traveling backwards, every past incident of my life seemed to glance across my recollection in retrograde succession; not, however, in mere outline as here stated, but the picture filled up every minute and collateral feature; in short, the whole period of my existence seemed to be placed before me in a kind of panoramic review, and each act of it seemed to be accompanied by a consciousness of right or wrong, or by some reflection on its cause or its consequences; indeed, many trifling events which had been long forgotten, then crossed into my imagination, and with the character of recent familiarity.

According to Noyes, this return to the memories of the past may be the result of the sudden loss of future time orientation. Aging persons approaching the end of their lives tend to withdraw their investment in the future and turn toward reminiscences of the past. Similarly, those individuals who are suddenly confronted with the termination of their lives may experience an increased investment in their pasts. This narrow focusing of vital energy on past events might be related to the intensity and vividness of the emerging early memories.

Noyes has pointed out the existential significance of this final life-review and emphasized the unique perspective upon life that it brings. At the moment of death an individual's existence becomes a completed and unalterable pattern. All through history death has been recognized as a climactic moment for this very reason; it represents the last opportunity to attain or defend the aims held highest. Dying individuals experiencing this final review passionately affirm the transcendent meaning of their existence and integrate it into the universal order which they embrace. This can be seen as a powerful assertion of the dying person's spiritual aspirations. In many instances the visionary experiences of some people were so gratifying that they had a strong desire to die and stay forever in the transcendental realms; they often showed resentment or even hostility for having been revived and awakened to everyday reality.

Usually the stage of *transcendence* evolves naturally from the life-review. Individuals surveying their existence from the point of view of good and evil can see it from an increasingly distant perspective. They can arrive at a point where they view their lives in their entireties and in every detail simultaneously. Finally even this limitation is overcome, and dying individuals experience what has been referred to as mystical, transcendental, cosmic, or religious consciousness, and what Abraham Maslow has called a "peak experience." In some instances the life-review does not occur and the individual suddenly confronted with death moves directly into the phase of transcendence. Victor Solow's death experience, which received wide publicity through his appearance on the Walter Cronkite show, can be used as an example. After his morning jogging on March 23, 1974, Victor Solow suffered a heart attack followed by cessation of the heartbeat and was resuscitated twenty-three minutes later, after a sequence of fortuitous coincidences. Solow described his experiences in an article in the *Reader's Digest*. Here is a condensed version of his account:

> For me, the moment of transition from life to death—what else can one call it?—was easy. There was no time for fear, pain or thought. There was no chance "to see my whole life before me," as others have related. The last impression I can recall lasted a brief instant. I was moving at high speed toward a net of great luminosity. The strands and knots where the luminous lines intersected were vibrating with a tremendous cold energy. The grid appeared as a barrier that would prevent further travel. I did not want to move through the grid. For a brief moment my speed appeared to slow down. Then I was in the grid. The instant I made contact with it, the vibrant luminosity increased to a blinding intensity which drained, absorbed and transformed me at the same time. There was no pain. The sensation was neither pleasant nor unpleasant but completely consuming. The

nature of everything had changed. Words only vaguely approximate the experience from this instant on.

The grid was like a transformer, an energy converter transporting me through form and into formlessness, beyond time and space. Now I was not in a place, nor even in a dimension, but rather in a condition of being. This new "I" was not the I which I knew, but rather a distilled essence of it, yet something vaguely familiar, something I had always known buried under a superstructure of personal fears, hopes, wants and needs. This "I" had no connection to ego. It was final, unchangeable, indivisible, indestructible pure spirit. While completely unique and individual as a fingerprint, "I" was, at the same time, part of some infinite, harmonious and ordered whole. I had been there before.

Walter Pahnke, who in 1966 made a comparative study of transcendental experiences of mystics and religious teachers through the ages, modified William James's and Walter Stace's criteria and defined the basic characteristics of these phenomena. His *mystical categories* reflect the most important common denominators of transcendental states. The *sense of oneness* or *unity* with other people, nature, and the entire universe is a necessary condition of cosmic consciousness. *Ineffability* is another important characteristic; the ineffable quality of the experience can be due to its uniqueness, the intensity of the accompanying emotion, or the inadequacy of our language to describe it. The next typical aspect of mystical experiences is *transcendence of time and space*. This entails a feeling that the experient is outside of the usual space-time boundaries, beyond the past and future, in eternity and infinity, or in a completely different dimension. *Noetic quality* is another important feature; individuals are usually convinced that they are in touch with a deeper truth about reality and the nature of existence. Experiences of transcendence are always accompanied by a strong *positive affect*. This can range from peace, serenity, and tranquility to an ecstatic rapture not dissimilar to a sexual orgasm of cosmic proportions. Accounts of mystical experiences are also characterized by striking *paradoxicality*. Many of the statements about such states appear to contradict each other and violate the basic rules of

Aristotelian logic. One more aspect of these experiences deserves special notice, namely the sense of *objectivity and reality*. An individual tuned into cosmic consciousness usually has no doubt that he or she is confronted with the ultimate reality, which is in a way more real than the phenomenal world as it is experienced in a more usual state of consciousness.

Transcendental experiences occurring in near-death situations and associated with clinical death have all the characteristics described by Pahnke's mystical categories. Noyes has added another characteristic feature—*loss of control,* relinquishing one's hold on reality, and submission to passivity. This surrender is usually accompanied, as in the second stage, by feelings of extraordinary calmness or ecstasy. These episodes of unusual states of consciousness can be accompanied by perceptual changes, in particular by vivid imagery.

An important complement to Noyes's studies are the fascinating research data collected by David Rosen, a psychiatrist from the Langley Porter Neuropsychiatric Institute in San Francisco. Rosen conducted a follow-up study of six of the eight survivors from suicide attempts off the Golden Gate Bridge and one of the two survivors from suicidal jumps off the San Francisco Bay Bridge. In his 1975 study he attempted to obtain information that would help clarify the magical attraction that the Golden Gate has for suicides,* but he also recorded and analyzed the nature of the subjective experiences during the falls and the long-term effects of this event on their lives. All these survivors, during and after their jumps, experienced mystical states of consciousness characterized by losing the sense of time and space and by feelings of spiritual rebirth and unity with other human beings, the entire universe, and God. As a result of their intimate encounter with death, some of them had a profound religious conversion; others described a reconfirmation of their previous religious beliefs. One of the survivors denied any suicidal intent altogether. He saw the Golden Gate Bridge as "golden doors" through which he will pass from the

---

* There are now over 580 recorded suicides that were committed by jumping off the Golden Gate Bridge since it was opened in 1937, making this bridge the number one location for suicides outside of Japan.

material world into a new spiritual realm. He claimed that his jump off the bridge was fulfilling a spiritual need and had more to do with parapsychology than psychology or psychopathology.

The subjective accounts of these survivors show a great similarity to Heim's material and reports of near-death experiences from other sources. The major difference is that the emphasis is on the transcendental phase, while the element of struggle and resistance is missing and the reliving of memories and the life-review is truncated or altogether absent. Rosen related these differences to the volitional nature of suicide, as compared to the unexpected and involuntary character of accidents. Individuals anticipating suicide would have faced the resistance to the termination of their life before they arrived at the decision to end it; similarly, some of the review and reckoning of life could well have taken place earlier.

Shortly after the completion of the writing on this book, Raymond A. Moody published his study of *Life After Life;* his observations are so important for our discussion that we will describe them at some length. Moody's background in both psychology and medicine, his direct personal interviewing of the survivors, and his objective approach uncolored by sensationalism make his book a very special contribution to the study of the death experience. He has collected material from 150 persons, and his observations fall into three different categories: Some of the death experiences come from persons who were resuscitated after having been thought, adjudged, or pronounced dead by their doctors; the second category contains reports from individuals who, in the course of accidents, severe injuries, or diseases, had a very close confrontation with physical death; the last category consists of accounts of persons who described their experiences of dying to other people present at their death-beds.

Moody personally interviewed over fifty persons in the first two categories in great detail and found far-reaching similarities among individual reports. He was able to isolate several basic characteristics of the death experience that occur with great constancy. Many of these seem to be elements that we encountered earlier during our discussion of perinatal and transpersonal phenomena in psychedelic sessions.

Most accounts involved complaints about the ineffability of the experience and the inadequacy of our language to convey its specific nature. In many instances the dying described that during a comatose state or after physical death they heard statements and even entire discussions about their condition made by doctors, nurses, and relatives (on occasion the accuracy of this perception could be verified by subsequent investigation). Feelings of peace and quiet, sometimes with a transcendental quality, occurred quite frequently. Many dying individuals reported hearing peculiar sounds similar to those described in the *Tibetan Book of the Dead* and to those occurring in perinatal LSD sessions. Some of these were distinctly unpleasant noises, such as loud clicks, roaring, ringing, buzzing, whistling, or banging; others involved beautiful chimes, soothing sounds, or even majestic music. Unusually frequent were descriptions of passing through a dark enclosed place, referred to as a funnel, cave, tunnel, cylinder, valley, trough, or sewer.*

Out-of-the-body phenomena, another common characteristic of the death experience, can take many different forms. Some individuals describe themselves as amorphous clouds, energy patterns, or pure consciousness; others experience distinct feelings of having a body which is, however, permeable, invisible, and inaudible for those in the phenomenal world. Sometimes there is fear, confusion, and a tendency to return to the physical body; sometimes there are ecstatic feelings of timelessness, weightlessness, peace, serenity, and tranquility. Some individuals in this state show concern about the fate of their physical bodies; others feel totally indifferent. There is no perception of smells, odors, temperature, or kinaesthesia; hearing and seeing seem to be perfected almost to the point of having no limitations. The similarities between these experiences and the Tibetan descriptions of the *Bardo* states are quite striking.

Many dying individuals have reported encounters with other beings,

---

* Although this was not specifically mentioned by Moody, one finds in these accounts many indirect allusions to the birth process: sliding down head first, concentric circles of the tunnel, absence of air in the enclosed space, breathing difficulties, scatalogical elements, etc.

such as dead relatives or friends, "guardian spirits," or spirit guides. Particularly common seem to be visions of a Being of Light, which usually appears as a source of unearthly light, radiant and brilliant, yet showing certain personal characteristics such as love, warmth, compassion, and a sense of humor. The communication with this Being occurs without words, through an unimpeded transfer of thoughts. In the context of this encounter or outside of it, the dying individual can experience a partial or total review of his or her life, which almost always involves vivid colors and a three-dimensional, dynamic form. The message from this experience seems to be the realization that learning to love other people and acquiring higher knowledge are the most important values in human life. In many reports there is a description of reaching a border or limit, and returning. This frontier can have a purely abstract form or be symbolically represented by a body of water, a gray mist, a door or a gate, a fence or a line.

The attitudes toward coming back seem to change during the process of dying. During the first few moments following death, there is usually a desperate desire to get back into the body and regrets over one's demise. After a certain depth is reached, and particularly after the encounter with the Being of Light, this changes into unwillingness to return. Some individuals do not know how they returned or attribute their return to their own decision to do so. Others feel that they were sent back by the Being of Light, or were brought back by love or the wishes or prayers of others, regardless of their own wishes.

Moody paid special attention to the problems persons who experienced the encounter with death have in communicating to others this special event which they themselves consider so profound, real, and significant. He points out that difficulties in describing these unusual states, together with the inability of others to understand and their frequently condescending or derisive attitudes, are responsible for us hearing so little about these relatively frequent episodes. This can be best illustrated by the fact that only in one case in the entire sample did the physician involved reveal any familiarity at all with near-death experiences!

The survivors of near-death situations and of clinical death developed, as a result of their experiences, new concepts of death. Many lost their fear of death and developed positive attitudes toward it; this was not associated with a desire for death or suicidal tendencies. Their doubts about the possibility of survival after death were dissipated; continuation of consciousness beyond physical demise became for them an experiential fact.*

One of the most important aspects of Moody's study is his discussion of the effects the death experiences had on the lives of these individuals. They felt that their lives had broadened and deepened. They developed serious interest in ultimate philosophical and spiritual issues, and started pursuing quite different values in life than before. Existence suddenly appeared much more precious, and much more emphasis was put on a full experience of the present moment, on the here and now. There were deep changes in the concept of the relative importance of the physical body and the mind; rarely, this was associated with the development of psychic abilities.

These findings are in full agreement with Walter Pahnke's conclusions regarding the consequences of mystical experiences occurring spontaneously or during religious practice, without the association with vital emergency. One of his categories describing mystical consciousness involved lasting, positive changes in feelings, attitudes, and behavior following the experience. The nature of these changes seems to be identical with those described by Moody. Russell Noyes arrived at similar conclusions in his analysis of a large number of near-death and death experiences. Rosen, studying the lives of survivors of suicidal attempts, also discovered lasting beneficial changes in their emotional state, thinking, and behavior. The most striking aspect of this transformation was a powerful upsurge of spiritual feelings, resulting in religious conversions or reinforcement of preexisting religious be-

---

* In spite of great similarities between Moody's findings and our own observations, there is one fundamental difference which deserves special notice. Moody emphasizes the lack of mythological elements in these new concepts of death, and of what he calls "the cartoonist's heaven of pearly gates, golden streets, and winged, harp-playing angels, or a hell of flames and demons with pitchforks." In our experience concrete archetypal images of deities and demons were equally frequent as the occurrence of the divine or demonic entities without form.

liefs. A sense of spiritual rebirth was associated with a new way of being in the world and perceiving it. The most significant practical consequence of this new orientation toward life was a decrease of self-destructive tendencies, increase of vitality, and joyful affirmation of human existence. One of the survivors described it in these words:

> I was refilled with a new hope and purpose in being alive. It's beyond most people's comprehension. I appreciate the miracle of life—like watching a bird fly—everything is more meaningful when you come close to losing it. I experienced a feeling of unity with all things and a oneness with all people. After my psychic rebirth, I also feel for everyone's pain. Surviving reconfirmed my belief and purpose in my life. Everything was clear and bright—I became aware of my relationship with my creator.

Temporary or lasting changes of this kind are very common in people who have had an intimate experiential encounter with death, whether it occurred in an accident, a suicidal attempt, a serious disease, or an operation; or in a symbolic form, such as during a psychedelic session, a spontaneous mystical experience, an acute psychotic episode, or in a rite of passage. This phenomenon seems to be of such fundamental practical and theoretical significance that it will be discussed in detail in the following chapters.

8.

THE POSTHUMOUS
JOURNEY OF THE SOUL:
MYTH AND SCIENCE

In the preceding chapters we have discussed in detail the death experiences and transpersonal phenomena occurring in psychedelic sessions, and have shown their similarity to the experiences associated with actual clinical death and with various near-death situations. We will now use these observations to explore the controversial problems of consciousness after death, afterlife, and the posthumous journey of the soul. There is no doubt that a deep belief in the beyond makes dying easier. That in itself is not a sufficient justification of these concepts for most modern Westerners, who are governed by a strong desire for knowledge and truth. In our culture the ultimate criterion for acceptance or rejection of an idea is its compatability with scientific observations and existing knowledge.

In psychiatric and psychological books the ideas of afterlife and of the spiritual journey after death have usually been treated as manifestations of primitive magical thinking or as an expression of an inability to accept the fact of impermanence and death. Until recently it was hardly ever considered that the descriptions of the posthumous adventures of the soul could reflect experiential reality rather than wishful fantasy. We are now beginning to learn that Western science might have been a little premature in making its condemning and condescending judgments about ancient systems of thought. Reports describing subjective experiences of clinical death, if studied carefully and with an open mind, contain ample evidence that various eschatological mythologies represent actual maps of unusual states of consciousness experienced by dying individuals. Psychedelic research conducted in the last two decades has resulted in important phenomenological and neurophysiological data indicating that experiences involving complex mythological, religious, and mystical sequences before, during, and after death might well represent clinical reality. In the following text we will make an attempt to reconcile the ancient knowledge and mythology of preliterate cultures with modern clinical and laboratory observations, and to offer a new approach to the understanding of the death experience.

The concept of afterlife has taken many specific forms in different cultures, but the basic underlying idea is the same—that death does not terminate human existence entirely and that in one way or another life or consciousness will continue after the body is no longer vital. Sometimes the image of the afterworld is very concrete and real, not dissimilar to earthly existence. More frequently the realms of the world beyond have special characteristics distinguishing them from anything known on earth. Whether or not the residing place of the soul is a familiar environment, the soul's journey to the afterworld is often believed to be a complex process of transitions and transformations through many different levels and realms.

Comparative studies of the concepts of afterlife and of the posthumous journey of the soul reveal striking similarities between cultures and ethnic groups separated historically and geographically; the recurrence of certain motifs and themes is quite remarkable. The idea of the final home of the righteous after death—heaven or paradise—appears in many different variations. In the Christian tradition there are two different ways of representing heaven: One reflects a theological and metaphysical concept of heaven as a state in which hierarchies of angels and saints enjoy the presence of God and contemplate His being. The symbolism associated with this conception combines the Hebraic image of a region in the sky with the Greek ideas of concentric celestial spheres and of the spiritual journey. The myth of the Golden Age and the Garden of Eden are the roots for the idea of paradise or the Garden of Love. The symbolism used for this concept involves a geographical location, elements of pristine nature, walls of gold, and roads paved with emeralds.

The Koran promises the faithful a paradise reflecting male Arab tastes. It has the form of a beautiful oasis with gardens, rivers, and luscious trees. Men are clad in silken robes and lie on couches feasting on fruit and wine; unlimited hosts of black-eyed houris serve the pleasures of faithful Muslims. Having satisfied the sexual desires of their clients, these women resume their virginal status. Classical Greeks believed in the Isles of the Blest and the plain of Elysium, located over the waters of the Atlantic at the world's end. The plain had an ideal climate with no rain, snowfall, or strong wind, and its fertile land bore honey-sweet fruit thrice a year. The Orphic mystics, who taught salvation as a release from matter and earthly bondage, saw the Elysian fields as a joyful resting place for pure spirits, at first located in an underworld of strange brightness, and later in the upper regions of the sky.

The Aztecs distinguished three different paradises to which souls went after death. The first and lowest of these, Tlalocan, land of water and mist, was a place of abundance, blessedness, and serenity. The happiness experienced there was of a very earthly variety. The dead sang songs, played leapfrog, and chased butterflies. The trees were laden with fruit and the land was covered with maize, pumpkins, green peppers, tomatoes, beans, and flowers. Tlillan-Tlapallan was the paradise of the initiates who were followers of Quetzalcoatl, the god-king symbolizing rebirth. It was referred to as the land of the fleshless; it was an abode for those who had learned to live outside their physical bodies and were unattached to them. The highest paradise was Tonatiuhichan, House of the Sun. It seems that this paradise was a place for those who achieved full illumination. They were the privileged ones who were chosen as daily companions of the sun and lived a life of pure delight.

In the Nordic tradition access to Valhalla was gained on the basis of martial prowess. Here warriors were engaged in splendid tournaments during the day and at night feasted together on pork and mead. Indian mythology abounds in images of heavens and paradises. According to the ancient Vedic tradition, Yama, the ruler of the dead, reigned in the realm of light in the outer sky. The lives of all the worthy deceased were free of pain and care; they enjoyed music, sexual fulfillment, and sensual pleasures. In Hinduism the regions above the clouds are places of beauty and joy and are inhabited by various deities; access to these regions is gained by a proper way of life and a correct performance of rituals. The Buddhist concepts related to the soul's resting place are to a great degree derived from Hindu mythology. Mahayana Buddhism has a graded hierarchy of paradises inhabited by deities and spiritual beings. However, these heavens do not represent the ultimate goal of Buddhist religion and philosophy. They are temporary stations for those who are not ready to give up personal desires and attachments and achieve total release from the bondage of personality.

The image of paradise as a place of the dead exists in many aboriginal cultures. Thus some North American Indian tribes such as the Ojibway, Choctaw, and Sioux believe that the deceased inhabit the region of the sunset or the happy hunting grounds. Some Eskimo peoples see their dead in the radiance of the aurora borealis, joyfully playing with the head of a walrus. The mythology of the Tumbuka in Malawi involves a spirit realm in the underworld where the departed are always young and never unhappy or hungry.

The concept of hell or purgatory, a place where the departed will be exposed to inhuman tortures, is equally ubiquitous. In the Hebraic tradition the dead go to Sheol, which is a great pit or walled city, "the land of forgetfulness," "the land of silence." There they live in dust, darkness, and ignorance, all covered by maggots and forgotten by Yahweh. Gehenna is a deep valley with burning fire where the wicked are tormented in flames. The Christian picture of hell involves hierarchies of vicious devils exposing the damned to torture by physical pain, suffocation, and fiery heat. It is located far underground, with entrances through dark woods, volcanoes, or the gaping mouth of Leviathan. The Book of Revelation mentions the lake that burns with fire and brimstone; it is the final destination of "the cowardly, the faithless, the polluted, murderers, fornicators, sorcerers, idolators, and all liars." Less frequently, cold and ice are described as instruments of torture. This is true for the medieval image of the cold hell and for the lowest circle of hell in Dante's Inferno. Freezing cold also characterizes Nifelheim, the Nordic underworld, ruled by the fierce and ruthless goddess Hel. The Islamic picture of hell bears a close similarity to that of the Judaeo-Christian tradition from which it was derived.

The Greek underworld, Hades, was a place of dreary darkness, described by Homer as "the hateful Chambers of Decay that fill the gods themselves with horror." It was located either in the deep underground or far in the west; the principal river of the underworld was the Styx, across which the dead had to be ferried by Charon. Those who had personally insulted Zeus were imprisoned in the bottomless pit of Tartarus and had to undergo agonizing torments. The suffering of Prometheus, Sisyphus, Tantalus, and Ixion was of truly heroic proportions. In Persian Zoroastrianism, hell is in the far north, in the depths of the earth. It is a dark place, foul and stinking, and teeming with demons. There the damned souls, "the followers of the lie," have to remain after death, in pain and misery, until the God of Darkness, Ahriman himself, is destroyed.

The Aztec underworld, Mictlan, was a region of utter darkness ruled by the terrible Lord of the Dead, Mictlantecuhtli. His face was covered by a mask in the form of a human skull. His black, curly hair was studded with starlike eyes, and a human bone protruded from his ear. In the Aztec tradition it was not the conduct of the deceased that determined one's fate after death but the occupation and the manner of death. Those of the dead who were not selected for one of the paradises were subjected in Mictlan to a series of magical trials. They had to pass through nine hells before they reached their final rest. These hells should not be considered as places to which the wicked went for punishment. They were regarded as a necessary point of transition in the cycle of creation. It was inevitable in the cosmic process that all created things plunge into matter and return back to light and their creator.

In Hinduism and Buddhism there are numerous types and levels of hell. Similar to the various paradises, they are not places where the deceased stay forever; they are merely transitional stages in the cycle of birth, death, and rebirth. The tortures experienced in these hells are at least as multiform, diabolic, and ingenious as those described in other traditions.

Another recurrent theme in eschatological mythology is the Judgment of the Dead. Christian art abounds in images of devils and angels fighting for the soul of the deceased and in depictions of the Last Judgment, with the just ascending into heaven and the damned devoured by the mouth of hell. In the Islamic religion two angels, Munker and Nakeer, come to examine and interrogate the dead. If they are found righteous they are refreshed by air and perfume and a door is opened for them toward paradise. Infidels are clad in garments from hell and infernal doors open for them; the heat and pestilential wind of hell envelop them, and the grave closes in on them and crushes their ribs. There they have to remain in agony until the day of resurrection. The Moslem tradition speaks also of the Sirat, which is a bridge over hell, "finer than a hair and sharper than a sword," which all departed must cross. Believers are able to keep their balance and cross successfully; unbelievers will slip and plunge into the infernal abyss. Crossing the bridge also plays an important role in the judgment of the dead of the Zoroastrian religion. A deity named "just Rashnu" weighs the evil deeds of the departed against their noble deeds. After this procedure the deceased undergo a special ordeal: They have to make an attempt to cross the Cinvato paratu, or "Bridge of the Separator." The just easily pass across the bridge to eternal bliss, while those who are found wicked are seized by the demon Vizarsh.

The earliest descriptions of the Judgment of the Dead are found in the funerary texts known as the *Egyptian Book of the Dead,* which date back to about 2400 B.C. The judgment scene, psychostasis, takes place in the Hall of the Two Truths or Hall of Maat. In the scale-pans of a great balance, the heart of the deceased is weighed against the feather of the Goddess Maat, symbolizing truth and justice. The scale is attended by the jackal-headed God Anubis, while the ibis-headed God Thoth, god of wisdom and divine scribe, records the verdict as an impartial judge. The triform monster Amemet (crocodile-lion-hippopotamus), Devourer of Souls, stands by ready to swallow those who fell through at the trial. The just are introduced by Horus to Osiris, who accepts them into the pleasures of his kingdom.

In the Tibetan version of the judgment scene, the administrator of truth and justice is called Dharma-Raja, the King of Truth, or Yama-Raja, the King of the Dead. He is adorned with human skulls, human skin, and a serpent, and holds the sword of discrimination in his right hand and the mirror of karma in his left hand. This mirror reflects every good and evil act of the dead; these are symbolized by white and black pebbles and weighed against each other. From the court six karmic pathways lead to separate *lokas,* realms in which the deceased will be reborn according to his or her credits and debits. Typical punishments in various hells of the lower world include tortures by heat and cold, hacking to pieces, affixing to the Spiked Tree, pouring of molten metal into apertures of the body, or detention in the terrible Avitchi Hell where those who are guilty of heinous sins endure punishment for ages that are immeasurable.

The fate of the departed is often represented as a path, a journey, or a specific sequence of events. Some of the descriptions appear to be rather naive, while others represent complicated and sophisticated maps of unusual subjective experiences. The Guarayo Indians of Bolivia believe that after death the soul has to choose between two paths. One is broad and comfortable, the other narrow and dangerous; the soul should not let itself be seduced by the seeming advantages of the easy road and should take the difficult one. It has to cross two rivers, one on the back of a gigantic alligator, the other on a tree trunk. Other dangers await the soul during this journey. It has to negotiate through a dark territory by the light of a burning straw and pass between two clashing rocks. After all perils are successfully overcome the soul arrives in a beautiful land with flowering trees and singing birds, where it will live happily for all eternity.

Similar, although more complicated, is the soul's journey to the spirit world in the tradition of the Huichol Indians in Mexico, as it has been orally transmitted from generation to generation and depicted in colorful yarn paintings, or *nearikas*. The first part of this path is straight, but at a point called "The Place of the Black Rocks," the path splits into two directions. From there the Huichol with a pure heart takes the right path; a Huichol who has committed incest or has had sexual intercourse with a Spaniard must go to the left. On the left road Huichols who have transgressed endure a sequence of agonizing ordeals; they are impaled on a large thorn, beaten by the souls of the people they have illicitly enjoyed in their lifetimes, burned by a purifying fire, crushed by clashing rocks, and forced to drink hot, foul-smelling water full of worms and slime. After this they are allowed to return to the separation of the paths at the Black Rocks. Here they may continue on the right path which will take them to their ancestors. On this portion of the journey they must symbolically appease a dog and a crow, two animals who are traditionally badly treated by the Huichols. They encounter a possum (coati) and have to prove that they have not eaten the meat of this animal that is sacred to the Huichols. Then they encounter a caterpillar, the symbol of the first sexual experience. At a wild fig tree the souls dispose of the burdens of sexual organs and obtain in turn the tree's fruit. After a great feast with figs, maize beer, and peyote, all souls join together and dance around Tatewari (Our Grandfather Fire).

The Huichol concept of the posthumous journey has certain elements in common with the descriptions of ancient Aztecs. According to the Aztec religion the dead had to undergo a series of ordeals that involved crossing a deep river guarded by a yellow dog, passing between two mountains that were joined together, climbing over a mountain of obsidian, being exposed to icy wind, being pierced by sharp arrows, and being attacked by wild beasts devouring human hearts. The Aztecs performed complicated rituals to ease the posthumous journeys of their deceased.

Two cultures in the history of humanity have manifested particular concern about and knowledge of the process of dying: Egypt and Tibet. The priests in these two cultures conducted elaborate rituals to ease the ultimate transition and developed sophisticated maps as guidelines for the posthumous journey of the soul. The written forms of these manuals became known in the West as the *Egyptian Book of the Dead* * and the *Tibetan Book of the Dead*. These two sacred texts are documents of great relevance in regard to the theme of this chapter.

The *Egyptian Book of the Dead* is a title referring to a collection of funerary texts which the ancient Egyptian scribes composed for the benefit of the noble dead. These texts consist of spells and incantations, hymns and litanies, magical formulas, and prayers. The *Book of the Dead* was the product of a long development of religious beliefs and ritual practice. Many of the sections can be traced back to earlier collections of funerary texts inscribed in hieroglyphs on the interior walls of certain pyramids in Sakkara (the Pyramid Texts) and later on the sides of wooden coffins (the Coffin Texts). The Pyramid Texts originated between 2350 and 2175 B.C. and are the oldest written records not only in Egypt but also in the entire history of mankind; however, the material they contain points to sources that are even more archaic.

From first to last, the texts reveal the unalterable belief of the Egyptians in resurrection and in the immortality of the soul. However, egyptologists have pointed out an apparent conflict in the heterogeneous material of the texts. On the one hand, great emphasis was put on the role of the Sun God and his divine retinue. The texts were supposed to provide magical means of facilitating the ascent of the departed to the sky, where he or she would enjoy blessed afterlife for eternity, accompanying the Sun God on the solar barge. Yet another, older tradition of the ancient mortuary god Osiris also permeates the

---

* The name, *Egyptian Book of the Dead,* is misleading. The texts do not form a comprehensive and connected work and do not belong to one historical period; they span a time period of several millennia. The title is actually a translation of the name given by Egyptian tomb-robbers to every roll of inscribed papyrus they found with mummies—*Kitab al-Mayyitun*—"book of the dead persons." The ancient Egyptian title was *pert em hru,* translated usually as "manifestation in the light" or "coming forth by day."

texts.* A dead person who was ritually identified with Osiris could be raised to life again. Thus the texts include rituals for use in embalming and funeral rites together with hymns, incantations, myths, prayers, and magic spells.

According to Egyptian mythology, the Sun God Afu-Ra traveled during the day in his boat across the sky. At sunset the solar boat passed through the chain of mountains in the west and during nighttime continued its journey through the Tuat, the other world and abode of the dead. A district of the Tuat called Sekhet Aaru, Fields of Reeds, was the kingdom of Osiris, where he lived with his court. Only those who passed the judgment in the Hall of Maat (see p. 164) were admitted to this realm. The Tuat had twelve regions, one for each hour that the solar barge spent in the other world at nighttime. Each region of the Tuat had a gate protected by three guardian deities and presented specific dangers for the solar crew. The companions of the Sun God had to struggle through places of blazing fire where heat, fumes, and vapors were destroying nostrils and mouths. A number of hideous beings, fantastic creatures, and monstrous serpents threatened them on their way. The most dangerous of these perils was Osiris's brother Set, in the form of Aapep, a gigantic serpent attempting to devour the solar disk. Every day Afu-Ra completed his journey through the Tuat, triumphed over all its dangers, killed Aapep with the help of the feline goddess Bastet, and rose in the sky through the eastern mountains to give heat, light, and life. The Egyptians assumed that the soul of the deceased underwent the same struggles and transformations as Afu-Ra.

Bardo Thödol,† the *Tibetan Book of the Dead,* is of much more recent origin than its Egyptian counterpart and seems to have more

---

* Osiris, one of four divine siblings of the Egyptian pantheon, was killed and dismembered by his evil brother, Set. His sister Nephthys and his wife-sister Isis found the parts of his body scattered in the Nile delta, reassembled them in a rawhide, and resurrected Osiris with the help of Osiris's son Horus. In a fierce battle that followed, Horus killed Set and avenged his father. The legend about the death and resurrection of Osiris is central for the understanding of his role in the Egyptian death mythology and in the death-rebirth mysteries.

† *Bardo Thödol* means literally "Liberation by Hearing on the After-Death Plane."

inner consistency and congruence. It was first put into written form in the eighth century A.D. by the Great Guru Padma Sambhava, who introduced Tantric Buddhism into Tibet. It integrates, however, elements of much older, secret oral traditions. *Bardo Thödol* is a guide for the dying and the dead, a manual helping the departed to identify various stages of the intermediate state between death and rebirth and to attain liberation. The Tibetans distinguish a total of six so-called intermediate states or Bardos. The first is the natural state of Bardo while in the womb. The second is the Bardo of the dream state. The third is the Bardo of ecstatic equilibrium while in deep meditation. The remaining three Bardos are associated with death and rebirth; these are described in detail in the *Tibetan Book of the Dead*. They are the Bardo of the moment of death, the Bardo of experiencing karmic illusions during the dream state following death, and finally the Bardo of the inverse process of sangsaric existence while seeking rebirth.

The first part of *Bardo Thödol*, called *Chikhai Bardo*, describes the psychic happenings at the moment of death. The three chief symptoms heralding imminent death are a bodily sensation of pressure ("earth sinking into water"), clammy coldness gradually turning into feverish heat ("water sinking into fire"), and a feeling as though the body were blown to atoms ("fire sinking into air"). At the moment of death the departed have a vision of the Primary Clear Light of Pure Reality. If they are not frightened by its overwhelming intensity, they can attain instant liberation. If they allow themselves to be deterred, they have another chance later, when the secondary clear light dawns upon them. If they miss this opportunity as well, they then become involved in a complicated sequence of spiritual events during which their consciousness becomes progressively more estranged from the liberating truth as they are approaching another rebirth.

In the *Chönyid Bardo*, or the "Bardo of the Experiencing of Reality," the departed successively envision a pantheon of Peaceful Deities enveloped in brilliant light of different colors, Doorkeeping, Wrathful, Knowledge-Holding Deities, and Yoginis of the Four Cardinal Points. Simultaneously with the overwhelming presence of these deities, the departed perceive dull lights of various colors, indicating the individual lokas, or realms into which one can be born: the realm of the gods (devaloka), the realm of the titans (asuraloka), the realm of the humans (manakaloka), the realm of brute subhuman creatures (tiryakaloka), the realm of the hungry ghosts (pretaloka), and the realm of hell (narakaloka). The attraction to these dull lights can interfere with spiritual liberation and indicate a proclivity to rebirth.

If the departed have missed the opportunity for liberation in the first two Bardos, they enter the *Sidpa Bardo,* or the Bardo of seeking rebirth. At this stage the departed are warned not to desire the miraculous karmic powers which they seem to manifest and not to get attached to them. Their Bardo bodies, which are not composed of gross matter, are endowed with the power of unimpeded motion and can penetrate through solid objects. They can appear or disappear at will, change size, shape, or number, and appear instantaneously in whatever place.

Happiness or misery experienced in the Sidpa Bardo depends upon the karmic record of the departed. Those who have accumulated much bad karma will be tormented in this Bardo by frightening events such as horrifying screams, flesh-eating *rakshasas* bearing weapons, terrible beasts of prey, and raging elemental forces of nature—clashing and crumbling rocks, angry overflowing seas, roaring fire, or ominous crevices and precipices. Those who have accumulated karmic merit will experience various delightful pleasures, while those with neutral karma will find colorless stupidity and indifference. An important part of this Bardo is the scene of Judgment (see p. 164) during which the King and Judge of the Dead, Yama-Raja, examines the past actions of the deceased with the help of his karmic mirror and assigns him or her to the appropriate fate.

During the Sidpa Bardo the experiencer will make frustrating attempts to reenter the dead body but finds it decomposed, cremated, interred, frozen, thrown into water, or given to birds and beasts of prey. At this point it is important for the deceased to realize that all of these experiences are only hallucinations, products of the mind, and essentially voidness. If this moment is missed rebirth will invariably follow, and it will take innumerable aeons before one comes out of the quagmire of misery. When the lights of the six lokas are dawning on the departed, an attempt can be made to close the door of the womb. The *Bardo Thödol* suggests several approaches to achieve this purpose: One can contemplate one's tutelary deity, try to realize that all apparitions are sangsaric illusions, meditate upon the clear light, focus on the chain of good karma, avoid attraction by visions of male and female figures in union, or seek detachment from the ambivalent forces of Oedipal bonds to one's future parents. If liberation has not occurred one will be maneuvered irresistibly by vivid illusions toward new birth. There various signs characteristic of individual places of birth or lokas occur. With proper guidance the deceased who has missed the many opportunities to attain liberation in the three Bardos can still influence the choice of the womb into which he or she will be born.

It is generally much less known that the Egyptian and Tibetan books of the dead had a counterpart in our own cultural tradition. Toward the end of the Middle Ages, the works usually globally referred to as *Ars Moriendi,* or the *Art of Dying,* belonged to the most widespread literary forms in many European countries, particularly Austria, Germany, France, and Italy. The intense interest in dying was greatly influenced by the general uncertainty of life in the Middle Ages. The mortality rate was excessive, with people dying by thousands in various wars and battles, during travels, mass starvation, epidemics, and from the unhygienic conditions of living. It was not exceptional that during the outbreaks of pestilence a quarter, a third, or even half of an entire population was exterminated. People were used to witnessing the deaths of their relatives, friends, and neighbors, and the ominous sound of the death bell was heard almost incessantly. Funeral corteges and processions with corpses were standard parts of everyday life rather than exceptional events. Mass burials, burning of cadavers, public executions, as well as immolations of heretics and alleged witches were conducted on a large scale. The far-reaching corruption and disintegration of the social, political, and religious fabric in Europe also contributed to the development of eschatological literature. Both the scholastic and the mystical traditions contributed to this genre, and many outstanding theologians considered its topic of sufficient importance to invest in it much of their time and energy.

In general the literature on *Ars Moriendi* falls into two broad categories: The first deals primarily with the significance of death in life; the second focuses more specifically on the experience of death, on the preparation for actual biological demise, and on the care for the dying.

The first group should be more appropriately referred to as *Ars Vivendi, The Art of Proper Living*. A recurrent theme in many of the works in this category is contemplation of death (*contemplatio mortis*) that leads to contempt for the world (*contemptus mundi*). The basic problem of human existence is best expressed in the Latin saying *mors certa, hora incerta;* nothing in life is more certain than death and nothing less certain than the hour of death. We should, therefore, live every moment of our lives as if it were the last. The fear of death is the beginning of all wisdom; it introduces into human life constant vigilance and a tendency to avoid harmful behavior. We should not be concerned about living as long as possible, but about living correctly. The works dealing with the contempt for the world depict in many symbolic images, metaphors, and parables the impermanence and nothing-ness of all worldly pursuits. Especially favorite targets for the *contemptus mundi* literature were the powerful, famous, and influential personages of this world. The members of the religious hierarchy—bishop, cardinal, and pope—and of the secular power structure—judge, duke, king, and caesar—appeared with great frequency. The fact that even these illustrious individuals are subject to the same mandatory life trajectory as everyone else was used as a devastating evidence for Soloman's statement, ''Vanity of vanities, all is vanity'' (*Vanitas vanitatum est omne vanum*). The strongest argument for the contempt of the world was the contemplation of the ugliness of death and realistic descriptions of the human body in various stages of putrefaction and biological decay.* One should not, there-

---

* Observations from LSD research throw a completely new light on the medieval preoccupation with death and with negative aspects of existence, which have usually been seen, in the framework of social pathology, as a manifestation of generally pes-

fore, strive for worldly pleasures, power, and riches, since all these turn into sadness at the time of death. Instead, one should focus one's individual attention on the transcendental realities.

The theme of death that was so powerfully expressed in a prosaic form in the literature on the contemplation of death and the contempt of the world also found its way into poetry in the form of numerous *Memento Mori* poems reminding humans of their mortality. Especially interesting were *polemic poems* (*Streitgedichte*) in which philosophical and religious problems of life and death were presented in argumentative dialogues between man and death, world and man, life and death, soul and body, or between the dying and the devil. In the poems called *Vado mori* (I am walking toward my death), dying representatives of different social groups or symbolic personifications of various human characteristics shared their feelings and reflections. These poems are in many ways predecessors to the texts used in the dances of death (*danses macabres, Totentänze*). The *danses macabres* that reached epidemic proportions in many European countries were the most dramatic manifestation of the preoccupation with death because of their unusual psychological power transcending the barriers of sex, age, and social class.

The second category of medieval works dealing with death involves texts focusing on the actual experience of dying and on the art of guiding and supporting dying individuals on their last journey. This is the literature on *Ars moriendi* or the *Art of Dying* in the narrower sense. Its beginnings can be traced back to the end of the fourteenth century, when the mortality rate reached critical proportions and it became physically impossible for priests to visit personally all the sick to prepare them for death. As a result of this many people died without

---

simistic attitudes hostile to life. It is interesting from this point of view to notice the strong similarity between the basic themes of the literature dealing with contemplation of death and the contempt of the world with the phenomenology of the existential crisis associated with the no-exit situation on the perinatal level (see p. 49). According to clinical experiences from LSD psychotherapy, deep experiential confrontation with the most frightening and revulsive aspects of human existence not only opens individuals to spiritual dimensions of their being, but can eventually result in a qualitatively different way of existing in the world.

clerical assistance, "in the middle of their sins." Under these circumstances concerned representatives of the church became interested in preparing the living for death. It was particularly the Franciscan and Dominican monks who taught and preached about death and the last affairs of human beings. *Ars moriendi* was originally conceived as a pastoral manual for young priests to prepare them for work with dying individuals. Later, when their number was not sufficient, the texts were translated into popular languages to make them available for lay people.

Although at first sight the number of death manuals seems truly overwhelming, many of them are actually modified translations of or variations on several original sources. It is possible to extract from the works on *Ars moriendi* several basic lines of thought and certain recurrent themes. Some of these were of a more formal nature and represented a more or less codified system of specific questions addressed to the dying which required "correct" answers, a standard set of concrete instructions and admonitions, and model prayers to God, Christ, Mary, and the archangel Michael. This aspect of care for the dying was most directly influenced by traditional Christian beliefs and was an immediate outgrowth of orthodox doctrines. Other parts of the texts, however, although they were also colored by traditional Christian symbolism, were related to the actual experiential aspects of dying. Of these, the phenomena usually referred to as the attacks of Satan (*Anfechtungen Satans*) deserve special attention. These were specific states of mind that the dying typically experienced in their last hours. Church authorities interpreted them as results of the devil's attempt to divert the souls from their way to heaven by interfering at this most strategic and crucial time. Most of the manuals discussed five major attacks of the devil: serious doubts regarding faith; desperation and agonizing qualms of conscience; impatience and irritability due to suffering; conceit, vanity, and pride; and greed, avarice, and other worldly concerns and attachments. In some texts unwillingness to surrender to the process of dying is added to the above five. These attempts of the devil were counteracted by divine influences that gave the dying a foretaste of heaven, a sense of being subjected to Supreme

Judgment, a feeling of obtaining higher help, and a promise of redemption.*

Another important aspect of the *Ars moriendi* literature involved concrete instructions for the dying and their helpers to guide them during the last hours. Most medieval death manuals concur that the preparation for death depends critically on creating the right disposition and right attitude in the dying person. It is very important not to instill false hopes in regard to recovery. All possible support should be given to the dying individual to help him or her face death and accept it. Confrontation of death was seen as absolutely crucial, and avoidance of this was considered one of the major dangers the dying person was facing. Some of the manuals explicitly stated that it is less objectionable and harmful if the helpers evoke fear in the dying that later prove unsubstantiated than if they allow him or her to use denial and therefore to die unprepared.

The Egyptian and Tibetan books of the dead, as well as the *Ars moriendi* literature, were necessarily influenced by the cultures and religious traditions from which they came and by the specific demands of historical time and location. However, an open-minded researcher will find these works to be unique sources of information about consciousness and the human mind. Many of the descriptions of unusual states experienced by the dying and some of the empirical principles postulated by these writings have recently been receiving unexpected validation from contemporary clinical and laboratory research. It is

---

* Closer examination of these descriptions reveals that this phenomenology of dying has all the basic characteristics of the perinatal experiences discussed earlier. Hopelessness, despair, sense of guilt, and feelings of inferiority are typical for the no-exit matrix. Irritability, aggression, impulsiveness, greed, possessiveness, lust, and elements of the Judgment belong to the death-rebirth struggle. Holding onto worldly investments and personal pride, as well as unwillingness to surrender to the process of dying, are the most difficult psychological impediments of the ego death and rebirth experience. Visions of the divine, experience of grace, redemption, salvation, and other elements of communication with the supernal realms are then characteristics of a completed rebirth process. These far-reaching parallels indicate that many of the descriptions in the manuals for the dying should be considered experiential maps rather than arbitrary symbolic constructs.

possible that in the not-too distant future they may be reformulated in modern terms.

Descriptions of spiritual journeys, whether those of aboriginal mythologies or their elaborate versions such as found in Tantric Buddhism, have in the past attracted very little attention from Western scientists. This situation was not noticeably influenced by the fact that actual subjective accounts of death and near-death experiences, as well as death-bed observations by physicians and nurses in a few existing studies, were in many ways similar to ancient and aboriginal descriptions of the phenomenology of death. We should mention at least two important exceptions: Carl Gustav Jung, as a result of his extensive studies in comparative mythology, his unusual intuitive capacity, and his own near-death experience, recognized the extraordinary value of the *Bardo Thödol* and similar texts describing post-mortem experiences for the understanding of the human mind. And in *Heaven and Hell* Aldous Huxley suggested, on the basis of his own psychedelic experiences, that such concepts as hell and heaven represent subjective realities that can be experienced in a very concrete and convincing way in unusual states of mind induced by drugs or various powerful nondrug techniques.

Clinical research with LSD has given us ample evidence supporting Huxley's idea. Individuals unsophisticated in anthropology and mythology experience—without any programming—images, episodes, and even entire thematic sequences that bear a striking similarity to the descriptions of the posthumous journey of the soul and the death-rebirth mysteries of various cultures. Psychedelic drugs have made it possible to develop a new understanding of the experience of clinical death and of the dynamics of the symbolic death-rebirth process that occurs in shamanic initiation, rites of passage, temple mysteries, and some schizophrenic episodes. Deeper phenomenological analysis shows that the extended map of the human unconscious derived from LSD research is indeed applicable to all these situations.

Some of the experiences of individuals approaching death are of a purely abstract and aesthetic nature. Karlis Osis showed in his study that visions of beautiful colors and ornamental patterns are quite common. The psychodynamic level of the unconscious is frequently involved in the process of dying. Dying individuals quite regularly experience various degrees of age regression and relive important memories, or review their entire lives. Sometimes they have to confront various intrapsychic or interpersonal conflicts, work through problems, and give up emotional attachments. Many important phenomena associated with dying seem to originate on the perinatal level. The experience of cosmic unity, heaven, or paradise occurs in close connection with the embryonic feelings of prenatal existence. The encounter with various images of hell coincides with the no-exit situation related to the first clinical stage of delivery. The concept of purgatory seems to occur when individuals are undergoing the death-rebirth struggle associated with propulsion through the birth canal in the second stage. In this context some individuals go through shattering experiences of the Judgment of the Dead. Typical scenes of salvation and redemption seem to coincide with the reliving of the moment of biological birth. The theme of descent into the underworld and that of the ascent, so typical for eschatological mythology, are related on this continuum to the transition from cosmic unity to hell (the beginning of delivery), and to the shift from the death-(re)birth struggle to the death-rebirth experience (completion of the delivery), respectively. Many additional aspects of the spiritual journey after death are related to transpersonal phenomena, such as the encounter with various wrathful and blissful deities, fights with demons, contact with ancestors, identification with different animals, extrasensory perception, astral projection, and, particularly, reliving of what appear to be past incarnation memories.

One important aspect of the observations from psychedelic research needs special emphasis. Not only do the LSD and DPT sessions contain sequences that are identical to those found in eschatological mythology, rites of passage, and death-rebirth mysteries, but these are frequently experienced in terms of specific symbolism associated with particular cultures. Thus the experiences of heaven, hell, or Judgment of the Dead in European and American subjects do not necessarily follow the canonic rules of the Judaeo-Christian religious tradition, as one would expect. On occasion unsophisticated individuals have described detailed sequences from Hindu, Buddhist, and Jain mythology, or complex scenes from the little-known *Egyptian Book of the Dead* showing the battles of the crew on the solar barge with its enemies in the darkness of the Tuat. Parallels with some of the experiences from the Tibetan *Bardo Thödol* are so striking that in the mid-1960s Leary, Metzner, and Alpert recommended the use of this sacred text as a guide for psychedelic sessions. Death-rebirth sequences can be experienced by some individuals in a Biblical framework as identification with Christ's suffering, death on the cross, and resurrection. Others, however, identify at this point with Osiris, Dionysus, or the victims sacrificed to the Aztec Sun God, Huitzilopochtli. The final blow mediating the ego death can also be experienced as coming from the terrible goddess Kali, from Shiva the Destroyer, from the Bacchants, or the Egyptian Set. The symbolism of a particular cultural framework attached to the experience can be quite specific and detailed; in many instances the sophisticated structure of such sequences transcends the education of the experiencer. Frequently the nature and origin of the manifested information remains a mystery in spite of our efforts at clarification. To follow Jung's example and call these phenomena archetypal provides a convenient label, but it does not solve the problem.

In what follows we will illustrate the parallels between the LSD state and the subjective experiences of real encounters with death by using two descriptions of episodes from the lives of individuals who experienced both situations. They show not only the phenomenological similarity between the symbolic and the physical encounter with death but also the fact that psychedelic experiences of death can change an individual's attitude and approach to an actual vital threat. The first example is the story of Beverly, a young student whom we met during our seminar entitled "LSD and the Human Encounter with Death." She volunteered her story during a discussion at this workshop, agreed to write it up for us, and gave us her permission to use it in this book. It is of particular interest because she took LSD on her own, outside of a therapeutic structure. The following is an excerpt from Beverly's letter:

Here is an account of the death-rebirth experiences that you asked about when at Naropa Institute. I will try to make this as detailed as possible, hopefully without being too lengthy or boring.

In August 1969, I took a tab of Sunshine acid. Previous to the experience I had been reading a lot of literature on philosophy, religion, and metaphysics, which may have had something to do with why this experience was of a "universal" nature rather than just "psychedelic," which had been the experience with LSD up until that time. What seemed to touch off the experience was the concentration on a mandala that had a maze of lines around a center which contained the words "It's Here." As you can imagine, being on acid, I started seeing it as a gateway to all sorts of fundamental revelations. All of my life I had been searching endlessly for something that was right here before my very eyes all along. It was as though I had been playing a joke on myself and it seemed humorous and relieving at the same time.

Then I saw images of gods or celestial beings and had a strong feeling of their presence. These beings seemed to be saying: "Come on, let us show you what it is all about," waving me on further and unraveling a Universe eternally evolving in the moment. At the same time, these beings felt like the core of the inner nature of everything, existing in and beyond all things simultaneously. I felt as though I was remembering something I had known before I was born, but had forgotten by identifying with the physical and mental world as total reality. This part of the experience was extremely uplifting, but then came the thought: "Well, if this is true of Life, what about Death?"

At approximately the same time we decided to leave my friend's house where we spent the first part of the experience; her parents were there and there was some paranoia about that. We went to the bus terminal and got on a bus heading for Philadelphia. When we were on the bus, it started to thunder and rain and the weather was very hot and humid. It felt as though I was on a continent in the midst of earthquakes and tidal waves, in complete chaos and destruction. Gradually the feeling that I was going to die along with everyone else started to prevail, which strangely enough had a sort of profound beauty to it. The bus started to drive over a bridge and, for some reason, I felt that death would come when the bus reached the middle of the bridge. It seemed that there was no way out of the situation and it would be too risky to panic openly on the bus and cause a big scene. Somehow, I still knew I had taken LSD and that it all could be due to that, although it did not seem in any way separate from reality. I remember just giving up and letting go to the experience whether or not I was going to die, for at that point I was not sure. Pictures of the bridge falling and the bus sinking to the bottom of the river started to spring up in my mind and I saw my body drown and my soul rise from it. At that point the bus reached the other side of the bridge and miraculously the rain stopped and the sun came out; everything seemed to be clean and glistening from the rain. I felt reborn and in a sense was, since this experience has had a profound effect on my consciousness and direction in life.

Two years after this experience with LSD, I was involved in an auto accident. After being thrown out of the car, a Volkswagen, it somehow spun around and the wheel rolled on top of my back. When feeling the pressure of the wheel becoming unbearable, I remember thinking that it would be all right if I died, and I believe this is largely due to my LSD experience and the knowledge of the continuation of consciousness or being after death learned from it. This greatly reduced any fear that was present and I just sort of relaxed and "let go" since there was no way out of the situation. At the moment of surrendering, I could feel the life force leaving my body, starting from the bottom of my feet, and moving upwards through my limbs and out of the head region. Then it seemed that the essence of "beingness" was in a realm of pure bliss and total liberation. There was no mind, thought, or emotion, and I felt once again I was home or in true Reality. Just knowing and pure Being.

It seemed there was an infinite amount of flashbacks, from the past up to the present, which were being observed in a very detached but intense way. The flashbacks predominantly had to do with people with whom I had strong family, love, and friendship bonds, a lot of whom I had lost touch with or stopped seeing, leaving with confused or unclear feelings. As the flashbacks progressed, the ties with the people were much stronger, until the last two had to do with family and a person who had been my "first love" and for whom I still had strong feelings though I had not seen him for three years (at that time) and he lived three thousand miles away. I remember he was sitting in a room of a friend's house with some people I had never met, and remember feeling good because I could tell he was happy. There seemed to be some concern for the well-being of others. Later, I called and verified this information which was exactly what he was doing that night.

When I opened my eyes again, the policeman bending over me looked like an angel. Realizing I could not move because of my back, I decided that the best thing to do would be to go unconscious. The next thing I knew was being in the emergency room and turning around to look at the clock on the wall which said exactly two o'clock; this immediately touched off the memory of the whole experience. There was an overwhelming urge to tell everyone that it was all right when you died, and I started babbling about karma and other similar things, which made the doctors think I was delirious. Also, I remember thinking at that time that if I was to be paralyzed from the accident, even that role on earth would provide immense learning situations to evolve through in life.

Ted, one of the persons dying of cancer who participated in our program of psychedelic therapy (see p. 69ff.), also experienced clinical death during a surgical operation and was returned to life.

In an advanced stage of his disease, Ted suddenly developed severe uremia. Several years earlier one of his kidneys had to be surgically removed because it was attacked by malignant growth. At this point the ureter of the remaining kidney became obstructed by infection, and Ted was developing symptoms of intoxication by his own waste products. The surgeons kept delaying the operation, apparently questioning the value of an intervention that would at best prolong his life for several additional weeks.

After Ted had spent eight days in progressively worsening uremia, we received an urgent telephone call from his wife, Lilly, at five o'clock in the morning. That night Ted had seen Stan in a dream and wanted to discuss an issue that he considered most important. We arrived at the hospital about an hour later; by that time Ted's condition had deteriorated considerably and he appeared to be in a coma. He was surrounded by several of his relatives, who tried to communicate with him; there was no reaction except for an occasional quite incomprehensible mumbling. It was apparent that Ted's death was imminent. While Stan was comforting Lilly and the relatives, trying to help them accept the situation, Joan sat down by Ted's side and talked to him gently, using her own Westernized version of the instructions from the *Bardo Thödol*. In essence, she was suggesting that he move toward the light and merge with it, unafraid of its splendor. At a time when everybody in the room seemed to have accepted Ted's death, a quite unexpected thing happened. At the last moment the surgical team decided to operate; without forewarning two male attendants entered the room, transferred Ted to a four-wheeler, and took him to the operating room. All the persons in the room were shocked by what appeared to be a brutal intrusion into an intimate and special situation.

During the operation Ted had two cardiac arrests resulting in clinical death, and was resuscitated on both occasions. When we visited him in the afternoon in the Intensive Care Unit, he was just recovering from anaesthesia. He looked at Joan and surprised her with an unexpected, yet accurate, comment: "You changed your dress!" Unwilling to believe that somebody who was apparently comatose correctly observed and remembered such a subtlety, we started inquiring about the nature of his experiences on the morning of that day. It became obvious that he had correctly perceived the people present in the room, their actions and conversations. He had even noticed that at one point tears rolled down Joan's cheeks. At the same time, however, he was involved in a number of unusual experiences that seemed to be unfolding on at least three levels. He listened to Joan's voice and responded to her suggestions. The initial darkness was replaced by brilliant light, and he was able to approach it and fuse with it. The feelings he described on experiencing the light were those of sacredness and deep peace. Yet, simultaneously, he saw a movie on the ceiling, a vivid reenactment of all the bad things he had done in his life. He saw a gallery of the faces of all the people whom he had killed in the war and all the youngsters he had beaten up as an adolescent hoodlum. He had to suffer the pain and agony of all the people whom he had hurt during his lifetime. While this was happening he was aware of the presence of God, who was watching and judging this life-review. Before we left him that day, he emphasized how glad he was that he had had three LSD sessions. He found the experience of actual dying extremely similar to his psychedelic experiences and considered the latter excellent training and preparation. "Without the sessions I would have been scared by what was happening, but knowing these states, I was not afraid at all."

Ted's experience allows for more than a simple demonstration of the formal parallels between the situation of dying and the phenomenology of the LSD state. He was a person who actually experienced both states and could make a comparison on the basis of his own subjective experiences. His explicit statement about the deep similarity between his experience of dying and the LSD sessions confirmed our own impressions, based on clinical observations in psychedelic sessions, study of anthropological and mythological literature, analysis of accounts of survivors of clinical death, and observation of several situations similar to Ted's.

This material suggests that the human unconscious is a repository for a wide variety of perinatal and transpersonal experiences that constitute the basic elements of the spiritual journey. The techniques and circumstances that can activate these matrices and transform their latent content into a vivid conscious experience involve psychedelic substances, sensory isolation or overload, sonic and photic driving, hypnosis, monotonous chanting and rhythmic dancing, sleep deprivation, fasting, various techniques of meditation and spiritual practice. On occasion some pathological states will have a similar effect; this is true for severe emotional and physical stress, exhausting diseases, intoxications, and certain injuries and accidents. For reasons that are not clear at the present state of research, the perinatal and transpersonal levels of the unconscious also become activated in naturally occurring psychoses, in particular in schizophrenia and manic-depressive disorders.

In individuals who are dying these elements in the unconscious can be activated by many different mechanisms. The specific triggers in individual cases will depend on the personality of the subject, his or her mental and physical condition, the type of illness, and the specific organs involved. The studies of Heim, Noyes, Rosen, and others have demonstrated that a sudden confrontation with death can result in an unusual subjective experience even if the organism itself is intact. In this case the only conceivable mechanism is psychological regression under the influence of severe emotional stress or shock. It is possible that a mitigated version of the same mechanism is also operating in persons facing a less imminent prospect of death. In dying individuals there exists, however, a variety of deep organismic changes, many of which can function as triggers of unconscious matrices. Many diseases interfere with proper nutrition and sleep, and are associated with various degrees of starvation and sleep deprivation. Frequently, inundation of the organism by toxic metabolic products is responsible for profound psychological changes. This is true especially in the case of hepatic and renal disease, since the liver plays an important role in the detoxification process of various noxious substances and the kidneys eliminate the waste products of the organism. Mental changes are particularly profound when the individual suffers from a progressive disease of the kidneys with subsequent uremia. A high degree of autointoxication can also result from disorders that are associated with disintegration of bodily tissues, as in cancer or wasting and degenerative diseases. Psychological concomitants of a physical disease are most easily understandable if the pathological process is affecting the brain; this occurs in patients with meningitis, encephalitis, head injuries, brain tumors, and other types of organic brain damage.

Anoxia, insufficient supply of oxygen to the tissues of the body, is of paramount significance as a trigger of unconscious matrices. In dying individuals anoxia is an extremely frequent condition. It can be caused by lung diseases reducing oxygen intake (emphysema, pulmonary tumors, pneumonia, tuberculosis, and others), by inadequate distribution of oxygen such as in anemia and cardiac failure, or by interference with the enzymatic transfer of oxygen on a subcellular level. It is well known from many different sources that a limited supply of oxygen or an excess of carbon dioxide produces abnormal mental states. Experiments with the anoxic chamber have shown that lack of oxygen can induce unusual experiences quite similar to LSD. R. A. McFarland has shown that the psychosomatic reaction to anoxia is directly related to the preexperimental personality of an individual. Neurotic persons have a much lower tolerance to this situation and tend to respond quite early with difficult psychosomatic symptoms. His findings show far-reaching parallels with the results of LSD research.

The so-called Meduna mixture containing 70% oxygen and 30% carbon dioxide can produce the whole range of experiences known from LSD experiences after brief inhalation.* The similarity is so close that this mixture can be used as a prognostic tool before LSD sessions; the nature of the subject's reaction to carbon dioxide predicts the response of that person to LSD. It can also be used before the session to acquaint the individual with the unusual states of mind experienced under LSD, or after the LSD experience, to work through residual problems that remained unresolved in the session. Maneuvers restricting the supply of oxygen have been widely used through all ages in the process of inducing unusual experiences. Thus certain aboriginal rituals use suffocation by mechanical means, near-drowning, or inhalation of smoke. According to some sources the original form of baptism involved a situation of near-drowning resulting in a profound death-rebirth experience. Pranayama, an Indian spiritual practice based on the science of breath, uses periods of hyperventilation alternating with prolonged withholding of breath to induce spiritual experiences. Other Indian techniques involve obstruction of the larynx by twisting the tongue backward; constriction of the carotid arteries; or prolonged suspension by the feet with ensuing long-term congestion of the blood in the head, resulting in brain anoxia. The Taoists advocate a technique of breathing during meditation where the intake of air is so slow and inapparent that a tiny feather placed in front of the nostrils remains unmoved.

It is possible that the similarities between LSD experiences and subjective concomitants of anoxia are more than accidental. Many hypotheses have been developed to explain the pharmacological and biochemical effects of LSD. Laboratory evidence exists indicating that LSD may interfere with the transfer of oxygen on the enzymatic level. Abramson and Evans, who studied the effects of LSD on Siamese

---

* In his 1950 monograph Meduna recommended repeated inhalations of this mixture as a treatment for emotional disorders.

fighting fish (*Betta splendens*), described a variety of specific vegetative, motor, and behavioral responses to the drug in these animals. The fish responded with increased pigmentation and caricaturelike postures and movements. In a separate study Weiss, Abramson, and Baron obtained similar effects using two inhibitors of tissue respiration, potassium cyanide and sodium azide, in nonlethal concentrations; some of these phenomena could be also induced by anoxia and asphyxia. Although the laboratory research concerning the inhibitory effect of LSD on tissue oxidation brought conflicting results, the possibility of such an effect is extremely interesting from the point of view of our discussion.

We have already mentioned that anoxia is rather frequent in dying individuals. In the study conducted by Karlis Osis on death-bed observations made by medical doctors and nurses, anoxia was described most frequently by attending physicians as the explanatory principle accounting for visions, apparitions, and other unusual experiences. If lack of oxygen and an excess of carbon dioxide can produce effects similar to LSD, then a combination of these factors could be responsible for some of the unusual experiences accompanying and following clinical death. In those instances where death is caused by the cessation of the heartbeat, the tissues of the body can survive for a certain time using the oxygen present in the blood and turning it into carbon dioxide. In the case of brain cells it takes several minutes before ischemia causes irreversible damage. If we believe that consciousness is associated with subcortical areas of the central nervous system, then this time period could be of even greater duration, since the cellular elements in more archaic parts of the brain are less sensitive to lack of oxygen and can survive longer.

Under these circumstances the deceased individual could experience various unusual states of consciousness similar to those induced by LSD or the Meduna mixture. Activation of psychodynamic, perinatal, and transpersonal matrices in the unconscious would result in experiences of life-review, divine judgment, hell, purgatory, heaven, or other elements of the posthumous journey of the soul as depicted in various traditions. The person in an unusual state of consciousness also experiences time in a way that is quite different from our everyday perception of clock-time. During several minutes of objective time persons under the influence of LSD can subjectively experience entire lifetimes, centuries, millennia, or even aeons. Dying individuals can relive their entire lives within several seconds, and in minutes of clock-time they can experience an entire cosmic journey. Under these circumstances one hour can be perceived as a second and one split-second can become eternity.

The most obvious objection to the concept of the "spiritual journey after death" is the possibility of an instant and permanent loss of consciousness at the time of clinical death, comparable to that occurring during general anaesthesia or following a brain concussion. The subjective accounts of survivors of clinical death indicate that there might be more than one alternative. Some individuals who have experienced physiological death have no memory of the event; others give accounts of most unusual adventures in consciousness. In certain instances of persons who have experienced clinical death more than once, some episodes had no subjective concomitants, while others were rich in content. Since the loss of consciousness under the influence of a general anaesthetic is so frequently considered to be a model of the situation occurring at death, we will mention a few observations from this area to show the complexity of the problems involved. In the dissociative anaesthesia induced by ketamine, individuals experience a variety of unusual states of mind while they appear to be unconscious to an external observer. Operations performed in this condition are possible not because consciousness is extinguished, but because it is drastically refocused. In our own psychedelic research LSD subjects have occasionally relived all the sensations from operations performed under deep anaesthesia of a conventional type. In other experiments patients were capable of reconstructing under the influence of hypnosis the conversations of the surgical team during an operation that had been conducted with general anaesthetics (Kenneth Godfrey).

Since there is more than a reasonable possibility that the experience of dying is a complex and ramified process, the efforts invested by archaic and aboriginal cultures in this issue would certainly seem to appear in a new light. In view of the psychological relevance of this event, it makes sense to learn as much as we can about the process of dying, to familiarize ourselves with the maps of the posthumous journey, and to obtain adequate training in the unusual states of consciousness that it entails. Many non-Western cultures provide occasions during which their people may become familiar with a broad range of nonordinary realities. In others the death experience is regularly rehearsed within the framework of rites of passage. In our world death takes most people by surprise and finds them totally unprepared.

Procedures that make it possible to experience profound sequences of psychological death and rebirth and various transpersonal phenomena might be more than training and preparation for dying and death. There are indications that these episodes of unusual states of consciousness in effect modify the way in which an individual will experience his or her biological death. We believe that the struggle and agony that are associated with dying in some persons are due to the fact that the physiological and biochemical changes in the organism activate painful unconscious material from the individual's history that has not been resolved and the imprints of the agony of birth that have not been worked through and consciously integrated.

An important observation from LSD psychotherapy supports this possibility. In persons who have had serial LSD sessions, the earlier LSD experiences usually contain much psychodynamic material and dramatic perinatal sequences. If the sessions continue these areas can be completely worked through, and all subsequent sessions are of a transpersonal, religious, and mystical nature. When these individuals are given inhalations of Meduna mixture in the course of their LSD therapy, their response to carbon dioxide will change depending on the stage of LSD treatment. In the free intervals between early LSD sessions, this mixture will evoke visions of abstract geometrical patterns and reliving of childhood memories. The same combination of gases administered later, at a time when these persons are working on the perinatal material, will trigger sequences of the death-rebirth struggle. In the advanced stages of LSD therapy, when the sessions are predominantly transpersonal in nature, an inhalation of Meduna mixture will induce transpersonal phenomena—various mystical and religious states, archetypal elements, or even past incarnation experiences. All these observations seem to support the point of view so clearly and succinctly expressed in the seventeenth century by Abraham a Sancta Clara, an Austrian Augustinian monk: "The man who dies before he dies, does not die when he dies."

As we have mentioned, unusual states of consciousness, similar to those produced by LSD, occur spontaneously in many dying individuals for reasons of a physiological, biochemical, and psychological nature. Such states are usually considered psychiatric complications and are routinely suppressed by the administration of tranquilizers. According to our experience a sensitive psychologist or psychiatrist can use at least some of them constructively, in a way not dissimilar to an LSD experience. With adequate support and guidance such episodes can prove to be very beneficial for the dying individual. This approach necessitates a dramatic shift in our value system, from the emphasis on mechanical prolongation of life to concern about the quality of dying and death.

A few words are in order here about the new relationship between religion and science that seems to be emerging from the study of unusual states of consciousness. The prevailing feeling is that the discoveries and developments of science have discredited the validity of religious beliefs. The basic concepts and assumptions of religions, if taken literally, appear naive and absurd to the sophisticated and scientifically minded. Astronomers have aimed gigantic telescopes at the sky and have systematically explored vast areas of the universe. There is no more uncharted space left for celestial spheres, hierarchies of angels, or God. Geological and geophysical data about the structure and composition of the crust and core of the earth have replaced the images of fiery underground caverns teeming with devils. What was attacked and discarded by contemporary science, however, was a primitive and naive belief that basic religious concepts have an objective existence in the three-dimensional physical universe as we experience it in usual states of consciousness. Observations from LSD research clearly indicate that in various special states of mind the bliss of paradise, horrors of hell, and ecstatic raptures of salvation can be experienced with a degree of vividness and a sense of reality that match or even surpass our everyday perceptions. The matrices for these experiences and a range of other religious and mystical phenomena appear to be an intrinsic part of the human personality. Recognition and exploration of these dimensions is thus indispensable for a deeper understanding of human nature.

9.

DEATH AND REBIRTH IN RITUAL TRANSFORMATION

In the preceding chapters we have described various observations made in the context of clinical research, as well as certain extreme situations of everyday life, indicating that a profound encounter with death can permanently alter the concept of death and the individual's attitude toward it. This seems to occur whether such an encounter happens in reality, as in dangerous accidents and in those instances that involve survival of actual clinical death, or in a purely subjective symbolic fashion, as exemplified by death-rebirth experiences in psychedelic sessions and spontaneous mystical experiences. In addition to changing an individual's feelings about the impermanence of human existence, such episodes can have a profoundly transforming influence on the person involved. According to various mystical traditions those who have experienced death or mortal peril and have returned to life are referred to as twice-born, illumined, or enlightened.

In most preindustrial societies and ancient civilizations, there have existed powerful rituals designed to transform and consecrate individuals, groups, and even entire cultures. These transformative events, termed *rites of passage* by anthropologists, are of fundamental importance to the discussion of the experience of symbolic death and rebirth. Rites of passage are those ritual events whose purpose it is to provide a context for the total redefinition of the individual. This process involves not only psychological and social variables but also basic philosophical and spiritual dimensions of human existence. Rites of passage occur at the time of important transitions in an individual's life or in the life of a culture. In terms of personal and biological history, they frequently coincide with major physiological transitions; they can take place at birth, puberty, first maturity (young adulthood, marriage, childbirth), second maturity, and death. At each of these points in life, the body, psyche, social status, and sacred role of the individual are going through some degree of change.* Rites of passage can also occur in the framework of shamanic and heroic initiation, initiation into a sacred society, calendrical festivals of renewal, geographical passage, and healing rituals. In these situations the individual or social group leaves behind one mode of being, and after passing through a period of liminality, moves into another and totally new existential condition. We will describe aspects of such transformative events, beginning with the classical form of rites of passage occurring when the individual moves from one life stage to another.

Arnold van Gennep, the author of the early study on rites of passage, has described these events in terms of three consecutive stages: separation, transition, and incorporation. In the first stage, *separation,* the individual is removed from his or her social network. The neophyte can be totally isolated or can share this unfamiliar condition with agemates who are in a like situation. The period of separation can be associated with grief reactions over the loss of the old way of being.

---

* When looking at Western culture from the point of view of life stages, we see that the time of major transitions from one stage in life to another is usually fraught with a negative value; this is certainly true for puberty, middle age, senescence, and, of course, dying. Even birth has taken on a certain negative cast in our culture, where the delivering mother is routinely relegated to the role of the sick and goes to a hospital to deliver her child. Another category to be considered as being liminal are people afflicted by diseases, especially those who have been designated as "terminally ill." Such persons are between life and death and therefore no longer viable social entities; from this point of view the dying are often viewed as social and economic burdens.

During the time of separation fear also plays an important role—fear of the unknown, fear of the unexpected, fear that can be projected onto the strangeness of this undefined world. And it is often fear that impels the neophyte to move beyond the ego, which holds onto what is predictable in life. During this time of separation a deep sense of community often develops. The special situation of seclusion combined with expectations and fear has the effect of binding the initiates together in this common experience through which they all must pass.

As the neophyte is learning the culture's mythology and cosmology, the preparation for more dynamic aspects of the rite of passage begins to unfold. The program for the arduous and frequently terrifying transition that is to be faced is communicated to the aspirant in the form of myths, tales, songs, and dances, or explicitly in terms of concrete mapping of the experiential territory that will be traversed. This dimension of the learning process is very important for the outcome of the initiation. The neophyte learns that this territory, though strange and perhaps ominous, has been and will be crossed by many others, not only by the sacred ancestors who have gone before but also by future generations to come. This knowledge has the potential of reassuring the initiate and can provide further impetus for surrendering into the archaic process.

In the second stage, termed *transition* by van Gennep, the neophyte moves from a time of intellectual learning into a time of experiencing the fiber of the myths. We must consider this phase both from the point of view of the external symbols and actions that frame the neophyte's experience and from that of the subjective experience of the aspirant who is going through the process. It is during this time of transition that various techniques are used by a culture to expand the consciousness of an initiate by reducing or eliminating the psychological defenses that separate the world of the supernatural from the world of everyday reality. Such techniques include sleep deprivation, fasting, body mutilation, sonic and photic driving, social isolation, hyperactivity, group pressure, suggestion, and, in some cases, psychedelic substances. Through a combination of the symbolic drama unfolding from within and external cultural symbols that frame the event, the neophyte is experiencing and ultimately learning in a deeply ramified way the core notion in all rites of passage—that one can suffer through the chaos of liminality and of dying, undergo an experience of total annihilation, and emerge from this process renewed and reborn. The learning here is profound; it involves not just the intellect but the entire psychobiological organism. A dialectical process occurs between external events and elements of the environment on the one hand, and the inner experience of the individual on the other; this meshing of unconscious contents emerging into consciousness with cultural symbols denoting renewal creates a situation of profound congruence and coherence within the individual.

The third stage in van Gennep's triad is that of *incorporation*. It involves the reintegration of the individual into his or her community. But the person who returns is not the same as the one who entered the initiation process. New conceptual frameworks and world-views, as well as redefined status and responsibilities, are enjoyed by the individual as he or she moves out of the initiation hut and enters another and higher mode of being.

A careful analysis of the external and internal symbolism occurring in rites of passage discloses that their essential elements are identical with those described earlier for perinatal phenomena. The parallels between the phenomenology of rites of passage and LSD experiences involving death and rebirth are far-reaching. The symbolism of each revolves around the same peculiar mixture of birth, sex, and death. The initiation hut is often called *vagina* or *womb*.* It is not uncommon that the same place is also called tomb, the place of burial. In some cultures, the term for gestation, burial, and initiation is the same. Conversely, tombs are sometimes built in the shape of wombs, and the dead are buried in a fetal position. Pregnant women can be referred to as dead and be considered reborn at the time they deliver their children.

In rites of passage as well as in perinatal sessions, the symbolism of

---

* Among the Iatmul, a New Guinea culture studied by Gregory Bateson, the entrance to the initiation hut is called *clitoris gate*.

spiritual death and rebirth is intermingled with concrete biological elements. Initiates are frequently stripped of all their clothes, their bodies shorn of all hair, and blood of sacrificial animals poured over their heads; it is not difficult to see these elements as an approximation of the situation of the neonate.* Furthermore, the use of fecal material and other revulsive substances is reminiscent of the scatological dimension of biological birth. Finally, the elements of torture and physical suffering, painful separation, and struggle for survival involved in many rites of passage bear a close resemblance to comparable phenomena that occur as part of the perinatal unfolding in psychedelic sessions. Sometimes the encounter with death can be staged in such a realistic fashion that the ritual enactment involves the danger of serious physical trauma or the risk of actual biological destruction.

Subjective symbolic phenomenology and external symbolic representation can be combined in ritual events in such a way that they augment each other and result in a powerful and overwhelming personal as well as collective experience. It is within these rites of transformation that the individual's personal boundaries widen to include not only the social organism but also supernal realms and sacred beings who inhabit the world beyond; this domain of experience has many parallels in the transpersonal phenomena that we have described in an earlier chapter. The introduction of the individual to the spiritual history of the culture, a cosmogony that is reiterated at every initiation, brings the neophyte into close relationship with the culture's archaic, sacred tradition and its relevance to his or her own psyche. It is the resacralization of the individual and the aspirant's introduction to the essential creative impulse in the cosmos that endow existence with

---

* The initiation rite practiced in connection with circumcision among some Bantu peoples in Africa can be used as a salient example of the deep association between symbolic death-rebirth and actual biological birth, as well as of the juxtaposition and overlap of birth, sex, and death symbolism. A boy who is to be circumcised is the object of a ceremony called "being born anew." The father sacrifices a ram and three days later wraps the child in the animal's stomach membrane and skin. Prior to this the boy has to climb in bed beside his mother and cry like a newborn infant. He remains in the ram's skin for three days; on the fourth day his father and mother have ritual intercourse. In this culture the dead also are buried in ram's skin and in the fetal position. (Eliade, 1958).

new meaning; at the same time, they also imbue with equal relevance the individual's death.

The similarity between rites of passage and perinatal phenomena can be seen not only in terms of their specific content but also in their overall structure and patterning. There is a clear parallel between van Gennep's stage of separation and the experience of loneliness, isolation, and alienation that is characteristic of the no-exit matrix on the perinatal level; the chaos experienced in this context further emphasizes this similarity. Van Gennep's stage of transition then corresponds to the experience of the death-rebirth struggle and subsequent transcendence. Finally, the stage of incorporation has its perinatal counterpart in the sequence of ego death and rebirth, reflecting the child's reunion with its mother. We can thus see rites of passage as structured events in which individuals can confront, experience, and express powerful energies associated with matrices deep in the unconscious. It seems plausible that in view of the nature of the psychological forces involved, elemental and uncontrolled manifestation and acting out of these energies could be destructive for the community. It is interesting to mention in this context the opinion of Arnold van Gennep, Margaret Mead, Mircea Eliade, and other outstanding anthropologists, according to which the absence of rites of transformation might be contributing to the social psychopathology observed in contemporary society. Many impulses of a basically destructive and antisocial nature, instead of being acted out with social sanctions in a safe and structured sacred context, leak insidiously into our everyday lives and manifest themselves in a number of individual and societal problems.

Another important area that involves all of the major experiential elements described in traditional rites of passage is *shamanic initiation.* The initiation trials of Siberian and Ural-Altaic shamans are very intense and dramatic events. The core experience of the shamanic journey is, again, a profound encounter with death in the form of ritual annihilation and resurrection or rebirth. Initiatory dreams and visions include descent to the nether regions, suffering and death, and ascent to heaven with resurrection. Siberian shamans maintain that during their initiatory illness they are dead for three to seven days in their tents (*yurts*) or in a solitary place. At this time demons and ancestral spirits take them to the underworld and expose them to a variety of tortures. Although there is considerable variation in the details of these ordeals among different tribes and individual shamans, they all share the general atmosphere of horror and inhuman suffering. The tortures involve dismemberment, disposal of all body fluids, scraping of flesh from bones, tearing eyes from sockets, or similar terrifying manipulations. After the novice shaman has been reduced to a skeleton and the bones cleaned, the pieces of his or her body are usually distributed among the spirits of various diseases. The bones are then covered with new flesh and the shaman aspirant might even be given new blood. In this transformed condition the resurrected person receives supernatural knowledge and the power of healing from various semidivine beings in human or animal form. The next important stage of the shamanic journey is the ascent to the heavenly regions by means of a pole, birch tree or magical flight for the purpose of consecration.

According to Mircea Eliade, a renowned authority on shamanism, shamans have contributed considerably to the knowledge of death and "funerary geography" and are the authors of many themes concerning the mythology of death. In most instances the land that the shaman sees and the personages that he or she meets are described in minute detail by the shaman during and after trance states. Through the repeated magical journeys of the shaman, the unknown and terrifying world of death assumes form and structure, and gradually becomes more familiar and acceptable. Little by little, the region of death becomes knowable and death itself is seen primarily as a rite of passage to a spiritual mode of being.

Initiatory death is always followed by resurrection and a resolution of the shaman's crisis; the shaman should be at home in both "objective reality" and the various regions of the supernatural world. In these mystical initiations the shaman must give religious significance to the symbolic suffering that he or she has endured and accept the experiences as meaningful ordeals. After initiation shamans are able to visit the world of spirits and communicate with them. They themselves behave like spirits, being able to leave their bodies and travel at will to cosmic regions. Accomplished shamans are healers, seers, priests, poets, and psychopomps for their people. They conduct healing ceremonies, direct communal ritual sacrifices, and play the role of escort for the souls of the dead during their journey to the other world.

Although the shamanism of the Siberian and Ural-Altaic peoples has in the past received the primary attention of anthropologists and ethnographers, similar practices and experiences, including initiatory illness, exist with some variations among peoples in southeast Asia, Australia, Oceania, Africa, and among Indians in North and South America.

This account of the initiation of a Avam-Samoyed shaman, recorded by A. A. Popov, can be used as an illustration of the experiences that open individuals to a shamanic career:

> Stricken with smallpox, the future shaman remained unconscious for three days, so nearly dead that on the third day he was almost buried. He saw himself go down to Hell, and, after many adventures, was carried to an island, in the middle of which stood a young birch tree which reached up to heaven. It was the Tree of the Lord of the Earth, and the Lord gave him a branch of it to make himself a drum. Next he came to a mountain. Passing through an opening, he met a naked man plying the bellows at an immense fire on which was a kettle. The man caught him with a hook, cut off his head, and chopped his body to bits and put them all into the kettle. There he boiled the body for three years, and then forged him a head on an anvil. Finally he fished out the bones, which were floating in a river, put them together, and covered them with flesh. During his adventures in the Other World, the future shaman met several semidivine personages, in human or animal form, and each of them revealed doctrines to him or taught him secrets of the healing art. When he awoke in his *yurt,* among his relatives, he was initiated and could begin to shamanize.

Mythology, the repository of a culture's sacred history, also reveals the relevance and universal nature of the experience of death and rebirth. Many ancient and contemporary cultures have dramatic stories about heroes who descended to the realm of the dead and, overcoming undreamt-of obstacles, returned to earth endowed with supernatural powers. Equally frequent are references to gods, demigods, or heroes who died or were killed and subsequently were brought back to life in a new role, rejuvenated or immortalized through the experience of annihilation. In a more obscure symbolic form, the same theme is sometimes represented by the hero being devoured and incorporated by a hideous monster and then either being regurgitated by the beast or making a miraculous escape.

In many places of the world these mythological themes became a conceptual basis for sacred mysteries in which neophytes experienced ritualized death and rebirth. The Babylonian and Assyrian rites of Tammuz and Ishtar revolved around one of the earliest examples of the allegory of the dying god, probably antedating 4000 B.C. The myth underlying the ritual procedure was the story of the Mother Goddess Ishtar and her descent into the underworld in search of the sacred elixir that alone could restore to life her dead son and husband, Tummuz. She herself was imprisoned in the house of darkness by the chthonic goddess Ereshkigal, the queen of the underworld, and was afflicted by various diseases. As a goddess of fertility, Ishtar in retaliation prevented the ripening of the crops and the maturing of all life upon earth. At the intervention of other gods, who were frightened by this situation, Ishtar was finally healed by the water of life and freed from the underworld. According to the esoteric interpretation the myth of Ishtar symbolized the imprisonment of consciousness in matter and its release through the life-giving and liberating effect of the secret doctrine. In the temples of Isis and Osiris of ancient Egypt, candidates of initiation underwent a complex sequence of ordeals under the guidance of hierophants in order to overcome the fear of death and gain access to esoteric knowledge about the universe and human nature. The mythological ground for the ritual transformation was the murder and dismemberment of Osiris by his brother Set, and his resurrection after a magical procedure conducted by his sister Nephthys and his wife and sister, Isis.

In ancient Greece mystery religions and sacred rites were abundant. The Eleusinian mysteries celebrated every five years in Attica were based on an esoteric interpretation of the myth about Demeter and her daughter Persephone. Kidnapped by the chthonic god Pluto, Persephone was compelled to spend six months of every year in the underworld. This myth, usually considered to be an allegory concerned with the seasonal cycles in nature, became for the Eleusinian initiates a symbol for the spiritual struggles of the soul.

The Orphic cult was based on the legend about the deified Thracian bard, Orpheus, who made an unsuccessful attempt to liberate his beloved Eurydice from the darkness of the underworld. Orpheus himself died a tragic death when he was torn to pieces by Ciconian women for interfering in the Bacchanalia. According to legend, his severed head, thrown into the river Hebrus, continued to sing and give forth oracles. The Bacchic and Dionysian rites centered around the mythological story of the young Bacchus, who was dismembered by the Titans and then resurrected after Pallas Athene rescued his heart. In the Dionysian rites the Bacchants sought identification with the murdered and resurrected god through drinking intoxicating beverages, rhythmic dancing, and eating raw animal flesh. The Samothracian mysteries of the Corybants or Cabiri were closely related to the Dionysian festivals. The ritualistic drama depicted the murder of Cadmillus by his three brothers.

The Phrygian mysteries were celebrated in the name of Attis, a god who emasculated himself under a pine tree, died, and was resurrected by the Great Mother Cybele.*

The ritual procedure practiced in Phrygia included a sacramental meal during which the neophyte ate out of a drum and drank from a cymbal. After having been smeared with the blood of a bull, he was fed entirely on milk. The mysteries of Adonis were annually celebrated in many parts of Egypt, Phoenicia, and Byblos. According to legend, Adonis was born from a myrrh tree, into which the gods had turned his mother, Smyrna. His birth was facilitated by a wild boar, who opened the maternal tree with his tusks. The wild boar, who thus functioned as a midwife for Adonis, became for him also an agent of death; Adonis died after having been gored and mortally wounded by this animal. In the mysteries of Adonis the neophyte passed through

---

* According to some mythologists, this legend represents the pagan roots of the Christian tradition of the Christmas tree.

the symbolic death of the god and was raised to life with the help of the priests. He entered into the blessed state of rebirth and redemption made possible by the suffering of Adonis.

In the Nordic tradition the murdered and resurrected god was Odin's favorite son, Balder. According to the myth, he was young and beautiful and was the only peaceful god in Valhalla. The trickster Loki, the personification of evil, stimulated the blind god of fate, Hoder, to shoot Balder with a mistletoe arrow, the only weapon that could hurt him. After much effort the heartbroken gods found a means of resurrecting their favorite. In the mysteries of Odin the neophyte drank sanctified mead from a bowl made of a human skull. As Balder, the initiate underwent a sacred ordeal in a complex of nine underground chambers and, at the end, was able to unveil the mystery of Odin, the most precious secrets of nature and the human soul. In the Druidic mysteries of Britain the boundary between symbolic and biological death was rather blurred. After having been buried alive in a coffin, the candidate was sent out to sea in an open boat in a symbolic enactment of the death of the Sun God. In this unusual ordeal many initiates lost their lives; those who survived the demanding ritual were referred to as reborn.

These examples are by no means an exhaustive account of the mystery religions. Similar ritual procedures focusing on death and rebirth have also existed in various forms in the Mithraic religion, in the Hermetic tradition, in India and Tibet, among various African tribes, in pre-Columbian and contemporary American Indian societies, and in many other cultures of the world. Similar rituals were also practiced during initiation into various secret societies of all ages.

Several specific examples of the events in the death-rebirth mysteries will show how closely they resemble the phenomenology of perinatal psychedelic sessions. Edward Schüré, in *The Great Initiates,* gave a vivid reconstruction of the process of initiation in the Egyptian mysteries of Isis and Osiris. According to him, the ritual ordeal started by passing through a narrow corridor of the secret sanctuary lit by torches. On the two sides of this sinister room, there were rows of frightening statues with men's bodies and animals' heads. At the end of this corridor there was a mummy and a human skeleton guarding a hole in the wall. The neophyte was given a little lighted lamp and entered this opening, which was so low that he had to crawl on hands and knees. Then the door closed behind him and he had to proceed in darkness through a very narrow passage. At the end there was a shaft which led to a ladder disappearing into a vertical hole. As the neophyte descended to the lowest rung, he found himself hanging above a terrifying abyss. As he was anxiously contemplating his grim predicament—impossible return above and mysterious blackness below—he noticed a crevice and a staircase on his right. He escaped from the abyss and the spiral staircase carved in the rock took him to a great hall with symbolic frescoes. The pastophor, guardian of sacred symbols, explained to him the meaning of the paintings.

The next stage of the trial started in a long, narrow corridor, at the end of which glowed a red-hot furnace. The door closed behind him and left him with the task of walking through the fire. As he gained enough courage and approached the fiery furnace, he saw it reduced to an optical illusion created by lighted interlacing resinous wood placed over iron latticework. A path through the middle allowed him to pass by quickly.

The test of fire was followed by the trial by water. The initiate was forced to go through a pool of black, stagnant water. After this two assistants led him into a dim grotto; there he was bathed, dried, and was scented with exquisite essences.

As he was resting he heard the music of harps and flutes. A Nubian woman, clad in a dark red robe and decorated with beautiful jewels, approached him as an embodiment of all feminine sensuality. If he surrendered to this temptation he failed the test and had to remain in the temple as a slave for the rest of his life. If he successfully passed through this last stage, he was led triumphantly into the sanctuary of Isis and had to pledge silence and submission in front of the colossal statue of the goddess.

In *The Obelisk in Free Masonry* John E. Weisse gave a description of the Eleusinian mysteries of ancient Greece. He depicted the initial atmosphere as one of utter chaos and horror, with blinding flashes of light and deafening rolling of thunder. According to him, the entire place seemed to shake and to be on fire, hideous specters glided through the air, moaning and sighing, and frightful noises and howlings were heard. Against the background of these infernal scenes, mysterious apparitions flew, representing the messengers of various wrathful deities—Anguish, Madness, Famine, Disease, and Death. As the trembling crowd of novices advanced amid this fearful spectacle, reflecting the torments of this life and those of Tartarus, they heard the solemn voice of the hierophant exhibiting and explaining the symbols of supreme divinity. Suddenly the scene changed and the images of horror were replaced by a serene light and various symbols of bliss. The phalanx of the Eleusinian initiates had thus experienced, in a short time and space, "the miseries of Earth, the tortures of Tartarus, and the happiness of Elysium."

In Schüré's account of the initiation into the mysteries of Isis and Osiris, the similarity between the various stages of this ordeal and psychedelic death-rebirth sequences is particularly striking. It involves tests by death, by fire, by foul water, and by sexual seduction. This clearly corresponds with the perinatal no-exit situation and the facets of the death-rebirth struggle involving fire, scatological elements, and sexual arousal. Weisse's description of the Eleusinian initiation could easily be an account of an LSD session with a major emphasis on the perinatal level. Both the confrontation with the most frightening aspects of human existence and the abrupt transition from extreme torture and anguish into transcendental bliss belong to the most common occurrences in psychedelic therapy.

The wide historical and geographical distribution of transformative rituals focusing on death and rebirth and their psychological relevance for individuals, groups, and entire cultures suggest that they must reflect important basic needs inherent in human nature. The study of those events and a deeper understanding of the death-rebirth process are thus of great theoretical and practical interest. Research in this area has been associated with specific problems. Much of the key information about the nature of these rites is usually considered sacred; it is kept secret and transmitted within small circles of initiates. If the material is revealed to the external world, it occurs traditionally in various cryptic forms. Reconstruction of the actual ritual procedures from historical descriptions or archaeological findings is very difficult and in many instances might be inaccurate.

Anthropologists who have studied ritual forms of contemporary cultures are confronted with the very difficult task of gaining access to the secret core of these procedures. Since most of these studies have been done in non-Western cultures, this was further complicated by cultural and linguistic barriers. With a few exceptions anthropological studies have focused in the past on the externally observable aspects of rites of passage rather than the subjective experiences of the participants.*

Psychedelic research seems to offer a unique approach to the future exploration of the process of ritual transformation. The parallels between LSD sessions and the ritual death-rebirth process are so striking that the former can be used as an experimental model of the latter. Using individuals from our own culture with known life-histories, who are willing to share their experiences, the researcher can overcome some of the difficulties intrinsic to historical scholarly approach and anthropological field-work. A deeper understanding of the transformative process, based on the synthesis of historical, anthropological, and experimental data, could have important implications for many different areas, including psychiatry, art, philosophy, religion, and education.

---

* In recent years many researchers have pointed to the fact that the subjective aspects of ritual events represent an important key to the understanding of the transformative process. They advocate that anthropologists should not only collect introspective data but should actually participate in the procedure and have a firsthand experience of the impact of the drugs or nondrug techniques involved. This orientation has been referred to as "visionary anthropology"; Carlos Castaneda, Michael Harner, Barbara Myerhoff, Marlene Dobkin de Rios, Joan Halifax, and Richard Katz are representatives of this approach.

10.

DIALECTICS
OF LIFE AND DEATH

Although the theme of death plays a dominant role in religion, mythology, and art of many non-Western cultures, it is quite surprising how little attention death has received in theoretical speculations of Western psychologists, psychiatrists, and philosophers. There have been, however, several important exceptions. The most interesting of these was Sigmund Freud, whose views regarding the psychological relevance of death underwent a dramatic change during various stages of his psychoanalytic research. In Freud's earlier writings there was an almost exclusive emphasis on sexuality. Death played a relatively minor role and did not have an independent representation in the human unconscious. Fear of death was interpreted as a derivative of separation anxiety or of castration fears, and was thus rooted in the conflicts of the pre-Oedipal and Oedipal stages of libidinal development. Most of Freud's followers accepted this point of view and contributed their own variations or modifications. Otto Fenichel, summarizing the findings in psychoanalytic literature, expressed doubt that there is any such thing as a normal fear of death. According to him, the idea of one's own death is subjectively inconceivable, and therefore fear of death covers other unconscious ideas. Sometimes these ideas are libidinal in nature and become understandable through the history of the patient. More frequently certain childhood experiences have turned fear of loss of love or castration into a fear of death. The idea of death may reflect fear of punishment for death wishes or fear of one's own excitement, particularly of sexual orgasm.

Freud himself changed his ideas about death rather drastically as a result of his clinical observations. Indications of such change can be found in his theoretical formulations published between 1913 and 1920 and especially in his analysis of Shakespeare's *The Merchant of Venice* ("The Theme of the Three Caskets") and in his essay entitled "Thoughts for the Times on War and Death." In these papers he showed a definite tendency to revise his earlier thesis that death does not have a representation in the human mind.

In 1920 Freud achieved a synthesis and integration of his divergent views of death and formulated a comprehensive biopsychological theory of the human personality. In *Beyond the Pleasure Principle* he postulated the existence of two categories of instincts—those that serve the goal of preserving life and those that counteract it and tend to return it from whence it originally came. Freud saw a deep relationship between these two groups of instinctual forces and two opposing trends in the physiological processes in the human organism, namely *anabolism* and *catabolism*. *Anabolic* processes are those that contribute to growth, development, and storage of nutriments; *catabolic* processes are related to the burning of reserves and expenditure of energy. Freud also linked the activity of these drives to the destiny of two groups of cells in the human organism—germinal cells, which are potentially eternal, and those forming the soma, which are destined to die. Earlier he had considered almost all manifestations of aggression as a form of sexuality and thus basically sadistic in nature; in the new conceptual framework he related them to the death instinct. According to this view, the death instinct operates in the human organism from the very beginning, converting it gradually into an inorganic system. This destructive drive can and must be partially diverted from its primary aim and be directed against other organisms. It seems to be irrelevant whether the death instinct is oriented toward objects in the external world or against the organism itself, as long as it can achieve its goal, which is to destroy.

Freud's final formulations concerning the role of the death instinct appeared in his last major work, *An Outline of Psychoanalysis* (1938). There the basic dichotomy between two powerful forces, the love instinct (Eros) and the death instinct (Thanatos), became the cornerstone of his understanding of mental processes—a concept which dominated Freud's thinking in the last years of his life. This major revision of psychoanalytic theory did not generate much enthusiasm among Freud's followers and has never been fully incorporated into mainstream psychoanalysis. Rudolf Brun, who has conducted an extensive statistical review of papers concerned with Freud's theory of the death instinct, found that most of them were clearly unfavorable to Freud's concept. Many of the authors have considered Freud's interest in death and the incorporation of Thanatos into the theory of instincts as an alien enclave in the development of his psychological framework. There have also been inferences that personal factors were the basis for this unexpected dimension in Freud's thinking. His later ideas have been interpreted by some as a result of his own pathological preoccupation with death, his reaction to the cancer which was afflicting him, and the demise of close family members. Brun in the aforementioned critical study has suggested that Freud's theory of the death instinct was also deeply influenced by his reaction to the First World War.

In his essay, "On the Psychology of the Unconscious," Carl Gustav Jung opposed Freud's concept of the two fundamental instincts of Eros and Thanatos. He also disagreed with Freud's thesis that the aim of Eros is to establish ever greater unities and preserve them and that the purpose of Thanatos is to undo connections and thus to destroy. Jung argued that such a choice of opposites reflected attitudes of the conscious mind and not the dynamics of the unconscious. According to Jung, the *logical* opposite of love is hate and that of Eros is Phobos (fear). However, the *psychological* opposite of love is the will to power, a force that dominated the theories of Alfred Adler.* Where love reigns there is no will to power, and where the will to power is paramount, love is absent. It was a concession to intellectual logic on the one hand, and to psychological prejudice on the other, that impelled Freud to name the opposite of Eros the destructive or death instinct. According to Jung, Eros is not equivalent to life, but for somebody who *thinks* it is, the opposite of Eros will naturally appear to be death. We all feel that the opposite of our highest principle must be purely destructive and evil. It is impossible for us to endow it with any positive life force, and we tend to avoid and fear it.

Jung's specific contribution to thanatology was his full awareness of how powerfully the motifs related to death are represented in the unconscious. He and his followers have brought to the attention of Western psychology the utmost significance of all the symbolic variations on the theme of death and rebirth in our archetypal heritage. This has been illustrated by numerous examples from various cultures and historical periods, ranging from the mythology of Australian Aborigines to alchemy.

The problems related to death also played a prominent role in Jung's psychology of the individuation process. He saw sexuality as the dominant force in the first half of human life, and the problems of biological decline and approaching death as the central focus in the second half. A preoccupation with the problem of death emerges under normal circumstances in the later decades; its occurrence in the earlier stages of life is usually associated with psychopathology. The process of individuation described by Jung results in the psychological completion of the personality and involves a resolution of the problem of death.

* Adler's life and work, according to his own account, were influenced by an encounter with death. At the age of five he was stricken with severe pneumonia, and his situation was declared hopeless by his attending physician. After recovering he decided to study medicine to be better able to defy death. Although Adler has not explicitly incorporated the fear of death into his theory, his own lifelong pursuits were influenced by this experience of vital emergency. The emphasis in Adler's therapy was on courage and the ability to face the dangerous aspects of life (Bottome, 1939).

The issue of death also has an important place in the thinking of the existentialists, particularly in the philosophy of Martin Heidegger. In his analysis of existence expounded in *Sein und Zeit* (*Being and Time*), death plays a central role. According to Heidegger, the awareness of impermanence, nothingness, and death permeates imperceptibly each moment of human life prior to the actual occurrence of biological death or an encounter with it. It is irrelevant whether the individual has actual knowledge of death, anticipates its advent, or is consciously paying attention to problems related to impermanence. Existential analysis reveals that life is "existence toward death" (*Sein zum Tode*). All ontological speculations must consider the totality of existence and thus also that part of it which does not yet exist, including the very end. The awareness of death is a constant source of tension and existential anxiety in the organism, but it also provides a background against which existence and time appear to have a deeper meaning.

It is important to note that Heidegger followed the recommendation of his teacher, Edmund Husserl, that philosophers should turn their attention away from the natural world and toward inner experience. In this way self-exploration is a basic necessity for our apprehension of the world and for our thinking about it. Heidegger claims to have described fundamental experiences that underlie and yet are beyond our everyday perception of the world and outside the reach of traditional scientific method. It seems to be the result of this approach that his views are so close to insights achieved in various unusual states of consciousness.*

In the last decade there has been an explosive increase of theoretical interest in the role death plays in the human unconscious. This has been closely related to clinical and laboratory studies of various unusual states of mind. With the use of psychedelic drugs, powerful

---

* It was mentioned in the discussion of perinatal experiences that the existentialist world-view seems to dominate the thinking and feelings of subjects who are under the influence of the no-exit matrix and are not able to find the only solution, which seems to be transcendence. The atheism of the existentialist philosophers confirms this relationship.

nondrug methods of altering consciousness, and some of the experiential techniques of individual and group psychotherapy, it is possible to activate levels of the unconscious that in the past were seldom available for direct observation.* Certain phenomena that used to be considered distortions due to the psychotic process when they occurred in schizophrenic patients are now produced with great regularity and constancy in normal volunteers by the above methods. Perceptive researchers who have studied these states from the phenomenological point of view cannot overlook the important role which experiences of death (and birth) play in this context. The observations from this field of research confirm, in the most general sense, what Freud, Jung, and some of the existentialist philosophers described, each in his specific way—that death is powerfully represented in the human unconscious.

Sequences of agony, death, and rebirth belong to the most frequent experiences in psychedelic sessions. They occur quite spontaneously, without any specific programming, and sometimes even to the great surprise of an unexperienced and uninformed subject. In many LSD sessions such sequences represent the central focus of the psychedelic experience. This illustrates not only the existence of matrices for such experiences in the unconscious and their powerful emotional charge, but also a strong need and tendency in human beings to exteriorize this deep material. This observation seems to explain the ubiquitous nature of various death-rebirth rituals and the importance attributed to them by initiates, religious groups, and entire cultures.

The parallels between LSD sessions and esoteric procedures focusing on the death experience are not only of a phenomenological nature. The physiological, psychological, philosophical, and spiritual

* Dramatic experiences of death and rebirth can be observed in encounter groups, marathon sessions, Gestalt practice, bioenergetic approaches, primal therapy, and hypnosis. They can occur occasionally in laboratory experiments with sensory deprivation, sensory overload, biofeedback, and various kinaesthetic devices. Many Western students of Oriental spiritual practices, such as Zen Buddhism, Vajrayana, or Kundalini Yoga, have experienced profound sequences of this kind as a result of their practice. Robert Masters and Jean Houston described several very effective exercises involving death-rebirth sequences in their book *Mind Games.*

consequences of well-resolved LSD experiences also bear a close similarity to the transformations described for initiates and neophytes of all ages who have faced death and returned to life. According to our observations, those individuals who have experienced death and rebirth in their sessions show specific changes in their perception of themselves and of the world, in their hierarchies of values, general behavior, and overall world-views. Those who prior to these experiences had various forms and degrees of emotional and psychosomatic discomfort usually feel greatly relieved. Depression dissolves, anxiety and tension are reduced, guilt feelings are lifted, and self-image as well as self-acceptance improve considerably. Individuals talk about experiencing themselves as reborn and purified; a deep sense of being in tune with nature and the universe replaces their previous feelings of alienation. Profound serenity and joy can dominate their mental lives. This is usually accompanied by a general increase in zest and a sense of physical health and good physiological functioning.

Some of these persons report that the death-rebirth process seems to have removed a subtle film from their senses which previously prevented them from experiencing reality fully. Sensory input in this new state feels very fresh and intense, almost to the point of being overwhelming; individuals can feel that prior to the experience of rebirth they had never really seen colors, smelled the variety of fragrances and odors, tasted the infinite nuances in food, or experienced the sensual potential of their bodies. Sexual activities can become freer, and potency in men, as well as orgasmic ability in both sexes, is often greatly augmented. Many individuals become intensely interested in nature and find a capacity for ecstatic experiencing of natural beauty, frequently for the first time in their lives. The same is true for the perception of art, particularly music; it is not infrequent that as a result of psychedelic experiences of this kind nonmusical persons develop vivid interest in music and others discover entirely new ways of experiencing it. Aggressive feelings and impulses are usually strikingly reduced and interpersonal and philosophical tolerance increases considerably. Individuals experience a new sense of empathy and warmth toward other people and perceive the world as a fascinating and basically friendly place. Everything in the universe appears perfect, exactly as it should be.

Individuals almost always experience a definite reorientation regarding time. They ruminate less on the traumatic aspects of the past and show less anxious anticipation of or wishful clinging to the future; these are replaced by an enhanced emotional emphasis on the here and now. The relationship between situations and things considered trivial and those seen as all-important usually changes drastically. Individuals tend to discover meaning and beauty in ordinary objects in their everyday environments. The boundary between the miraculous and the banal disappears. Values that were previously pursued with unusual determination and investment of energy are perceived as irrelevant. Excessive striving for power, status, and material possessions appears as childish and symptomatic of spiritual blindness. The most profound wisdom is found in the simplicity of life. This reduction of unrealistic ambitions is frequently combined with an increased ability to accept one's own limitations as well as one's role in the world.

Another common occurrence following a complete and well-integrated death-rebirth experience is a great increase of interest in philosophy, religion, and mysticism. New spiritual feelings are usually of a cosmic or pantheistic nature; the individual can see many additional spiritual dimensions to human life and sense the presence of a spiritual creative force behind the phenomena of everyday reality. Many persons have also experienced an awakening of intense interest in Oriental or ancient religions and philosophies. For some these new interests took a purely intellectual form; for others they were associated with a deep commitment to systematic spiritual practice. In many instances individuals found a new ability to understand universal religious symbols, the metaphors of holy scriptures and other sacred texts, and the language of certain complicated philosophical essays. If the experience of death and rebirth is followed by feelings of cosmic unity, individuals usually see the world and themselves in terms of spiritual energy involved in a divine play and tend to perceive ordinary reality as essentially sacred.

These transformations are usually very pronounced for several days or weeks after a profound and well-resolved LSD session involving the death-rebirth experience. Changes are frequently so striking that LSD therapists refer to them in their clinical jargon as "psychedelic afterglow." Sooner or later they tend to decrease in intensity; under the influence of the demands and pressures of the social environment, many subjects more or less lose touch with their cosmic feelings. However, the new philosophical and spiritual insights into the nature of reality that the experient discovered tend to persist indefinitely. With discipline it is possible to use the profound knowledge acquired in the death-rebirth process as a guideline for restructuring one's entire life. Some individuals are thus capable of creating a situation for themselves in which not only the cognitive insights but also the new spiritual feelings are potentially available much of the time.

It would represent a dangerous oversimplification to present the death-rebirth process with a one-sided emphasis on its potential benefits without pointing out the serious risks involved in this area. LSD sessions involving perinatal material not only can facilitate the most profound positive transformations but also are a potential source of the most frequent complications observed in the course of the LSD procedure. Poorly resolved sessions with perinatal elements can result in deep inhibited or agitated depressions with suicidal tendencies, destructive and self-destructive impulses, paranoid states, or grandiose and messianic manifestations. Allusions to some of these dangers are also frequently found regarding the transformative process in various rites of passage. According to mystical literature, oral traditions of aboriginal cultures, and various mythological accounts, physical disease, insanity, and even death are the dangers that threaten a careless and inexperienced seeker or spiritual adventurer. Adequate preparation, support, and guidance are indispensable for entering these territories of the human mind.*

In psychiatric patients the therapeutic effects associated with the ex-

---

* The beneficial, as well as the adverse, effects of LSD sessions involving activation of perinatal matrices have been described in detail in *Realms of the Human Unconscious,* by Stanislav Grof. The practical guidelines for maximizing the potential benefits and minimizing the risks of the psychedelic death-rebirth process will be outlined in a future volume.

perience of death and rebirth are so important that we will explore this area in some detail. It seems that perinatal matrices represent deep roots for the most salient aspects of many psychopathological syndromes. Such crucial symptoms as anxiety, aggression, depression, tension, and guilt, as well as feelings of helplessness and inadequacy, appear to be anchored in the perinatal level. Similarly, in many instances we can trace a preoccupation with various physiological functions or with biological material, hypochondriacal concerns, and a variety of psychosomatic symptoms to the elements of the death-rebirth process. This was true for ordinary or migraine headaches, neurotic feelings of lack of oxygen and suffocation, cardiac distress, nausea and vomiting, various dyskinesias, and muscular tensions, pains and tremors.

It was a rather common occurrence in LSD psycholytic therapy that patients who had moved beyond the psychodynamic level altogether did not resolve many of their psychopathological symptoms until they had worked through the material related to perinatal matrices. It appeared necessary to work through the no-exit matrix in order to reach a lasting resolution—not just a temporary remission—of claustrophobia or an inhibited depression. Frequently, severe suicidal urges disappeared completely when patients worked through and integrated perinatal material. Several individuals who completed the death-rebirth process independently reported that their previous suicidal tendencies had actually been unrecognized cravings for ego transcendence. Since this insight was not available to them at that time, they chose a situation in objective reality that bore a close similarity to the ego death, namely physical destruction. The experience of psychological death and rebirth tended to eliminate or greatly reduce suicidal tendencies and ideation. Powerful aggressive and self-destructive impulses were consumed in the many dramatic experiential sequences of the death-rebirth process. In addition, following the ego death individuals saw human existence in a much broader spiritual framework; no matter how difficult their life situations and circumstances were from an objective point of view, suicide somehow no longer appeared to be a solution.

In our work with alcoholics and heroin addicts, we made observations that were quite similar to those we made of suicidal individuals. The underlying dynamics are quite similar, and, from a certain point of view, alcoholism and addiction appear to be forms of gradual suicide.

LSD patients who experienced profound feelings of cosmic unity frequently developed a negative attitude toward the states of mind produced by intoxication with alcohol and narcotics. In the Spring Grove studies, where the number of LSD sessions was restricted, there was a definite tendency among both alcoholics and heroin addicts to discontinue their habit following a single high-dose LSD session. In a more open-ended treatment situation in the Psychiatric Research Institute in Prague, where it was possible to administer serial LSD sessions, complete working through of the perinatal material resulted in several instances of lasting abstinence and deep restructuring of the alcoholic's or addict's personality.

The insights of these patients concerning the nature of their habits resembled those of persons with suicidal tendencies. After they had discovered and experienced feelings of cosmic unity in their sessions, they realized that the state they had really been craving was transcendence and not drug intoxication. They recognized a certain superficial similarity and overlap between alcohol or heroin intoxication and the unitive feelings activated by LSD, and began to see that their desire to seek these drugs was based on confusing these two conditions. The elements that these states seem to have in common are the diminution or disappearance of various painful emotions and sensations, emotional indifference toward one's past and future, and an undifferentiated state of consciousness. On the other hand, however, many essential characteristics of the unitive state are not part of the experience of intoxication by alcohol or narcotics. Instead of inducing a state of cosmic consciousness in its entirety, these drugs produce a caricature that seems close enough to mislead the individual involved and seduce him or her into systematic abuse. Repeated administrations then lead to biological addiction and damage the user physically, emotionally, and socially.

After the experiences of ego death, abuse of alcohol or narcotics as well as suicidal tendencies are seen as tragic mistakes due to an unrecognized and misunderstood spiritual craving for transcendence. The presence of strong feelings of this kind, as improbable as they might seem to those familiar with the behavior patterns and life-styles of addicts and alcoholics, can be illustrated by statistics from psychedelic therapy. In the Spring Grove research, alcoholics and heroin addicts had the highest incidence of mystical experiences of all the studied groups, including neurotics, mental health professionals, and individuals dying of cancer.

Aggression and sadomasochism are also deeply influenced by the symbolic encounter with death. Activation of the destructive potential in the individual is one of the most important aspects of the death-rebirth struggle. Scenes of aggression and mass destruction, as well as sadomasochistic orgies, are constant components of the perinatal unfolding. In this process experients mobilize and discharge enormous amounts of destructive energies; the result is a dramatic reduction of aggressive feelings and tendencies. A typical concomitant of the experience of rebirth is a sense of love, compassion, and reverence for life.

Manifestations of acute psychotic states frequently resemble the experiences in various transformative events of a ritual nature that have been described earlier. Many schizophrenics experience ordeals of extreme physical and mental suffering, a deep awareness of the absurdity of existence, and numerous sequences involving death, annihilation of the world, or even cosmic catastrophes. These hellish tortures and encounters with demons are sometimes followed by experiences of rebirth or re-creation of the world. Similarly, destructive and self-destructive tendencies, preoccupation with biological material and scatological interests, as well as focus on the triad of death-birth-sex, are quite common in these individuals. It seems that an important part of the schizophrenic process is the activation of the perinatal level of the unconscious by internal or external factors of an unknown nature. Whereas in ritual events and psychedelic therapy the deep contents of the unconscious are deliberately activated in a structured and protected environment for spiritual or therapeutic purposes, in schizophrenics this occurs in an elemental fashion and in most instances to the detriment of the individual involved. New understanding of the schizophrenic process has recently resulted in therapeutic endeavors aimed at guiding such individuals through their experiences to a higher level of integration instead of inhibiting and controlling psychotic symptoms.*

The material from clinical research with psychedelic drugs, anthropological and historical data related to rites of passage, and the study of the schizophrenic process make evident the significance of death in human psychology and psychopathology. The reason for the psychological relevance of the issue of death is not the intellectual awareness of our impermanence and the knowledge that we have to die, but the existence of powerful repositories for the experience of death in our unconscious. Subjective as well as objective exploration of these realms is complicated by the fact that under normal circumstances massive defenses wall off perinatal forces and protect the ego from their full impact.

Individuals who have experienced death and rebirth in their sessions realize retrospectively that the awareness of death has accompanied them all through their lives in a mitigated fashion, or in the form of many of its derivatives. Under normal circumstances the subliminal awareness of death underlies a variety of human attitudes and behaviors. When the defense system that usually buffers the ego from the perinatal level starts failing or partially breaks down, these elements emerge into consciousness and give rise to various neurotic and psychosomatic symptoms. A total breakdown of the resistances then results in psychotic episodes in which the content of the perinatal matrices totally consumes the ego and becomes the individual's experiential world.

One of the most frequent ways of defending oneself against the painful impact of perinatal elements is what LSD subjects refer to as a

---

* The interested reader will find more information about the parallels between schizophrenia and the initiatory process and about the new approaches to schizophrenia in the books and papers of R. D. Laing, John Perry, Maurice Rappaport, and Julian Silverman. The implications of LSD research for the understanding of schizophrenia and some of the pioneering experiments with psychedelic therapy of psychotic patients will be discussed in a future volume.

"treadmill" approach to existence. Individuals living their lives in this way feel deeply dissatisfied with themselves and their present situation, and most of their thinking is oriented toward the past and the future. They keep reviewing their pasts, regretting their former decisions, toying with what would have been better alternatives, or evaluating their histories in moral terms. Their dissatisfaction with the present leads them to compensatory wishful fantasies or exaggerated concrete plans concerning future achievements. Whether or not they succeed in accomplishing what was supposed to bring them satisfaction, their distress and lack of fulfillment continue and require the formulation of more ambitious goals and plans. This constant orientation toward future achievement has been referred to by existentialist philosophers as the forming of "autoprojects." This cycle is never-ending and only perpetuates frustration because the persons involved do not correctly recognize the nature of their needs and are focusing on external surrogates, whether it be money, status, fame, or sexual pursuits. It is thus possible to spend an entire lifetime being driven toward various activities that never bring the expected final satisfaction. This is frequently associated with feelings of the meaninglessness of existence and inability to enjoy the fruits of one's own efforts. A person caught in a vicious circle of this kind usually suffers from an urgent sense that human life is too short in view of everything that could be experienced and should be accomplished.

A person who has gone through psychological death and rebirth realizes that a positive feeling about life and a deep sense of the meaning of one's own existence are not contingent on complicated external conditions. They represent a primary organismic state and a way of being in the world that is independent of the material circumstances of life, with the exception of some drastic extremes. If this fundamental affirmation of life is present, then even the simplest life conditions can be experienced as worthwhile. When this positive life feeling is not present, then external success of any kind and any scope cannot provide it; it has to occur within a process of deep self-exploration and inner transformation.

Although the death-rebirth phenomenon is most likely to occur in specially designed and structured frameworks, such as rites of passage or psychedelic therapy, occasionally profound death-rebirth experiences can unfold spontaneously or be triggered by ordinary events in everyday life. That profound death-rebirth sequences can occur without specific programming and without the use of powerful mind-altering techniques indicates to a much greater degree than some of our own observations the existence of matrices in the human unconscious that give rise to such phenomena. Since the spontaneous occurrence of death-rebirth experiences is so relevant for our discussion, we will illustrate this point by an account of an episode which occurred in the life of a well-known psychologist. The incident that he describes in retrospect happened when he was twenty-one years old; it had a powerful and lasting influence on his personal as well as professional life.

It started out when I was at a party in San Francisco. A woman whom I had met that evening suggested that we take a drive. As we were approaching the Golden Gate Bridge she mentioned that she was driving a Mercedes Sunroof. She said that sometimes when she was crossing the bridge, she would roll back the sunroof, lean back in her seat, and look up at the sky; she had very nearly killed herself doing this. As we came to the bridge she rolled back the roof and told me to lean back in my seat and look up at the sky and stars. I can remember seeing out of the periphery of my vision the cables going up to the first large upright on the Golden Gate. I was following all the uprights up; the vertical lines were brightly illuminated and looked like golden strands reaching up toward the stars. As we came to the first upright, my eyes followed it, and then I had the sensation of being drawn out of my face, out of my mouth, drawn up to a point that was level with the uprights on the bridge. I experienced a feeling of expansiveness, like I was mushrooming out. I also remember coming down on the other set of uprights and feeling myself being pulled in like a genie into a bottle and being drawn back down into my body. The sensation of lightness and flight was a very beautiful experience. I then realized that I was sitting in the car looking out through the top of a sunroof. As we approached the second upright I began to feel a tremendous sense of exhilaration and lightness and could again see in the periphery of my eyes the cables reaching up toward the second upright on the bridge. I again started being drawn out and had the very distinct sensation this time of actually being pulled outside of my body, feeling myself rising up until I could look from the top of the bridge back down to the traffic below me. I had the sensation of accelerating very, very rapidly and continuing on beyond the bridge uprights. I began to ask questions like what's going on here, and what am I doing, what's happening. I immediately got answers to those questions, and then I had a feeling of increasing exhilaration and increasing expansion, and the sensation of not even asking questions before they were answered. I continued having this feeling of exhilaration and expansion until I felt a silent white explosion and I experienced myself expanding in a kind of soft white light. I had the feeling that I reached infinity and knew everything there was to know, of having all questions answered.

That's what I was experiencing; the rest I am about to say now was what was related afterward by the girl. She said to me that when we approached the first upright, I let out a moaning sound and she looked over. When I came to the second upright, I suddenly screamed; she said it was not a scream of pain, but of exaltation. I had a very entranced, fixed look on my face and my body was very stiff. Another part of what I was experiencing at that point is that when I was in this clear, white-light space I had the sensation that I was able to hear a kind of slowing down, a cosmic kind of droning sound. Apparently what was happening in the car that related to this was that when I screamed she turned to me and lifted her foot off the accelerator; as she let off the accelerator, the sound of the car engine slowed down. My insight in this state was that I had died. I was absolutely and totally convinced that I had died, that it had come like a flash, that there had been a car accident, that I was dead, because everything in my Christian tradition had told me that you only saw God after you had died. At this point I was experiencing and somehow *knowing* that I was in the presence of God and concluded somehow that I must be dead.

Suddenly, at the thought of death, I became very frightened. I remember the sensation of fear which was constricting. I felt as though I were a genie being sucked back into a very small, cold bottle. I felt myself drawing together until I was like a hard, cold marble of lead and then found myself back inside my body, very much inside, feeling arthritic, cold, and cramped. I looked over at the girl who was driving and there seemed to be miles between us in space. The spatial dimensions of the car seemed enormous, and she had turned into a kind of stony gray, cold figure, very much a death figure. Everything about me seemed inanimate, dead, and cold. My thought at that point was that I had died, that there had been a very violent car accident and that I had made the transition very suddenly into an after-death state. I thought that in order to convince myself that I was dead, I would have to go through the car hitting the bridge, the crunching of metal, and the metal ripping my flesh. Suddenly, when I realized that I didn't have to make the transition with fear and with tearing, I felt myself being escorted back up and into this white light again, and there was a feeling of peace, of ecstasy. And at that point, she told me that I started to sob, began to cry and said: "Why me?" not "Why have I died?" but "Why me, why have I been allowed to see this?"

The study of death is of crucial importance for the understanding of mental processes. There is no doubt that a genuine comprehension of religion, mysticism, shamanism, rites of passage, or mythology is impossible without intimate knowledge of the death experience and the death-rebirth process. This information is also essential for a deeper insight into the nature of mental diseases, particularly schizophrenia. Avoidance of the perinatal and transpersonal levels of the unconscious necessarily results in a superficial and distorted image of the human mind, an incomplete understanding of emotional disorders, and limited possibilities for therapeutic intervention.

The realization of the psychological significance of death need not be fraught with negative connotations. A profound symbolic encounter with death under supportive and properly structured circumstances can have very beneficial consequences and be instrumental in overcoming negative concepts of death and fear associated with it. It can contribute to better emotional and physical functioning, fuller self-actualization, and a more satisfying and harmonious adjustment to the life process.

Death and life, usually considered to be irreconcilable opposites, appear to actually be dialectically interrelated. Living fully and with maximum awareness every moment of one's life leads to an accepting and reconciled attitude toward death. Conversely, such an approach to human existence requires that we come to terms with our mortality and the impermanence of existence. This seems to be the innermost significance of ancient mysteries, various spiritual practices, and rites of passage.

Rabbi Herschel Lymon, who volunteered for our LSD training program, described his unique insight into this dialectic relationship between life and death. During reentry from his LSD session, in which he experienced a shattering encounter with death and subsequent feelings of spiritual rebirth, he remembered a famous statement made five hundred years ago by Leonardo da Vinci. At the time when he was dying, Leonardo summarized his feelings about his rich and productive life by saying: "I thought I was living; I was only preparing myself to die." Rabbi Lymon, describing the death-rebirth struggle in his LSD session, paraphrased Leonardo's words: "I thought I was dying; I was only preparing myself to live."

BIBLIOGRAPHY

Abramson, H. A., and Evans, L. T. "LSD-25: II. Psychobiological Effect on the Siamese Fighting Fish." *Science* 120 (1954): 990.

Arendsen-Hein, G. W. "Dimensions in Psychotherapy." In *The Use of LSD in Psychotherapy and Alcoholism,* edited by H. A. Abramson. New York: Bobbs-Merrill, 1967.

Barrett, W. *Death-Bed Visions.* London: Methuen, 1926.

Bateson, G. *Naven.* 2nd ed., Stanford, California: Stanford University Press, 1958.

Bierce, A. "An Occurrence at Owl Creek Bridge." In *Great Modern American Stories, An Anthology,* edited by W. D. Howells. New York: MSS Information Corp., 1972.

Bonny, H., and Pahnke, W. N. "The Use of Music in Psychedelic (LSD) Psychotherapy." *J. Music Therapy* 9 (1972): 64.

Bottome, P. *Alfred Adler, A Biography.* New York: Putnam Press, 1939.

Brun, R. "Ueber Freuds Hypothese vom Todestrieb." *Psyche* 7 (1953): 81.

Budge, E. A. Wallis: *The Egyptian Heaven and Hell.* La Salle, Ill.: Open Court, 1974.

————. *The Book of the Dead.* New Hyde Park, N.Y.: University Books, 1960.

Capra, F. *The Tao of Physics.* Berkeley, Calif.: Shambhala, 1975.

Champdor, A. *The Book of the Dead: From the Ani, Hunefer, and Anhai Papyri in the British Museum.* New York: Garrett Publications, 1966.

Clarke, E. H. *Visions: A Study of False Sight.* Cambridge, Mass.: The Riverside Press; Boston, Houghton, Osgood & Co., 1878.

Cobbe, F. P. "The Peak in Darien: The Riddle of Death." *Littell's Living Age and New Quarterly Review* 134 (1877): 374.

Cohen, S. "LSD and the Anguish of Dying." *Harper's Magazine* 231 (1965): 69,77.

Crosby, C. *The Passionate Years.* New York: Dial Press, 1953.

Delacour, J. B. *Glimpses of the Beyond.* New York: Delacorte Press, 1974.

Eissler, K. R. *The Psychiatrist and the Dying Patient.* New York: International Universities Press, 1955.

Eliade, M. *Rites and Symbols of Initiation: The Mysteries of Death and Rebirth.* New York: Harper and Row, 1958.

―――. *Myths, Dreams, and Mysteries.* New York: Harper and Row, 1960.

―――. *Shamanism: Archaic Techniques of Ecstasy.* Bollingen Series, vol. 76. New York: Pantheon Books, 1964.

Evans-Wentz, W. E. *The Tibetan Book of the Dead.* London: Oxford University Press, 1957.

Feifel, H., ed. *The Meaning of Death.* New York: McGraw-Hill, 1959.

Fenichel, O. *The Psychoanalytic Theory of Neurosis.* New York: Norton & Co., Inc., 1945.

Fisher, G. "Psychotherapy for the Dying: Principles and Illustrative Cases with Special Reference to the Use of LSD." *Omega* 1 (1970): 3.

Fremantle, F., and Rinpoche, Chögyam Trungpa. *The Tibetan Book of the Dead.* Berkeley, Calif., and London: Shambhala, 1975.

Freud, S. "The Theme of the Three Caskets." In *Collected Papers* 4. London: Hogarth Press, 1925.

―――. "Thoughts for the Times on War and Death." In *Collected Papers* 4. London: Hogarth Press, 1925.

―――. *Beyond the Pleasure Principle.* Edited and translated by James Strachey. New York: W. W. Norton, 1975.

―――. *An Outline of Psychoanalysis.* New York: Norton Press, 1949.

Garfield, C. A. *Psychothanatological Concomitants of Altered State Experiences: An Investigation of the Relationship between Consciousness Alteration and Fear of Death.* Ph.D. dissertation, University of California, 1974.

Gennep, A. van. *Rites of Passage.* Translated by Monika B. Vizedon and Gabrielle L. Caffee. Chicago: University of Chicago Press, 1961.

Godfrey, K. Personal communication.

Grof, S., Pahnke, W. N., Kurland, A. A., and Goodman, L. E. "LSD-Assisted Psychotherapy in Patients with Terminal Cancer." A presentation at the Fifth Symposium of the Foundation of Thanatology, New York City, November, 1971.

———. "LSD and the Human Encounter with Death." *Voices* 8 (1972): 64.

———. *Realms of the Human Unconscious: Observations from LSD Research.* New York: E. P. Dutton, 1976.

Hart, H. *The Enigma of Survival.* Springfield, Ill.: Charles C. Thomas, 1959.

Heidegger, M. *Sein und Zeit.* Halle, East Germany: Max Niemager, 1927.

Heim, A. "Notizen ueber den Tod durch Absturz." *Jahrbuch des Schweizer Alpenklub* 27 (1892): 327.

Hunter, R. C. A. "On the Experience of Nearly Dying." *Amer. J. Psychiat.* 124 (1967): 84.

Huxley, A. *Island.* New York: Bantam, 1963.

———. *The Doors of Perception* and *Heaven and Hell.* New York: Harper and Row, 1963.

———. "Visionary Experience." Lecture from a series of talks entitled "The Human Situation," Los Alamos, 1962. Available as a record, copyright L. Huxley, A.-102.

———. *Brave New World.* Bantam Modern Classic. New York: Harper and Row, 1968.

Huxley, L. A. *This Timeless Moment.* New York: Farrar, Straus & Giroux, 1968.

Hyslop, J. H. *Psychical Research and the Resurrection.* Boston: Small, Maynard and Co., 1908.

James, W. *The Varieties of Religious Experience.* New York: Longmans, Green & Co., 1929.

Jung, C. G. "Two Essays on Analytical Psychology," *Collected Works of C. G. Jung,* vol. 7, Bollingen Series 20. Princeton: University Press, 1953.

———. *Memories, Dreams, Reflections.* New York: Pantheon, 1961.

Kast, E. C. "The Analgesic Action of Lysergic Acid Compared with Dihydromorphinone and Meperidine." *Bull. Drug Addiction Narcotics,* App. 27 (1963): 3517.

———. "Pain and LSD-25: A Theory of Attenuation of Anticipation." In

LSD-25: The Consciousness-Expanding Drug. Edited by D. Solomon. New York: Putnam Press, 1964.

————, and Collins, V. J. "A Study of Lysergic Acid Diethylamide As an Analgesic Agent." *Anaesth. Analg. Curr. Res.* 43 (1964): 285.

————. "LSD and the Dying Patient." *Chicago Med. Sch. Quart.* 26 (1966): 80.

Kübler-Ross, E. *On Death and Dying.* London: Collier-Macmillan Ltd., 1969.

————. *Questions and Answers about Dying and Death.* New York: Macmillan, 1974.

Kurland, A. A., Pahnke, W. N., Unger, S., Savage, C., and Goodman, L. E. "Psychedelic Psychotherapy (LSD) in the Treatment of the Patient with a Malignancy." Excerpta Medica International Congress Series No. 180. *The Present Status of Psychotropic Drugs* 180. Proceedings of the Sixth International Congress of the CINP in Tarragona, Spain (April 1968): 432.

————, Savage, C., Pahnke, W. N., Grof, S., and Olsson, J. "LSD in the Treatment of Alcoholics." *Pharmakopsychiatrie, Neuropsychopharmakologie* 4 (1971): 83.

Laing, R. *The Politics of Experience.* New York: Ballantine Books, 1976.

Leary, T., Metzner, R., and Alpert, R. *The Psychedelic Experience: A Manual Based on the Tibetan Book of the Dead.* New Hyde Park, N.Y.: University Books, 1964.

Maslow, A. *Toward a Psychology of Being.* Princeton, N.J.: Van Nostrand, 1962.

————. "A Theory of Metamotivation: The Biological Rooting of the Value-Life." In *Readings in Humanistic Psychology,* edited by A. Sutich and M. A. Vich. New York: The Free Press, 1969.

Masters, R., Houston, J. *Mind Games: The Guide to Inner Space.* New York: Viking Press, 1972.

McCabe, O. L. *An Empirical Investigation of the Effects of Chemically (LSD-25) Induced "Psychedelic Experiences" on Selected Measures of Personality.* Baltimore: Dissertation Monograph, 1968.

McFarland, R. A. Fatigue and Stress Symposium, January 1952, Operations Research Office Technological Memorandum, ORO-T-185.

Mead, M. "Ritual and the Conscious Creation of New Rituals." Prefatory statement prepared for the participants of the Fifty-Ninth Burg Wartenstein Symposium on *Ritual: Reconciliation in Change,* sponsored by the Wenner-Gren Foundation. Gloggnitz, Austria, July 1973.

Meduna, L. J. *Carbon Dioxide Therapy.* Springfield, Ill.: Charles C. Thomas, 1950.

Melzack, R., and Wall, P. D. "Pain Mechanisms: A New Theory." *Science* 150 (1965): 971.

―――. *The Puzzle of Pain.* New York: Basic Books, 1973.

Moody, R. A. *Life After Life,* Atlanta, Ga.: Mockingbird Books, 1975.

Munk, W. *Euthanasia or Medical Treatment in Aid of an Easy Death.* New York: Longmans, Green & Co., 1887.

Noyes, R. "Dying and Mystical Consciousness." *J. Thanatol* 1 (1971): 25.

―――. "The Experience of Dying." *Psychiatry* 35 (1972): 174.

―――., and Kletti, R. *"The Experience of Dying from Falls."* *Omega* 3 (1972): 45.

Origenes Adamantius (Father Origen): *De Principiis—On First Principles.* Translated by G. W. Butterworth. Gloucester, Mass.: Peter Smith, 1973.

Osis K. *Deathbed Observations by Physicians and Nurses.* New York: Parapsychology Foundation, 1961.

Pahnke, W. N., and Richards, W. A. "Implications of LSD and Experimental Mysticism." *J. Religion & Health* 5 (1966): 175.

―――. "The Psychedelic Mystical Experience in the Human Encounter with Death." An Ingersoll Lecture. *Harvard Theol. Rev.* 62 (1969): 1.

―――, Kurland, A. A., Richard, W. E., and Goodman, L. E. "LSD-Assisted Psychotherapy with Terminal Cancer Patients." In *Psychedelic Drugs.* Edited by R. E. Hicks and P. J. Fink. New York: Grune and Stratton, 1969.

―――, Kurland, A. A., Unger, S., Savage, C., and Grof, S. "The Experimental Use of Psychedelic (LSD) Psychotherapy." *JAMA* 212 (1970): 1856.

―――, Kurland, A. A., Unger, S., Savage, C., Wolf, S., and Goodman, L. E. "Psychedelic Therapy (Utilizing LSD) with Terminal Cancer Patients." *J. Psychedelic Drugs* 3 (1970): 63.

Perry, J. W. *The Far Side of Madness.* Englewood Cliffs, N.J.: Prentice-Hall, 1974.

Pifister, O. "Schockdenken und Schockphantasien bei höchster Todesgefahr." *Ztschr. für Psychoanalyse* 16 (1930): 430.

Poe, E. A. "A Descent into the Maelström." In *The Complete Tales and Poems of Edgar Allan Poe.* New York: Modern Library, 1938.

Popov, A. A. *Tavgijcy: Materialy po etnografii avamskich i vedeevskich targicev.* Moscow and Leningrad: Trudy instituta antropologii i etnografii, 1, 5, 1936.

Rainer, R. *Ars Moriendi: Von der Kunst des heilsamen Lebens und Sterbens.* Koeln-Graz: Boehlau Verlag, 1957.

Rappaport, M., Hopkins, K., Hall, K., De Belleza, T., and Silverman, J. *Selective Drug Utilization in the Management of Psychosis,* NIMH Grant Report, MH-16445, March 1974.

Richards, W. A. "Counseling, Peak Experiences and the Human Encounter with Death. An Empirical Study of the Efficacy of DPT-Assisted Counseling in Enhancing the Quality of Life of Persons with Terminal Cancer and Their Closest Family Members." Ph.D. dissertation, School of Education, Catholic University of America, Washington, D.C., 1975.

Richards, W. E., Grof, S., Goodman, L. E., and Kurland, A. A. "LSD-Assisted Psychotherapy and the Human Encounter with Death." *J. Transpersonal Psychol.* 4 (1972): 121.

Rosen, D. "Suicide Survivors; A Follow-Up Study of Persons Who Survived Jumping from the Golden Gate and San Francisco-Oakland Bay Bridges." *West. J. Med.* 122 (1975): 289.

Saunders, C. M. "The Treatment of Intractable Pain in Terminal Cancer." *Proc. Roy. Soc. Med.* 56 (1961): 195.

———. *The Management of Terminal Illness.* London: Hospital Medicine Publications, 1967.

———. "The Need for In-Patient Care for the Patient with Terminal Cancer." *Middlesex Hospital Journal* 72 (1973), no. 3.

Savage, C., McCabe, O. L., and Kurland, A. A. "Psychedelic Therapy of the Narcotic Addict." In *The Drug Abuse Controversy.* Edited by C. Brown and C. Savage. Baltimore: National Education Consultants, 1972.

Schüre, E. *The Great Initiates.* West Nyack, N.Y.: St. George Books, 1961.

Sherwood, J. N., Stolaroff, M. J., and Harman, W. W. "The Psychedelic Experience: A New Concept in Psychotherapy." *J. Neuropsychiat.* 3 (1962): 370.

Silverman, J. "Shamans and Acute Schizophrenia." *Amer. Anthropol.* 69 (1967): 21.

———. "Acute Schizophrenia: Disease or Dis-Ease." In *Readings in Psychology To-Day.* San Francisco: CRM Books, 1972.

Simonton, C. O., and Simonton, S. S. "Belief Systems and Management of the Emotional Aspects of Malignancy." *J. Transpersonal Psychol.* 7 (1975): 29.

———. "The Role of the Mind in Cancer Therapy." Lecture at symposium entitled *Dimensions of Healing* at the UCLA, October 1974.

Solow, V.: "I Died at 10:52 A.M." *Reader's Digest* (October 1974): 178.

Stace, W. T. *Mysticism and Philosophy*. Philadelphia and New York: J. P. Lippincott, 1960.

St. Christopher's Hospice. *Annual Report,* 1971–2.

Toben, B. *Space-Time and Beyond*. New York: E. P. Dutton, 1975.

Tolstoy, L. N. "The Death of Ivan Ilyitch." In *The Novels and Other Works of Lyof N. Tolstoy*. New York: Charles Scribner's Sons, 1923.

———. *War and Peace*. New York: Modern Library.

Toynbee, A. et al. *Man's Concern with Death*. New York: McGraw-Hill, 1968.

Turner, V. W. *The Ritual Process: Structure and Anti-Structure*. Chicago: Aldine Publishing Co., 1969.

Unger, S. et al. "LSD-Type Drugs and Psychedelic Therapy." *Res. Psychother*. 3 (1968): 521.

Wasson, V. P. In an interview in *This Week,* May 19, 1957.

Weiss, B., Abramson, H. A., and Baron, M. D. "LSD XXV: Effect of Potassium Cyanide and Other Oxidase and Respiratory Inhibitors on the Siamese Fighting Fish." *Arch. Neurol. Psychiat*. 80 (1958): 345.

Weisse, J. E. *The Obelisk in Free Masonry*. New York, 1880, quoted in M. P. Hall's *The Secret Teachings of All Ages*. Los Angeles: The Philosophical Research Society, 1968.

———. *The Vestibule*. Port Washington, N.Y.: Ashley Books, 1972.

Wunderlich, H. G. *The Secret of Crete*. New York: Macmillan, 1974.

INDEX